DETERMINED
and with
COURAGE

☆ HEADING WEST ☆

Volume 1

Marlin L. Patterson

WESTBOW
PRESS®
A DIVISION OF THOMAS NELSON
& ZONDERVAN

WestBow Press books may be ordered through booksellers or by contacting:

WestBow Press
A Division of Thomas Nelson & Zondervan
1663 Liberty Drive
Bloomington, IN 47403
www.westbowpress.com
844-714-3454

Front cover photo
By Granddaughter and her husband, Samantha and Lance Goodwin also
granddaughter Kristy Woolford, With Loryann Balls at the camera.

Contact with the author:
marlinlpatterson@gmail.com

ISBN: 978-1-6642-7206-4 (sc)
ISBN: 978-1-6642-7207-1 (hc)
ISBN: 978-1-6642-7205-7 (e)

Library of Congress Control Number: 2022912776

Print information available on the last page.

WestBow Press rev. date: 10/10/2022

AUTHOR'S NOTE

This story has a little different format as it gives the reader a feeling and understanding of the daily routine of early pioneer life. It allows the reader to live the life of those the story is about. The story also will give the reader good feelings of giving, sharing, working and loving your neighbor and others and the things around you.

The stories of people working with animals in this book are not fiction, they are true experiences of the author, members of his family and close friends. These stories have been incorporated in this book to help the reader realize the intelligence of birds and animals. One needs to recognize the ability of other creatures as they can learn our language and can think on their own, remember past experiences, and what to do to help us in many ways. They can tease and play games with us, but can we learn their language?

Up until the late 1930's to early 1940's Horses were still used in farming. Families were using horse and buggy as the means of transportation. So there was a close working relationship with man and horse as well as with other animals. Many families, if they had place to keep them, had a cow or two to supply the needs of their families. This was the case with our family during the II World War. We got along real well as a family and had plenty to eat. Naturally we had a love for our animals and when we had to sell or part with one, there were often tears in our eyes of having to part with them.

Marlin L. Patterson

J ed jerked and sat up in bed, awakened by the rooster crowing out in the chicken coop. He had overslept the time he had planned to be up and moving. Today was a very special day in his life. Today, he was headed west to find his father. His father had left home three years previous, leaving his wife and two children to fend for themselves while he went west to seek a fortune in gold and a new place for his family to come and join him.

Jed jumped out of bed, quickly dressed, and put on his boots. He stepped out into main room of the house, which was the home of his sister, her husband, and soon a precious new baby. He had been living with them for the past month since finishing his apprenticeship with the neighbor down the road. He had taken on this apprenticeship to learn a trade that held a soft spot in his heart. It was in carpentry, woodwork, and wood carving. He loved this work and had spent many hours, evenings, and stormy days sitting by the fireplace and carving. Sometimes it was an animal, a bird, or a flower. He loved to see what he could create and how real he could make each look. But, for now, his love for woodwork would be on hold; he needed to find his father.

Jed moved about the room and gathered the last of his things to put into his packs to be placed on his packhorse. He tried to be really quiet as he moved about, but he was not quiet enough.

His sister, Elizabeth, had heard him and came out to help him and get him some breakfast.

"Oh, Jed, I wish you wouldn't go! I am really going to miss you. With Mama gone and Father being gone so long, you're the only family I have left. Are you sure you won't change your mind?"

Jed stepped over to her, placed his hands on her shoulders, and looked into her eyes. He said, "Elizabeth, you know I must go and try to find our father. He doesn't know about Mother's passing. He needs to know, but remember, Sis, that I love you and that you and Jonathon and your new baby will constantly be on my mind.

"I have to find him. That last letter we got from him told us he had struck gold somewhere in Arizona and that he would be in touch with us to let us know where. We know he is thinking of us since he sent some money, and we should hear from him again when he gets some land and builds a home for us. I would love to be there to help him build that home. He doesn't know about Mama, your marriage, or the fact that he's going to be a grandpa. It will certainly break his heart when he learns about Mama, but he will be happy to know about your baby. I'm determined to go find him and be of help to him."

Elizabeth said, "I know you are determined to go. You're just as determined as Papa was when he left to go find that gold. I'll hurry and fix your breakfast while you finish your packing."

Jed finished collecting his things and placed them by the front door and started for the barn to saddle his horse, Blaze, and get the packsaddle on his second horse, Chip.

Jonathon was up and offered to help. As they readied the horses, he said, "Jed, I realize you're only seventeen, and you have a good head on your shoulders and should do well in whatever you choose to do. Think well in all the decisions you need to make, but don't forget that you don't have to make them all on your own. There is a God in heaven who is always ready to help you. All you have to do is call on Him, and answers will come that will help you."

They led the horses to the house and tied them to the small hitching rail near the front door.

As they entered the house, Elizabeth said, "That didn't take long. Wash up and come sit at the table; your breakfast is ready."

Jonathon offered a prayer for the food and made an additional request to God to protect Jed in his travels. As they ate, they reminisced about the good times. They talked about all the things that Jed would see and do while traveling.

Jed said he would be in touch with them when he found their father.

Jonathon mentioned his interest in owning a good farm and having cattle.

Jed assured them that he would be on the lookout for such a place to make them happy. When he finished eating, Jed stood up and announced that there were roads to be traveled that day. He had best be on his way.

All his things had been piled by the door: his cooking pot, frying pan, utensils, food, bacon, beans, rice, lard, flour, salt, pepper, extra clothing, bedroll, rain slicker, canvas to cover his pack, heavy coat, gloves, rifle, pistol, extra shells and of course a number of tools to do woodwork.

Elizabeth looked at Jed and asked, "How about matches and an emergency fire starter?"

Jed looked at her and gave her a loving wink. "Yes, my dear." He had put a lot of thought into what he needed to take. He'd made a long list and had checked the items off as he'd put them in the pile by the door, including the tools. He had canvas pack bags for each side of the packsaddle, and he was careful to load them evenly for weight and proper balance for traveling. The things he would need most often were placed on the top and were easy to get to. He also filled two canteens of fresh water. He would carry one on his riding horse, and he hung the other one over the packsaddle.

Elizabeth remembered something she wanted Jed to take with him. It was the small family Bible his mother had kept at her bedside. She hurried to get it.

When she got back, she handed him the Bible, and with tears in her eyes, she explained the great value it had been to their mother. She told him she hoped it would mean as much to him. She told him to read it daily and said she knew it would be a blessing to him.

He said, "You should keep it for yourself, my dear, because it was our mother's."

Elizabeth told him that she had her own personal Bible and that it would mean a lot to her to have him carrying their mother's Bible with him. She knew it would be a great help to him to have it.

He thanked her very kindly and gave her a hug and a kiss on the cheek. He shook hands with Jonathon and then rechecked his saddle and packsaddle to make sure all was secure. He realized tears were welling up in his eyes. He gave Elizabeth a final hug and a kiss on the cheek, mounted Blaze, and headed down the lane. He turned and gave a final wave before he went out of sight.

Lots of thoughts went through his mind. *Am I doing it right? Is this too big a challenge? Will I be all right? Will I be safe? Will the money in my pack be enough to last me to Arizona? If not, I can always get a job doing something to earn enough to move me closer to my destination.*

For the first mile or so, his mind kept going over things and reviewing all he had prepared to take. *Is it enough?*

When he'd gone to the barn to prepare the horses that morning, fog had hung low to the ground. A light mist had been falling. The mist was gone now, and the clouds in the sky were fading away. The sun was peeking over the clouds on the horizon. It looked like it was going to turn out to be a good day.

Johnsonville, Illinois, had been home to him since he was born. As he rode, he thought of the community he had been reared in. It was comprised mostly of Mormons who had not followed the thousands of others who had traveled west, starting in the winter of 1846. To the best of his understanding, many wagon trains were headed west. His family had not joined in with this group of Mormons, but they had found them to be good people and honest in their dealings. Their family had thought well of the Mormons, and they were treated as if they were one of their group. What good memories he had of his seventeen years.

But what about Father? Is he well? This thought would push him down the road and trails until he could meet his father again.

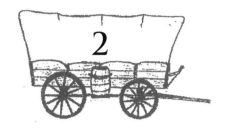

2

The first day of travel went smoothly. Everyone he met along the wagon roads he followed was friendly. At noon, he passed close to a farmer's home as the farmer was heading into the house for dinner. The farmer hailed him to come in and have dinner with them. He was a little reluctant because he knew it would take a little longer, but he graciously accepted. It turned out to be an enjoyable experience, and Jed's horses got a little longer rest. He needed to allow his horses a little more rest time because they hadn't been doing a lot of walking, and they needed to be toughened up slowly.

As they were eating, the farmer and his wife and two small children asked Jed lots of questions about where he was headed. They could tell that he must be traveling some distance. The children were excited to ask questions as well. They were cute and very mannerly.

After a pleasant but simple meal, he offered his

thanks and headed out the door. He thought of the little carved animals and birds in his pack. He had not thought about why he would carry them with him, but he had brought them along anyway. He went to his pack and took out a little animal for the little boy and a bird for the little girl. They were so excited to have such a wonderful gift.

He watered his horses at the farmer's water trough, thanked the family again, and headed down the road. By evening, he approached Centralia, a nice-looking little town that seemed quiet and peaceful. With only about an hour of light remaining, Jed pulled off the road and found a little draw with a clump of trees that offered a lot of green grass for the horses and a little water from runoff in the bottom. It was a good camping spot. He removed the saddles and tethered the horses.

Jed found some nice dry wood and started a small fire that couldn't be detected from any distance. After eating fried bacon and the bread Elizabeth had packed for him, he rolled out his bedroll, tucked himself in, and spent his first night out on his road west.

He was awakened the next morning by the chirp of birds in the trees. He listened for a few minutes since it was not yet fully light. The horses were settled down and peaceful. Finally, he rolled out of his bedroll and began to fix some breakfast. He had a little more bacon and the rest of the bread. He had a drink from his canteen and untied the horses and led them to water. They drank their fill of water, and then he saddled and loaded them and covered the campfire with a good layer of dirt. They were on the road.

The day went well until just before noon when a group of riders approached from the west. They pulled up, stopped him, and roughly inquired where he was headed.

Jed explained that he was heading up the road to visit a friend.

They asked what was in his packs.

Jed explained it was just some clothes and personal things since he hoped to go to work for this friend.

They grumbled for a minute or two, but he didn't know what they said. He assumed it wasn't good. One of the men said, "I think I see them coming. We've got to get out of here." The group of men spurred their horses and were gone.

In a few minutes, Jed saw more horses coming. The second group came up to him, reined up, and asked if he had seen a group of hard-looking men.

Jed told them about the group who had just passed.

They told him the first group had robbed a store a few miles back down the road and beaten the store's clerk pretty badly. The posse was out to catch them, and they took off in a full gallop after the outlaws.

A short time later, Jed pulled off to a shaded area to take a break and rest the horses. He loosened their cinches and tethered them out to graze.

Jed sat on a log and chewed on some beef jerky and took an occasional drink of water. After he had eaten, he picked up a dry tree limb and began to carve with his pocketknife. It was such a pleasure giving those children a carved piece, and he had better keep his supply up. When he left home, he thought he would be giving up carving for a long while—at least until he was settled down again. He sat there for twenty minutes or so and carved out another small animal to add to his supply. When the animal was finished, Jed put away his pocketknife, went to the horses, and put the carved animal in the pack. Taking the horses one at a time, he tightened their cinches and put the bridle on his riding horse, and they were soon back on the road.

The afternoon went well, but he kept watching the sky to the west. The clouds seemed to be building and getting darker. If this continued, there would be a thunderstorm that evening. Close to evening he passed through the little community of Posey. It was so small that they didn't have a livery stable. He hoped he could make the next town, which he was told was another five miles down the road.

It was getting darker, so he put the horses into a trot, which they maintained for nearly two miles. They pulled up in front of the livery barn just as it started to rain. Luckily for Jed, there was room for his horses and a place for him to roll out his bedroll for the night. He got the horses unloaded and into stalls and gave them hay. He inquired of the liveryman of a place where he might get something to eat.

The liveryman recommended a good one just across the street and a couple of doors down.

Jed pulled his hat down tight to keep it from blowing

off and headed out into the rain. The restaurant was pleasant, and the food was really good. When he finished eating, he headed back to the livery stable. It was still raining fairly hard. When he got back to the barn, he put his bedroll on one of the bed frames that had ample straw on it to make it really comfortable. It wasn't long before he was fast asleep. Jed had a comfortable night's rest. The next morning, it had stopped raining, but there were still heavy clouds around.

Jed went back to the eatery for breakfast and then saddled his horses and loaded the packhorse. It started to sprinkle as he was getting ready to leave. He stood in the doorway for a few minutes and studied the sky. He decided to head down the road. He put the canvas over the packsaddle and tied it down. He put on his rain slicker, mounted, and headed down the road.

Throughout the day, there was a light rain, but Jed was able to stay dry. At noon, he stopped at a grove of trees along the road and ate some more jerky. He put some beans and water in a sealable container to soak until evening, and then he would put them on the fire to cook.

When he made camp that night, the clouds had pretty well cleared from the sky. He readied the horses for the night and started a fire. The wood was a little damp, but after a while, it was burning well enough to put the beans on. In his small pan, he boiled some rice and then fried some bacon. The rice and bacon made for a nice meal.

About two hours after dark, he checked on the beans and found them to be getting tender. He banked his fire and crawled into his bedroll. Before the fire would burn out, the beans would be done. He slept well, waking just once during the night, and he could hear the crunch as the horses cropped grass. He could appreciate good horses, and if there was anything amiss in the area during the night, they would whinny and wake him up.

In the morning, the birds were chirping, which woke him up. It had just started to get light. For fifteen minutes, he contemplated his day. The best he could figure out was that the town of O'Fallon was just a short distance from where he was camped. By noon, he would be at the Mississippi River. Jed had never seen it before and was eager to see a really big river. He would take a ferry across, and then he would see the largest town ever to his way of thinking.

He crawled out of his bedroll, got dressed, and checked his beans. They had finished cooking, and with the bacon, they were delicious. He decided to eat the leftover rice from the night before and some of the beans. The fire had gone out during the night, and he rekindled his fire. It didn't take long for the beans to warm up. In short order, Jed had finished his breakfast and cleaned things up. He got the horses ready and loaded and was on the road. After two miles, he was going down the main street in O'Fallon. From there, it was fifteen more miles to the Mississippi River.

About two miles short of the river, Jed stopped for lunch. He had purposely put the container with the beans next to the horse's hide to keep them warm. They were warm enough to eat anyway. After the horses had rested, and he had eaten, Jed tightened the cinches and headed for the river.

What a sight the Mississippi River was! Jed had never seen that much water in one place. The small lakes back home were nothing compared to this. Wow! It took a little while to locate the ferry and get across. The horses were a little fussy while boarding, and he had to stay with them and talk to them to keep them calm. After leaving the ferry, they took the riverbank road up into the city of St. Louis. Wow! Jed had never seen so many horses and buggies and wagons in his entire life—and to see them all at once in one place.

Jed saw an honest-looking man walking along the street. He pulled up his horses and asked the man for directions to head west out of the city.

The man was very helpful and gave him good directions.

Jed asked how things were in the big city.

The man said that since the cholera had subsided, things were going really well.

Jed hadn't heard of cholera, and he asked how it affected those who got it.

The man said that people were dying at the rate of up to one thousand people each day. All work stopped except for building caskets and digging graves. But now that it was over, all seemed well.

Jed thanked the man for his friendship and the directions and asked the man if he had any young children. The man looked at him kind of funny and then said he did.

Jed asked how many.

The man said he had two young girls and one little boy.

Jed dug into his pack and took out two carved birds and one animal and gave them to the man.

The man thanked Jed and said he knew his children would be very happy with them.

Jed started his horses up the street and gave the man a hearty wave goodbye. He followed the instructions he had been given, and in less than an hour, he was on the outskirts of town. It interested to him see the big city. He saw all the businesses in the downtown area, and all of the homes were so close together. They didn't even have room for a barn to keep a cow, pigs, or even a few chickens. He wondered how they could exist without those necessities. He just shook his head and wondered.

Homes with barns and small fields had gotten farther apart, and he started to look for a place where he could camp for the night. It wasn't long before Jed came to a place that looked promising. It was a little higher than the road, and it had a group of trees and some brush along one side. There also was a little trickle of water coming down through the trees. Jed thought this was a nice place that gave him privacy as well. Jed knew it would be great place to camp.

He unloaded the horses, took them to water, and then tethered them out in the grassy area to graze. He started a small fire to warm up the beans. He also had some dried fruit that Elizabeth had sent with him. He decided to do something special with the dried fruit. He took his small saucepan, put in some dried fruit, added some water and a little sugar, and set it near the fire to simmer while he ate his beans. After they had simmered for forty-five minutes, he added a little cold water and began to eat the fruit. They really tasted good for a change.

After he had eaten, he washed up his utensils, banked his fire, and crawled into his bedroll. It wasn't long before he was asleep. About two hours later, he was awoken by the clattering of his cooking gear. He sat up, reached into his pants, and lit a match. In the darkness, he could see two shining eyes looking at him. A raccoon had been rummaging around in his food pack. Jed quickly scared off the raccoon by throwing a couple of chunks of wood at him. Jed stoked up the fire again, got back into bed, and went back to sleep.

Jed was awakened by the chirping of the birds in the trees at first light. This was his signal to be up and at it. He followed his morning routine of breakfast, watering the horses, and saddling and loading. About an hour later, he came to another big river. He asked a man walking along the road what river it was.

The man said it was the Missouri River, which dumped into the Mississippi River just north of St. Louis. Jed was fortunate that the road he was on led him to the ferry. He didn't have as much trouble loading the horses on this ferry as he did on the ferry crossing the

Mississippi River. He guessed they were getting used to things. He had the feeling that his horses trusted him since they were together twenty-four hours each day, never being very far apart—not even at night.

After leaving the ferry, it was a steady uphill trek for an hour. At the top, Jed pulled over for the noon rest. After staking the horses out to graze, he started a small fire and fried some bacon and cooked a little rice. He rested for a while after eating.

As Jed sat in the shade of a large sycamore tree, he picked up a dry stick, studied it for a few minutes, and decided to carve a bird. He shaped it like a cardinal. It had the feather top notch on top on its head and looked very real. These animals and birds he carved were one or two inches in size. It relaxed Jed to carve. After he finished his cardinal, he got the horses, put away his bird and his lunch things, and tightened the cinches. He was back on the road.

Jed entered an area of small rolling hills. He was amazed at the beauty he saw. The trees were so beautiful and green. He thought about the beauty of the earth, and he was enjoying it. In the middle of that afternoon, he arrived in O'Fallon, Missouri. As he rode through town, he enjoyed seeing all the stores. Jed was amazed at how many saloons there were in these towns. He had never been in a saloon before and had no desire to do so. He had never heard of any good coming out of one. There always seemed to be a hitching rail in front with a whole bunch of horses tied there. The men he had spoken to about saloons said the men went there to enjoy themselves. He thought, *"If that is enjoyment, I don't want any"*.

Toward evening, he came to the little community of Wentzville. It was a quiet place, and he supposed it was different because of the nationality of the people who had settled there. Jed knew when one or two families would find ground they liked, they would stop and build homes. A short while later, other families would come across people speaking their language and want to be close to them. Communities of the same nationality would form. They seemed to be a friendly sort, and as he passed by, they would wave and say hello.

After another hour's ride, he found a nice camping spot to spend the night. It had water, green grass, trees, and bushes. He went through his routine of unloading the horses and caring for them. He started a fire to prepare something to eat. After eating, he had some time to kill before he got into his bedroll. He took out his sharpening stone and sharpened his pocketknife. He found a nice piece of wood and decided it would make a good raccoon. His hands got busy, and it wasn't long before he had two beady eyes looking up at him. He was amused at the expressions he was able to put in the faces of his carvings. It seemed that each piece of wood had some animal or bird inside of it that wanted to get out. When he finished his raccoon, he put it away, banked his fire for the night, and turned in.

The next morning, he could hear drips hitting the canvas that covered his bedroll. He slowly pulled back the canvas and saw a light rain falling. Jed thought it might turn out to be a miserable day. Jed was in the habit of taking care of things before going to bed and was prepared to face a storm in the morning. He dressed, put on his boots and rain slicker, and crawled out into the dampness of the morning. He uncovered the dry wood he had stashed and started a fire. It wasn't long before he smelled the bacon frying. What a sweet aroma it was.

Jed stirred up a little flour and baking powder and fried three pancakes. They were cooked in a little bit of bacon grease and were fried to perfection. He brought in the horses. They had found some shelter from the light rain and were not too wet. He had a cloth he had brought for this purpose and rubbed the horses down and saddled them. With all things properly packed, he swung into the saddle and moved out onto the road. The clouds were not heavy, and he really didn't expect much rain during the day. The horses were eager to move out and warm up from the cool rain.

The day went well, but there were periods of light rain. At noon, he found a thick grove of trees that offered shelter from the rain. The afternoon was uneventful. He hadn't even passed anyone on the road. Everyone seemed to be staying in where it was dry. That evening brought Jed into the small town of Williamsburg. There was a livery barn where he and his horses could stay dry. He was able to put up his horses and have nice place to lay out his bedroll.

Jed ate at a little eatery across the street from a saloon. He had taken a table that was near the front window. While he ate, he heard gunshots from across the street. Three men rushed out and mounted their horses. As the horses swirled away, two other men ran out and fired their guns at them. Two of the men fell from their saddles and landed in the mud. The third man got away.

Someone shouted that both men in the street were dead. Other men straddled their horses, and ten men went after the man who had gotten away. Jed had heard that there had been drinking and gambling in the saloon, and one man at the gambling table had been killed. Jed was so glad that he was an innocent bystander, and he didn't understand what men would do for fun!

After the town settled down, Jed headed back to the livery barn.

The liveryman hadn't been able to see what had happened, but Jed told him what little he had seen and heard. After they visited for a few minutes, Jed went over and laid out his bedroll crawled in, and quickly went to sleep.

The next two days passed without anything unusual happening. The rain stopped, and the skies were clear. With the sun out, it made each day something Jed looked forward to. The second evening found him near the town of Boonville. He camped just outside of town. His campsite was near a rushing stream that looked like it might have some fish in it. Jed dug into his pack and found his fishing line and hooks. He cut himself a willow for a pole, attached his line and a hook, found some grubs for bait under an old tree, and cast his line in the water.

In just a few minutes, there was a tug on his line. After a second tug, he jerked it out. Along with the line came a nice-sized trout. Jed thought if there was one fish, there ought to be another. So back in went his line, and a few minutes later, he had a second fish. Jed cleaned his fish and started a fire. He put some bacon fat in the frying pan, rolled the fish in flour, and placed them in the pan. He sprinkled them with a little salt, and in a few minutes, he turned them over. The fish turned golden brown and separated from the bones when he put them on his plate. As he sat down to eat, he thought about how lucky he had been in his travels.

Jed sat back and thought about his sister and her husband back in Illinois. He wondered how they were getting along. It would be about another month before their baby would be born. He wished he could be there to welcome the new little baby into this life. His thoughts went to his mother. What a brave woman she had been, having bid her husband goodbye as he set out to find gold and a new home for the family.

But what about his father? Was he doing well and taking care of himself? He had mentioned in his letter that he had met a family who lived in the little town where he got supplies. He would go to church with them on Sundays. He enjoyed the church and the people. The family would always invite him over for Sunday dinner. They had four daughters and two sons. The oldest daughter was Jed's age, and the youngest daughter was five years old. He was hoping to buy property near them. He wanted to build a home for his family. Jed knew it would be at least three or four months, and maybe longer, before he would find him.

It was well after dark when he crawled into his bedroll and fell asleep.

Morning arrived with the chirping of birds in the trees. Jed got up quickly, fixed a breakfast of bacon and pancakes, washed his dishes, and stored them away. He loaded the horses and headed down the road as the sun came up. Jed knew it was going to be a beautiful day.

The horses walked a little faster each day and got in a few more miles. This gave Jed a good feeling about the trip he was undertaking.

Jed stopped for a short while at the Lamine River and had lunch. There wasn't a ferry available to cross, but he rode along the river to find where others had crossed. The water didn't look very deep, but quicksand in the river could suck a horse down and drown them all. After going upstream, he turned back down and searched for a safe place to cross. Jed finally found what he needed. A small road led down to the water and came up on the other side. He must have missed a turn on the main road. Jed slowly put the horses into the water, and they waded across with no difficulties. Not long after that, he came across a road that was used more.

Jed passed a number of small farms that appeared to be quite prosperous. A mile or two down the road, he came upon a wagon that had broken down. A father and mother with two young boys had gone to town for supplies and were returning to their home. The reach in the wagon had broken and had turned the rear wheels loose, and they had come out from underneath the wagon box. One child had been thrown from the wagon and had broken his arm. The other child was bruised and crying. The father and mother were shaken up, and the father was checking what he could do to fix the wagon and get his family home.

Jed dismounted and talked with the farmer. Jed had done some wagon work while serving as an apprentice, and he knew exactly what needed to be done. He took his ax out and cut down a small tree. He cut the length he needed and returned with it. The team was removed from the wagon and tied to a small tree.

Jed went to work shaping a new reach, which runs between the front and rear axles of the wagon to hold the wagon together. It didn't take Jed long to shape a new one. The next problem that Jed had was to get the wagon box up in the air so they could move the rear wheels and reach into place. Jed returned to the stand of trees and cut two more pieces, one to be a long lever and the other the vertical block to pry over.

The mother helped steady the box, and the farmer

moved the rear wheels into place while Jed lifted the box with the lever. The wagon was soon back together.

The farmer hitched the team of horses back to the wagon, and the family was ready to head home. They were so thankful to Jed for his great help, and they invited him to stay and eat with them. Jed rode alongside the wagon and talked to them as the wagon rumbled along.

When they got to the little farm, the little boy's broken arm was examined. They found it to be in proper alignment, but it needed a splint to protect it. Jed immediately went to work cutting one. In a few minutes, he had it ready to place.

The mother wrapped the arm, placed the splint, and wrapped it again. The pain was beginning to subside, and the boy felt better. Jed remembered his carvings and selected one for each little boy. When he presented them to the children, they were excited and hugged Jed.

The parents were so pleased, and the mother prepared a light meal.

As they started to eat, the farmer said, "We were so busy fixing the wagon and getting home that we didn't introduce ourselves properly. And we don't know your name. My name is Jasper Aikens, my wife is Hannah, and our two boys are Jimmy and Johnny. And your name is?"

Jed answered, "My name is Jed Sandalin. I am very happy to meet you folks. I'm sorry it had to be like this."

The boy with the broken right arm struggled to feed himself but did not complain.

After supper, Jasper said he needed to take care of the livestock and milk the cow.

Jed offered to help.

Hannah said, "You have been such great help to us today. Why don't you stay with us tonight, and you can be back on the road in the morning. We don't have any more beds in the house, but I'm sure you can find it comfortable with your bedroll on some hay in the barn."

Jed didn't take long to make up his mind. He said, "You're just like family, and I would be glad to take you up with that offer." He went with Jasper and led his horses to the barn. He unsaddled them and put the packs in a dry, safe place.

Jasper told him to turn his horses out into the pen on the south side of the barn. When Jasper finished milking the cow, they fed the five hogs and a few chickens. They also gathered the eggs. With the eggs and a bucket of milk, they returned to the house.

Hannah strained the milk into crock jars, covered each with a cloth, and had Jasper take them out to cool in the springhouse.

While the men were doing the chores, Hannah had made a pudding and brought some fresh cream in from the springhouse. She made whipped cream for the pudding. They sat in the large room in the house and visited. They asked all about Jed, his family, and where was he going.

He asked they had come from and how long they had been in Missouri.

The little boys were starting to fall asleep on the floor, and Jed announced that he should go so he could get a good night's rest.

Hannah reminded them about the pudding and whipped cream. The boys brightened, and Jed said that it sounded wonderful. Hannah dished up the pudding with a generous portion of whipped cream on top. This made Jed miss his home even more.

When all had finished their pudding, Jed thanked Hannah for the special treat. He said good night and headed for the barn. Jed had a good feeling about helping a young family in need. He thought about the value of his three-year apprenticeship in woodworking. Jed found his bedroll, undressed, and slipped into bed. It was a little while before he fell asleep.

True to his role in life, the cocky rooster in the chicken house offered a wake-up call at first light. To Jed, it was sweet music to hear the crow of a rooster. Jed thought about what this day might bring. He heard the screen door open and knew Jasper was on his way to the barn to milk and to do his morning chores. Jed was rolling up his bedroll when Jasper came into the barn. "Good morning, Jasper."

Jasper responded, "Good morning there, young man."

Jed carried his bedroll over to his packs and saddles and stepped around Jasper as he put a little ground grain into the manger for the milk cow.

Jasper opened the door to let the cow into the barn

and said, "Looks like it is going to be a beautiful day. There doesn't seem to be a cloud in the sky."

"That will suit me just fine. I do enjoy a good clear day," Jed answered. "Is there anything I can do to help?"

"You remember where the grain bin is and how much grain we fed the chickens last night? I give the chickens about the same amount in the mornings. Also, you might check the amount of water in their watering pan. It needs to be at least halfway full to take them through the day."

Jed went to the grain bin, got the feed for the chickens, and went to the chicken house. He scattered the grain on the floor and checked the water. The pan was three-quarters full, which would be fine for the day. As Jed walked around the farmyard, he enjoyed what he saw. *Jasper must be a good man. Everything is neat and in good order.* He returned to the milking barn as Jasper finished milking the cow. Jasper turned the cow back out to the pasture and closed the door. Jasper suggested Jed throw a little hay over to his horses so they might eat while they went up to the house for breakfast.

Jasper had to stop at the springhouse to bring down some table scraps and a bucket of skimmed milk for the pigs. He said he would take the milk up to the house and bring back the hog feed. A few minutes later, Jasper fed the hogs by adding a gallon of ground grain into the milk in their trough.

On the way back to the house, Jasper told Jed that

he was able to purchase a small hand grinder to grind the grain. The animals got more out of ground grain than the whole grain. The grinder came with a pair of stones to make flour.

Jed marveled at how efficient Jasper and Hannah were and how neat their home was. He made a mental note of the things he saw. He would like to have a home and farm like theirs someday. They stopped at the springhouse, strained the milk, and put it in a crock jar. The jar was placed in a wooden trough of cold water. A trickle of cold spring water was flowing through the trough. They could put containers in the water and keep the milk and other foods cool.

Jed told Jasper how impressed he was with his efficiency.

Jasper looked up at Jed and smiled.

They stopped at a wash bench on the little porch and washed their hands and faces before entering the home. Hannah was busy getting breakfast on the table. She called out to Jimmy and Johnny to hurry.

As the boys came into the room, Jimmy apologized for being late. He said that getting dressed was harder with his arm in a sling.

Johnny had helped Jimmy put on his shirt and put the sling back in place.

Jed asked Jimmy how his arm was feeling.

Jimmy said it felt pretty good, but it hurt a few times during the night. He thought it was starting to get better.

They all sat down at the table, and Jasper asked if Hannah would say grace.

Hannah offered a short and sweet prayer to thank their heavenly Father for the food and for Jed's help. "May Jed be protected as he travels this day. Amen!"

Jed had to hold back his tears. He thanked Hannah for her thoughtfulness. Jed noticed the nice breakfast on the table. *Hot biscuits, fried eggs, bacon, gravy, and milk? Wow. This is great.*

The conversation centered on the many things that lay ahead of Jed and the experiences that he might have.

When they finished, Jed thanked Hannah for the wonderful breakfast and told them he had to get his horses and things ready to get on the road.

Jasper offered to help Jed get his horses packed and ready. The two men headed to the barn. The horses were caught, saddled, and loaded. The two men walked back to the house, and Hannah and the boys came out to say goodbye. Hannah handed a cloth bag to Jed.

"What's this?" Jed asked.

Hannah told him it was some extra biscuits and some strips of bacon. She had fixed extra so he would have some to take with him. She gave Jed a hug and said she had never met anyone who seemed so much like a brother to her. She had tears in her eyes.

This show of affection prompted the boys to hug Jed as well. They also thanked him for the carved animals.

Jed turned to Jasper, clasped his hand, and thanked him for his hospitality and friendship.

Jasper said, "You need not thank us! It was you who helped us when we were in such a bad fix. What we have done for you does not really cover what we owe you. If you ever come by this way again, promise that you will stop for a visit."

Jed promised that he would. He walked around his horse, stepped up into the saddle, waved goodbye, and headed up the lane. He heard the little boys calling goodbye to him as he turned onto the road.

4

The next day, the sun was well up in full view as Jed continued his westward journey. He was reviewing his experience with the Aikens family the day before. They were so like his family, with an air of kindness and love about them. Jed thought it would be great if the world were filled with people like that!

A rabbit jumped out of the grass ahead of the horses and scampered across the road. It startled the horses, and they shied sideways on the road and almost threw him out of the saddle. He realized his mind had been too far away from business. He calmly spoke to the horses, patting Blaze on the neck and assuring him that it was just a silly rabbit. As he rubbed the horse's neck, he could feel the tension leaving.

In a few minutes, things were back to normal. In a little over an hour, he forded another stream. He stopped the horses in the middle and let them drink. He also took out his own canteen and had a drink.

When the sun was straight up, he made a rest stop.

A small clump of trees offered shade and grass. He tied the horses so that they could graze and loosened the cinches. He took out the bag with the biscuits and bacon and found a note that expressed again Hannah's thanks for his help. He thought, *What a sweet woman she is.* He took out a biscuit, put a strip of bacon in the center, and began to eat. It tasted so good. The biscuits tasted as good cold as they did when they were fresh out of the oven.

After his second biscuit with a strip of bacon, he settled back to rest. He thought of the little boys, which prompted him to sit up and reach for a piece of wood. He took out his pocketknife and begin to carve. Seeing the rabbit on the road gave him an idea. His hands worked smoothly and quickly, and a rabbit came to life. In less than half an hour, the rabbit was finished. It was time to get back on the road.

Jed went to the horses, put away the lunch bag, and stowed the rabbit with the other carved animals. He tightened the cinches, took a drink from his canteen, and stepped into the saddle. His afternoon went well, and the horses kept up a good pace.

Toward evening, he passed through the little community of Mayview. A few dogs came out, wagging their tails and barking, but the horses didn't seem to mind. The sun was below the horizon as Jed started looking for a campsite. Up ahead, he saw a small ravine with trees and a stream meandering down the middle. It looked inviting.

He rode up the ravine about two hundred feet and

found a place where he could have privacy for his camp. The horses were unloaded and tethered out to graze. He didn't bother building a fire that evening. It was warm enough, and he still had a couple of the biscuits and some bacon to eat. They would certainly taste better if they were eaten before they dried out. He had a cold camp that night. He gathered a little wood and piled it close to where he would make a small fire to cook breakfast. He laid out his bedroll, undressed and crawled in.

As he waited for sleep to overtake him, his mind wandered to his father. *Where is he? What is he doing? How is he? I wonder if he has grown a beard like most men do when living alone out in the wild.*

At first light, Jed's natural alarm went off. The birds were singing in the trees. He quickly got out of bed, dressed, and rolled up his bedroll. He went to the pack and dug out the things for pancakes and bacon. He got a little fire burning, fried the bacon, and saved some of the grease.

When Jed finished eating, he cleaned his utensils and packed them away. He went for the horses, took them to water, and saddled and loaded the packhorse. He mounted up and was back on the road.

Jed's day went well, and he stopped once for lunch and to rest the horses. He met quite a few people on the road that morning. Some would give a hearty hello, and others would just kind of grunt and nod their heads.

That afternoon, he passed through Independence, Missouri. He had heard stories about how the Mormons had been mistreated there, and he couldn't understand why that would be so. It seemed so unfair.

A few miles north of Independence, he decided to spend the night. Jed went about his routine of setting up camp and fixing supper. During the night, he was awakened by the sound of gunshots. He sat up in his bed and listened. He heard shouting and horses pounding down the road. Jed felt relief in knowing that his camp was a little off the road. When it was quiet, he went back to sleep. After breakfast and packing, he was back on the road.

About a quarter of a mile down the road, Jed came upon a man walking toward him. Jed stopped and asked the man what had happened in the night.

The man looked at him and asked who he was and why he was asking.

Jed explained that he was camped up the road and was awakened in the night by gunshots, yelling, and horses.

The man told him that someone had tried to steal some of his horses. The horses were running around the corral and whinnying. He jumped out of bed, grabbed his gun, ran to the door, and fired a couple of shots. He yelled at the thieves, and they jumped on their horses and left.

Jed told him he was glad they didn't get anything, wished the man well, and headed down the road. He decided to be more careful and keep his pistol under his pillow at night. The area around Independence—with Kansas City to the west and Gladstone to the north—was more densely populated. With the greater population, he was likely to come across people who might be up to no good.

He decided to look for a stable, a livery barn, or a farmer's barn to stay in at night. That would give him a little more protection. He would just need to keep his eyes open for safer places to stay.

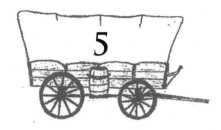

A **few more** miles down the road, Jed was surprised to come to a large river. A ferry had just returned bringing a couple of wagons across. Jed asked the operator what river it was.

The man looked at him with surprise and told Jed it was the Missouri River.

Jed told him that he was from Illinois and was not familiar with how that river flowed through the country. He had already crossed it twice before.

The man asked where he was headed.

He told him he was headed up to Omaha and hoped to join a wagon train and cross the Great Plains to the west. He explained his hope of finding his father.

The man asked if he had any idea where his father was.

Jed told him about the letter and how he thought he was somewhere in Arizona.

The ferryman told Jed he would like to wait a little

while in hopes of another customer or two before crossing the river again.

Jed told him that would be OK. He would just tie his horses up in the shade and wait. When Jed was about to sit down, he noticed a nice stick. He picked it up, studied it for a little bit, and decided to carve a blue heron. He had seen quite a few of these birds around the marshes and streams, and he sat down and began to whittle.

It was not long before a lone rider came up and spoke to the ferry operator. Evidently, a lone rider never made it worthwhile for a trip across. The rider and the ferryman visited for a few minutes, and then a wagon came down the road.

As Jed finished carving the bird, the ferryman waved for him to board the ferry. He jumped up, untied his horses, and led them aboard. He noticed a man, a woman, and a small child on the wagon. Jed made conversation with the family. The little girl was sweet. Jed had a natural love for children and teased her. He had her laughing and playing with him. He reached into his pocket and took out the blue heron. He asked if she knew what a blue heron was.

She did. At their home, down below the barn they had a pond and often there would be a blue heron there trying to catch polliwogs or little catfish to eat.

Jed handed her the carved bird.

She admired it. When he asked if she would like to have it, she squealed with delight and asked her mother if it would be OK.

Her mother said it would be fine.

The girl showed it to her father, and he looked it over.

The mother said, "Sarah, what do you tell this kind man?"

The little girl turned to Jed and said, "Thank you. Thank you!" She held the bird to her cheek.

Jed explained that Sarah was his mother's name and that he thought it was the most beautiful name.

Jed stepped back to his horses to assure them as the ferry bumped against the dock. The lone rider unloaded first, then the wagon, and then Jed and his horses.

The wagon turned onto a road heading east along the river. The little girl was standing next to her mother and waving at Jed.

Jed stepped into the saddle and headed up the road. *That was a nice little family.* The road took him over some rolling hills and away from the river bottomland. He passed by a lot of small farms, and then he came to a small community where the homes were quite close together. It amazed him that people could live so close together and not raise their own animals for meat and have gardens. He thought, *What is this world coming to?*

The amount of traffic on the road was considerable for that time of day.

As Jed passed the little town of Gladstone, the sun told him it was time to take a break, have some lunch, and rest the horses. A little farther up the road, he found a small grove of trees with plenty of grass and a small pond with clean-looking water. He stepped down from his horse and led both horses to the water. When they had their fill, Jed loosened the cinches on the saddles and staked them out to graze.

He decided to eat some beef jerky and dried fruit for lunch. He had plenty of cool water in his canteens. As Jed ate, his mind began to think about Elizabeth and Jonathon back in Illinois. He surely hoped things were going well for them. He really loved his sister and thought Jonathon was a good husband. When he found his father, the two of them could build a nice home for Elizabeth and her family and then a smaller home for himself and his father to live in. His father certainly wouldn't spend all his time at his mining claim.

Two young boys came racing their horses up the road, putting the whip to them, and trying to get all the speed out of horses. Jed could tell it was a race for fun. Jed watched them until they went over a small rise in the road. He remembered when he used to race his horse with a neighbor before he took the apprenticeship with the carpenter. He took another drink of water and looked for a piece of wood.

With knife in hand, Jed went to work, but he didn't have a clue about what to carve. As the shaving started to fall away, it came to him. He would carve a wild turkey. A day or two back, he had seen a flock of wild turkeys in a field. The head gobbler looked so proud with his tail feathers all fanned out and his head tucked back. That turkey just strutted around, guarding his flock and daring anything to molest his hens or their young chicks. After about thirty minutes, the turkey was finished. It was time to get back on the road. He put his turkey in the pack with the other carvings and put the remaining jerky away. He tightened the cinches, put away the tethering ropes, stepped into the saddle, and headed north.

The afternoon was uneventful. He passed a number of people with spirited horses pulling buggies, wagons, and all kinds of loads. He watched the people as they passed by. Late in the afternoon, he hailed a kind-looking man who was coming toward him. The man stopped, and Jed asked if there was a livery stable up ahead.

The man explained that there was a livery barn in the small town of Dearborn, which was about three miles up the road. The man asked where Jed was heading, and Jed told him of his intentions. The man told him to watch himself since a couple of groups of unruly young men were roaming the roads and trying to do harm to unsuspecting travelers. He told Jed that he should get off the road and try to hide if he saw a questionable group approaching. The man wished him well and went on down the road.

The time went fast, and Jed arrived in Dearborn. It was a nice little town with stores, an eatery, a saloon, and a livery barn. Jed pulled up in front, and the proprietor came out to greet him. The man asked if he would like to put his horses up for the night. Jed explained his intentions and asked the price. It would be one dollar per horse, which would include hay. Jed asked about a place to roll out his bedroll.

The proprietor had a place, and there would be no extra charge.

Jed accepted the deal and was shown the stall for the horses, a place to put his saddles and pack, and the spot for his bedroll. There was already hay in the manger.

After Jed put away his things, he asked the man about the best place to eat in town.

He told Jed the one he liked best and reminded him to tell the waitress that old Charlie over at the stable had sent him over. "They'll set you a good meal and will give me a cup of coffee for sending you over." Charlie winked and smiled.

Jed headed over to the eatery and was greeted by a jolly and chubby young waitress. There were only a few people in the establishment, and after she had taken his order, she came back and sat down at the table across from him.

Katy's mother was the owner and the cook.

Jed told her that Charlie had sent him over, and Katy laughed and told him that Charlie was her uncle. She really loved him. Katy's mother called to Katy when his order was ready. She jumped up and went to get it. She brought it all back on one large tray and set it all out in front of Jed. He had steak, potatoes, apple pie, and a large glass of milk.

Katy sat down on the other side of the table and asked, "Does it taste all right?"

Jed smiled. "It tastes just the way my mother used to fix it."

Katy looked at her mother and gave her a wink and a little nod. Katy asked a lot of questions.

Jed's answers were short because he was really enjoying his meal. It was hard to eat and talk at the same time.

Katy told him about her family and many other things.

Jed listened and smiled as he finished the pie and the cold milk. He pushed himself back in his chair and said, "That's the best meal I have had since I left Illinois."

That broadened the smile on Katy's face, and she thanked Jed for the compliment.

Jed paid for his meal and asked what time they opened in the morning.

Katy said that they were always open by six thirty.

Jed told her he would see her again in the morning and headed back to the livery stable. He talked to Charlie for a few minutes before going to his bedroll. Jed slept very well, and he heard a rooster crowing at first light.

It was too early for the eatery to be open, but Jed got up anyway. He took his horses to the watering trough, saddled them, and got the packs on. He was ready to be on the road after breakfast. He looked across the street, and people were moving around in the eatery. He figured they must be open. He walked over and went in.

Katy was taking a food order from a customer. She looked up and gave him a little wave.

Jed felt good to be recognized.

Katy took the order to the kitchen and then came to Jed's table. "What are you going to have this morning, young man?"

"I believe I'll have biscuits with gravy, two fried eggs, a couple strips of bacon, and a glass of cold milk."

Katy looked at him for a minute and said, "No coffee?"

Jed explained that he had never acquired a taste for it. He drank milk when he could get it or water, and he was happy with that.

She said, "You are different, aren't you?"

Jed told her he was very happy with the way he was. He gave her a smile, and she went to take his order to the kitchen.

In ten minutes, she was back with his breakfast. There were two very large biscuits, a plate filled with rich, thick gravy, two eggs, and bacon.

"Wow. It looks great," he said.

She said, "I think you'll enjoy it too." She went to wait on another customer.

Jed enjoyed his big breakfast. He thought, *If I ate like this all of the time, I would be chubby like Katy.* That was no put-down of Katy; it was a compliment to her mother.

Katy came over and asked, "Did you enjoy your breakfast?"

He said, "I certainly did, and it was almost too much. I am stuffed." He gave her the money for the meal plus a tip, thanked her for the two wonderful meals, and said, "Please tell your mother I really enjoyed the good food. She's a great cook."

Katy thanked him and wished him well in his travels.

Jed crossed the street, finished getting his horses ready, stepped into the saddle, and rode out into the street. He headed north for another long day in the saddle.

After three hours, he noticed a small group of men on horses. They were headed his direction. His intuition warned him these might be the ruffians he had been warned about. He quickly studied the area. A couple hundred feet ahead of him, there was a lane that turned off on the right. It looked like it led toward a farmer's place. He hurried his horses, and they turned down the lane. He stopped behind some bushes and talked softly to the horses to keep them quiet.

When the riders passed by, he could hear them cursing and threatening anyone who would go near them. One of the men said they were going to find themselves a Mormon and have a hanging.

Jed thought, *How low and dumb can a man get? They must have been drinking booze.* Their words were slurred, and they slouched in their saddles. They were dirty and very unkempt.

After fifteen minutes, he felt safe enough to go back to the road. He looked to the south, but the men were nowhere in sight, which gave him relief. As he headed north, he thought he better look behind him often to be sure the men didn't turn around and come back in his direction. If the men came up behind him, he wouldn't know it until it was too late to find cover.

From what Katy had told him, he should be pretty close to St. Joseph, Missouri. It was a larger town, and he would have more protection in the city.

As he went up over a rise in the road, he could see the city off through the trees. This gave him relief. Jed entered the city and headed up a street. He didn't know how to get through town. He stopped the first person who looked trustworthy and asked directions.

The man was kind and gave him careful directions that would be easy to follow.

Jed thanked him, and they each went on their way. It was well past noon, and his breakfast had worn off. He needed to take a rest and eat. The horses also needed a rest. On the outskirts of town, he stopped under some trees. He staked the horses out so that they could graze a little and rest their legs. He dug into his pack for some jerky. There wasn't very much left, and his bacon supply was getting low. He needed to stop at a store soon to replenish his food supply.

After eating and carving another bird, he was ready to hit the road. The horses needed water, but it wasn't long before he saw a small creek. He pulled over and let them drink. The afternoon went well, and he only passed a few people on the road. They were kind and spoke to him as they passed by.

As the sun was getting low, he was concerned about his safety. He looked for something special and noticed a little hill on his left. It dropped away on the west side.

It looked pretty good, and the ground dropped away to form a little basin. It was low enough that a man or a horse would not be seen from the road. A little stream passed by on the lower side. It looked to be ideal. He decided it would work for him.

He stepped down from his horse, unsaddled, took the horses to drink, and staked them out to graze. As he was finishing with the horses, he noticed a couple of grouse near the edge of the basin. That looked like a pretty good supper. He eased back to his pack and slowly pulled out his rifle. It was a small caliber, and it wasn't really loud when it fired. The sound wouldn't carry very far with the number of trees around. Jed edged over to a tree with a fork in it, levered a shell into the chamber, aimed at the head of one of the grouse, and slowly pulled the trigger. The gun went off, and so did the bird's head. It began flopping in the grass as the other grouse took flight over the little hill. He put his gun back in the pack, picked up the bird, dressed it out, and hung it from a branch. He made a small campfire with dry wood that wouldn't create much smoke. Any smoke would disappear in the leaves of the trees.

Jed cut two small limbs with forks on them, stuck them in the ground on each side of the fire, and got a straight stick to use as a spit to roast the grouse. The fire was putting off plenty of heat. He put the grouse on the spit and placed the spit in the forks. In a couple of minutes, the grouse sizzled and popped.

Jed turned his attention to getting the rest of the things ready for his supper. He sprinkled some salt and pepper on the bird and turned it over. He took out his frying pan, mixed up some flour with water, baking powder, and a touch of salt, molded four round balls of dough, placed them in the greased frying pan, and placed the frying pan on some rocks near the fire. The biscuits would soon start to rise and bake. Every couple of minutes, he turned the roasting bird to keep it from burning.

The trick was to keep the fire at just the right temperature for the roasting bird and his biscuits. In about twelve minutes, his biscuits were evenly browned, and he set them back to stay warm. The meat on the legs and wings of his bird were starting to pull away from the bones. The breast area needed more time to cook.

In a few minutes, he used his fork to take some meat from one of the legs, blew on it to cool it, and then took a bite. The meat was tasty. He worked slowly on the meat from the legs and wings until he had cleaned them. He also ate a biscuit with bacon grease instead of butter. It tasted good, but it was not quite as good as the meals at Katy's restaurant.

When the breast was cooked, he set the whole bird on the spit to cool. After it had cooled, he made himself a sandwich from some of the breast meat. It was really good, and he enjoyed it. He put the other two biscuits and the balance of the breast meat away for tomorrow's lunch. It was dark, and he went to sleep.

At first light, his alarm—the birds—went off. He thought about the day ahead of him. According to the information he had gained from people he had met on the road, he wouldn't make the Iowa border that day. He rolled out of his bed, dressed, and got his fire going. This morning, he would have fried bacon and pancakes.

He finished eating, cleaned up his utensils, put out his fire, and covered it with dirt. Jed went to his horses, took them to water, and saddled them up. With the packs on and tied down, he was ready to be on the road.

As he stepped into the saddle, he thought, *This was a right good camp. I wish all of my campsites were as good as this one.*

6

The rock and sway of the saddle almost put Jed to sleep. He didn't see a soul on the road for nearly two hours. He finally saw an elderly man coming toward him. The man was driving a small team of blacks on an old wagon. Jed stopped his horses in front of the old man. This signaled that he would like to talk for a minute.

The old man pulled up and stopped, looking at Jed for a minute or so. He finally said, "Where ya headin', young feller?"

Jed told him of his intentions of going on up to Omaha to try to join up with a wagon train heading west and how he hoped to find his father who had gone west in search of gold about three years ago.

"Ya don't say, about three years ago now, ya think?' the man asked.

Jed told him it was three years ago this spring.

"What was your father's name there, lad?"

"His name is Jacob Sandalin, goes by Jake," explained Jed.

The old man scratched his head. "Yes, I think I remember him passing by this way. He was riding a large pinto mare, leading a packhorse that looked a lot like yours there, Yes, I do remember him. I thought he was a good man. He said he had left his good wife, a teenage son, and an older daughter at home. I believe he said it was from back in Illinois. That's your daddy, you say? I'll declare, such a small world, ain't it?"

Jed was almost speechless. "Wow, you met my dad? This is great." Jed explained that they had received a letter from his dad a few months back and that he was somewhere in Arizona and had a good mining claim. He told the old man about his mother's death and his sister's marriage and how she was expecting a baby soon. He also explained that his dad's letter didn't say exactly where he was, but there were a couple of clues in his letter. "Yes, and I am that teenage son you referred to."

The old man tipped his hat and said, "I'm just as tickled as peach pie to meet you, son. What's your name?"

"Jeremiah Sandalin, but I go by Jed. What's your name?"

"Joseph Sippy. I go by Joe. People here abouts just refer to me as Old Joe, and that's fine with me."

Jed asked the old man how far it was to the next decent store.

"There's a little store up the road a short piece, but I

wouldn't buy any bacon from him. His bacon is always rancid and just not fit to eat. If I were you, I'd wait until the next store, which is ten or eleven miles up the road. He sells good bacon, and he doesn't charge an arm and a leg for it either."

Jed expressed his pleasure about meeting him and told Joe he needed to be moving on.

"It's been my pleasure to meet you, young un. You take care of yourself and tell that daddy of yours hello for me, won't ya?"

Jed assured him he would, tapped his horse with his heels, and headed on up the road. After a few minutes, Jed looked back toward the old man.

Old Joe was sitting sideways in the wagon seat and looking back at Jed.

Jed gave a wave of his hat, and the old man returned the wave.

The next couple of miles went fast because he had a destination that was in immediate reach. As he rounded a curve in the road, he saw the first store that Old Joe had told him about. It was a very run-down place to be sure. Even if old Joe hadn't told him about this place, he surely would not have stopped. He had another seven or eight miles to go to the next store.

In the next seven miles, he only saw one other man on the road. He was riding an old plow horse that really showed its age. He felt sorry for the old horse having to carry this heavyset man. The man kind of grunted when they passed each other. Jed had given the man a cheery hello, but the man hardly looked up.

At noon, Jed reined the horses off the road for a break. There was a fairly large pond on the right side of the road, and a few trees offered some shade. As the horses drank, Jed heard a lot of bullfrogs croaking, and he could see a few small catfish swimming among the cattails in the shallow water. When the horses had their fill, he led them over to some grass and tied them so they could graze. He took out the rest of the grouse and biscuits from last night's supper, sat in the shade, and ate.

When he was finished, he found a piece of wood and started carving. Because of the croaking frogs in the pond, that's what he decided to carve. He had never carved a frog before, but he had seen plenty of them in his life. The frog came easy for him. When the frog was finished, he put his knife back in his pocket, walked over to the packhorse, and put the frog in with the other carvings. He readied his horses, stepped up into the saddle, and went back on the road.

Jed figured it probably wasn't too much farther to the store. After a mile and a half, Jed came to a rise in the road and saw the store. Jed thought it was a nice-looking place! He could tell someone cared about life and the things around him. The store was neat, and on the front porch, there seemed to be a lot of merchandise and wares on display. It was obvious that the man stocked most of the things that people needed to buy, which made a lot of sense.

He pulled up in front and slowly eased out of the saddle. He tied his horses to the hitching rail and kept his eye on the merchandise. He loved seeing all the things that the store had to offer. He looked around a little a bit and then walked into the store. He was impressed by all the things that were there.

The proprietor greeted him with a cheery hello and a broad smile. "What can I get for you?"

Jed told him he was traveling west and needed a slab of bacon, a little flour, some dried fruit, and some beef jerky. "While you are getting that, I just might find something else to buy."

The storekeeper asked, "How big of a slab of bacon?"

"A small one because I am traveling alone."

"How much flour?"

Jed answered, "Five pounds will do."

The storekeeper had some dried apples, prunes, and peaches.

Jed looked in the small barrels. "I'll take a scoop of each."

"How much jerky would you like?"

Jed said, "A large scoop will do." A glass case on the counter had some fresh-looking rolls. "I don't believe I have ever seen bread rolls for sale in a store before. They look really good."

The storekeeper told him that his wife baked them nearly every morning, and the rolls were her specialty. He loved her rolls.

Jed told him he would take four.

The storekeeper took out the four rolls, wrapped them in paper, slid them into a paper bag, and rolled the top of the bag down tight.

Jed asked if he had a family

The clerk told him he had his wife and a twelve-year-old daughter. "Anything else I can get for you?"

Jed said he thought that was about all he could get into his pack.

The storekeeper told him his total was $8.45.

Jed paid the man and started to pick up his purchases.

The storekeeper told Jed he would help him out with his things. As they were walking out of the store, the storekeeper asked Jed where he was heading.

Jed explained all about his plans. As Jed was packing the supplies away, he asked the clerk about his daughter. Did she have anything special she really liked?

The man told him she loved birds, and cardinals were her favorite.

Jed looked into his pack, took out the cardinal he had carved a few days back, and handed it to the man. "Give this to your daughter as a gift from me."

The man admired it and thanked Jed for such a fine-looking bird.

Jed went around his horse and mounted.

The storekeeper wished him luck and a safe and successful journey.

Jed waved goodbye to the man and headed back to the road.

Jed guessed he would have another three hours on the road before would need to look for a camping place. His mind went to the bread rolls in his pack. They looked so good, and he was tempted to stop and eat one as he rode along. He decided he could wait until he stopped for the night.

The next three hours passed rather slowly. He only saw one wagon with a man and a woman. He had thought he would see a lot more wagons in Iowa. He kept his eyes peeled for a possible campsite. He finally found an area that looked good, but when he rode down into the area, it didn't appeal to him because there was no water.

After half a mile, he heard the trickle of a stream. He left the road and went up over a little hill, which was only about a hundred feet off the road. A stream fell down through some rocks, and there was plenty of room for the horses to graze, for his campfire, and for his bed. It was completely out of sight of the road.

Jed unsaddled the horses, led them to water, and staked them out to graze. He started his fire and fried some bacon. He used the last couple of strips from home and cut a couple of strips from the new slab. He also got out the fresh rolls. They sure looked good. When the bacon was done, he sliced one of the rolls in half, put a couple of strips of bacon between them, and started to eat. He fixed the other two strips of bacon in a roll, which made a good meal. The new bacon was really good. Old Joe had been right; the man sold good bacon and rolls. With a little time left before darkness, Jed carved another cardinal. He finished it up by the light of the campfire, put it away, and crawled into his bedroll. Sleep came quickly.

At first light, the birds woke him up. He thought for a few minutes and then rolled out of bed. He had bacon and pancakes. After cleaning up and packing things away, he went for the horses. He took them to water and then saddled and loaded the packs. With his routine down pat, things seemed to move along fast. Soon, he was back on the road. He estimated that he would cross into Iowa at noon.

Time went fast, and he only passed a couple of riders on horseback. The sun was about straight up when he saw a small sign on a post: "Entering the State of Iowa." He was rather excited to reach another milepost on his trip. He found a nice place to pull off the road for a rest and a bite to eat. There was water for the horses and grass. He ate one of the rolls and some dried prunes and peach slices. The dried peaches were much to his liking.

After drinking some cold water from his canteen, he was comfortable. He picked up the piece of wood he had found down by the creek. He looked it over and decided to carve a chipmunk holding a pine cone. It was his first chipmunk holding a pine cone. The chips flew, and he was engrossed in his work.

As he finished, a rough voice hollered, "What are you doing here, young man?"

Jed dropped his knife and the chipmunk and jumped up. "Who, uh, who are you?"

The man said, "I'm asking the questions. Who are you? And what are you doing here?"

Jed's voice was shaking, but he answered, "My name is Jed Sandalin, and I am resting my horses and taking a break myself. Am I doing something wrong?"

The man said, "I am not sure. Where did you come from—and where are you headed?"

Jed settled down some and answered, "I come from over in eastern Illinois, and I am headed west to Arizona to find my father."

"What proof do you have that you are telling the truth?"

Jed handed him the letter from his father.

The man read the letter and handed it back to Jed. "Which way did you come from?"

Jed explained that he had just come north from St. Joseph and was headed to Omaha to catch up with a wagon train.

Jed noticed a sheriff's badge under his leather vest. "Has something happened around these parts that you think that I might have been a part of?"

The sheriff answered, "Yes. A couple of hoodlums tried to steal some things from a poor farmer up the road. They hit him a couple of times and slapped his wife and threw her down on the floor of their little home. They took a few things but nothing major. Young man, you look to be honest, and I don't think you would ever give an old couple any harm."

Jed asked, "Will the couple be OK? Is there anything I could do to help them out?"

The sheriff said, "They were bruised up a little, but I think they will be able to manage OK."

Jed said, "I sure hate to hear things like that. Why can't people take care of themselves and not cause harm to innocent people?"

The sheriff looked Jed over for a minute and said, "I see you're not wearing a gun."

Jed said, "I have never carried a gun in a holster, and I hope I don't have to. I have no intentions of shooting at someone, but I guess if I had to protect myself or someone else, I would do it. I am a good shot, but I'm not fast at drawing a gun."

The sheriff chuckled and asked Jed about his knife and the carving.

Jed picked them up, put away his knife, and handed the carving to the sheriff.

The sheriff took the carving and looked it all over. "Hey, you do pretty good work there, my boy. What do you do with all of your carvings?"

Jed explained that mostly gave them to children.

The sheriff told Jed he had a young boy at home who was sick a lot and wasn't able to get out of the house much. The sheriff then asked if he might buy that chipmunk from him.

Jed explained that the chipmunk wasn't for sale, but he would be very happy to give the chipmunk to his son. Perhaps it would cheer up his son a little.

The sheriff smiled and told Jed that he would accept it as a gift for his son. He told Jed he must be on his way. He really needed to track down those two young hoodlums and make them pay. The sheriff stepped into his saddle, turned his horse, and headed to the road. He wished Jed a safe journey and warned him to keep an eye out for those two.

Jed put his lunch things away and took the horses

to water before getting on the road. The afternoon went well, but he did keep his eyes open to watch for those young men. He wondered what he would do if they came up to him along the way. The only thing he knew to do was play it by ear, be honest, and not to do anyone any harm if he could help it.

That evening, he found himself in Percival, Iowa. There was a small livery stable in town, and he decided to spend the night inside for a change.

The stableman was really just a young boy, probably three years younger than himself, but he seemed to know his business. Jed asked about a stable for the night, and the young man told him it was eighty cents for each horse with hay. Jed asked about a place to lay out his bedroll.

The young man told him that there were a couple of wooden bed frames in the back with straw-filled ticks. They made a comfortable bed, but that would be twenty cents extra.

Jed took him up on it and asked about a restaurant.

There was one just down the street.

Jed paid the boy, stabled his horses, and put his saddles and packs down by his bunk.

As he walked to the restaurant, he noticed that the sky had gotten pretty dark over on the west side of the Missouri River, which was about fifteen miles away. He saw some lightning. They would probably get a thunderstorm that night.

The restaurant was clean and tidy. An older lady took his order, and the food turned out to be good. It was not quite as tasty as the food where Katy worked. After he finished, he paid the waitress and walked back to the stable.

The clouds had rolled in, and the storm had arrived. He was really glad he wasn't camped out in the woods. As the storm blew in, it got dark fast. In about twenty minutes, the storm hit with a bolt of lightning and a loud clap of thunder. He hoped the barn would hold up.

As it started to rain, the young man closed the big sliding doors.

Another man came riding in and man asked to stable his horse and have a bunk. A lantern on the wall gave some light in the barn. The man unsaddled and rubbed down his horse.

Jed spoke to him, and they talked about the storm.

The middle-aged man was pleasant to talk to. He prepared his bed and crawled in. He had to be on the road at first light and was going right to sleep. Jed crawled into his own bed and listened to the rain pounding on the roof until he finally dozed off.

Jed awoke the next morning to the stirring of the middle-aged man. Jed asked why he was in such a hurry.

He was trying to catch a certain wagon train in Omaha before it pulled out. The wagons were due to leave tomorrow morning. In order to catch them, he had a day and a half's travel. He felt that he could make it, but he couldn't let any grass grow under his or his horse's feet. He just hoped that his horse would survive the trip.

Jed asked if he was going to eat before leaving.

The man informed had food in his saddlebags and would eat on the go. He rolled up his bedroll and saddled his horse. He opened the big door wide enough for his horse to walk through and came back for his horse.

Jed mentioned that he was also headed to Omaha. "Maybe I will see you up there."

The man led his horse out and headed up the road.

Jed was eager to get to Omaha to join a wagon train—but not at the expense of his horses.

7

J ed got dressed, walked over to the door, and looked
out. The rain had stopped, and there were only a
few clouds in the sky. It looked like it was going to be a
good day. He checked the hay supply, and the manger
was clean. He put more in for them. They nickered at
him as if they were saying thank you.

He rolled up his bedroll and placed it on the packs.
He would saddle the horses after he returned from
breakfast. It was nearly full light, and he walked to the
restaurant. He sat down at a table, and the waitress
took his order. He ordered biscuits, gravy, bacon, and
a glass of milk.

The waitress looked him and said, "You must still
be a growing boy."

He smiled and said, "I'm pretty much grown, but I
just like the finer things in life."

She chuckled and took his order to the kitchen.

A few minutes later, she brought his meal to him.
"Where are you heading so early in the morning?"

He briefly explained his plans.

Another customer walked in, and she went to take his order.

Jed paid for his meal, thanked her, and walked back to the stable.

He quickly saddled up, put the packs into place, lashed them down, and led his horses out in front. He stepped into the saddle, touched his heel to his horse's side, and headed up the road. The roads were a little muddy from the storm. The rain was being absorbed fairly quickly, and the horses were able to move along at a good pace.

After about two hours, Jed saw two or three covered wagons. This made Jed anxious. Where would they be heading? And would they be in the same wagon train that was heading out of Omaha? These were questions to ask when he caught up to the wagons.

An hour later, he caught up to them. The oxen pulling the wagons were moving slower than the horses. The wagon in the rear had just an older man walking alongside his oxen and a woman, no doubt his wife, sitting on the seat.

Jed stayed in pace with them for a few minutes, passed the time of day, and then moved on up to the next wagon. This wagon had a young man walking by his oxen and his young wife on the seat with a baby. Jed said hello and asked about their baby.

The mother responded, "It is a boy, and he is two months old."

Jed could tell that both parents were proud of their baby.

Jed moved up to the lead wagon and saw a middle-aged man walking beside his oxen. His wife and a young girl were on the wagon seat, and Jed guessed the girl was about thirteen years old. A boy on the opposite side of the wagon rode a horse. They also had a milk cow tied to the back of the wagon. Jed said hello and acknowledged the young girl and boy. He asked where they were headed.

The father said they were headed for Omaha and had hopes of signing on with a large wagon train headed for Utah.

"Are you folks Mormons?" Jed asked.

"Yes, and we are proud to say that we are."

Jed told them he was not a member, but he had been raised around Mormons and had great respect for them and their religion. "I am Jed Sandalin, and what are your names?"

The man said his name was Adam Myers, his wife was Trudy, their daughter was Priscilla, and their son was Jake.

Jed nodded to each as the father gave their names. "Young man, you have a great name. It is the same as my father's, and I have great respect for him."

Adam explained that the young man behind them was his younger brother Abe his wife, Joan, and baby, Ronald. The last wagon was his parents, Joseph and Ruby Myers.

Jed expressed his pleasure in meeting them. He said

that they might be with the same wagon train leaving Omaha because he was also headed west. He would be going south to Arizona to be with his father. Jed said he would move on and would look for them in Omaha. He moved ahead of them, and his horses settled into their normal pace. After he rounded a curve, he never saw them again.

An hour and a half later, he pulled off from the road for a rest and lunch.

He watered his horses, staked them out to graze, and sat down to eat. He had one of the good rolls, some jerky, and a few dried prunes. He had a drink of water and settled back to carve. He decided on a bullfrog this time. He hadn't carved one of those for a few days. A frog took a little less time because it didn't have as much detail.

When Jed finished the frog, he put it away and said, "Well, guys, are you ready to go again?"

The horses raised their heads and nickered at him.

Jed took that as a yes and got them ready to go.

That afternoon, he only passed a few people on horses and a wagon going in his direction. The wagon was a farmer heading to a neighbor's place. They had a brief conservation as he passed.

The sun reached the horizon, and Jed pulled over for the night. He cared for the horses, started a small fire, fried some bacon, and boiled rice. It wasn't much, but it satisfied his hunger. By the time Jed had put away his things, it was dark. He rolled out his bedroll and crawled in.

The birds awoke Jed in the morning. He was excited for his day. In less than three hours, he would be in Council Bluffs, Iowa. He would ferry across the river to Omaha and look for the Mormon camps. The wagons assembled there to form the trains that headed out over the plains.

He rolled out of bed, dressed, and rolled up his bedroll. He started a small fire to cook his bacon and pancakes. After he ate, he cleaned up, took the horses to water, and saddled them.

An hour after getting on the road, he passed four covered wagons. Their occupants were breaking camp and getting ready to get back on the road. Jed waved to them and kept on going down the road.

An hour later, the road dropped down to the Missouri River. He could see Council Bluffs on the east side of the river. Omaha was across the river. Jed was excited to be reaching the first major point on his trip. As he came into Council Bluffs, he saw a sign for the ferry, and he turned down the heavily traveled road.

In a few minutes, he was at the ferry landing. The ferry was just returning to the Iowa side. A couple of wagons and a man on a horse were waiting to cross. The ferry tied up to the landing and unloaded one wagon and two riders on horses.

The ferry operator signaled those waiting to come aboard. The man on his horse went on first, and the two wagons followed. Jed led his horses onto the ferry and tied them to the rail. As the ferry made its first small jerk in the water, the horse of the man up front started to act up. The horse tried to rear up a couple of times, but he was snubbed short and couldn't get his front feet very high. He jumped from side to side a couple of times and then settled down. The rider talked to his horse and rubbed his neck and shoulders. They were on the river for fifteen minutes.

Jed led his horses to the place where people waited to cross. He looked around for a local person. He needed to find out where the Mormon encampment was. He approached a man who was walking by and asked him how to find it.

The man was kind and explained how to get there.

Jed thanked him and headed out.

From the ferry to the encampment, it was about a forty-five-minute ride.

As Jed pulled into the staging area, he asked the first man he saw if he could direct him to the man in charge.

The man pointed out a tent and told Jed to ask for Brother Roberts.

Jed thanked him and headed over to the tent. When he arrived, he saw a couple of men talking. He stepped down from his horse and waited.

When the men finished their conversation, a man turned to Jed and asked if he could do something for him.

Jed said he was looking for Brother Roberts.

The man said, "Well, that's me—and who are you?"

Jed gave his name and said he was hoping to join up with a wagon train.

Brother Roberts asked if he was a Mormon.

Jed told him that he wasn't but had been raised around the Mormon people and respected them and their way of life.

Brother Roberts asked if he had any training with cattle, horses, oxen, or a trade.

Jed was pleased to tell him he had been raised on a farm and had completed a three-year apprenticeship in woodworking, carpentry, and building wagons.

Brother Roberts was impressed with his training and experience. He told Jed he was sure that his talent could be used. He asked when Jed would like to leave.

Jed told him that he was alone and wanted to leave as soon as possible.

Brother Roberts explained that he had a group of wagons that was nearly ready to leave. They were just waiting for a few more wagons and a few more provisions for the journey.

Jed explained that he had met four wagons, but he did not know their intentions. They would probably be pulling in later this evening or in the morning. Jed told him there were three more wagons about a day behind that group of wagons, and they were definitely planning on joining a train.

Brother Roberts added Jed's name to the list and would find a place for him on the next train out. "By the way, if you'd like to make a camp for yourself, you can find a place over there in those trees."

Jed thanked him and led his horses over to the place that Brother Roberts had pointed to. When he got there, he tied up his horses and introduced himself to those in a camp close to where he tied up his horses. The group was helpful and explained the lay of things and other helpful information.

Jed went back to his horses, unloaded the packs, and took off the saddles. He led them to water and staked them out to graze. The grass had been grazed some, but there would be enough for his horses for a day or two. Jed dug into his pack and took out some jerky and dried fruit. As he ate, he looked around at the people. *They must be from a number of countries.* He saw English, German, Swedish, Norwegian, and Dutch people. The mixture of people had joined together to travel nearly a thousand miles. Jed thought that many of them were untrained in handling oxen and horses and camping. Maybe he could help them.

None of the four wagons he had seen showed up the next day. He guessed their plans were not taking them to the Salt Lake basin. Late the next evening, the three wagons pulled into the camp.

Jed went over to greet them. He shook hands with Adam, said hello to Trudy and Priscilla, and told them he was glad to see they had made it OK. He showed them where to find Brother Roberts. Jed walked past Adam's wagon, and Abe greeted him warmly. Jed asked how the baby was doing. Joan said he was doing just fine. Jed greeted Joseph and Ruby. "Glad you made it up to Omaha." They were a little surprised that he knew their names.

He left them to get checked in with Brother Roberts

and walked back to his camp. He had gathered a little wood and started a small fire to fry some bacon for his supper. The Myers camp wasn't too far away from his camp.

The next morning, Brother Roberts called a meeting for all heads of families who would be driving teams or oxen or riding horses. Brother Roberts explained the rules for the wagon train. Anyone who did not follow directions and the rules would be invited to withdraw from the train. If there were any issues that could not be quickly resolved, the wagon would be expected pull out and be on their own to face Indians or other problems without the protection and help of the others. He passed out a list of provisions for each person. They were expected to go over their list and take inventory. If they did not have something, they would have today and tomorrow to obtain them. If they were unable to obtain what was necessary, they would have to forgo going out with this train.

When he had finished with all of the instructions, he motioned for a man to come up to the front. "This is Brother Jeremy Hyde. He will be your wagon master. He has traveled west twice previously and is here to see that all of you make it to the valley safely. He knows the trail well, and you can trust him. You will learn to love him because he is a very kind and caring man. I will turn the time to him to talk to you and answer any questions you might have."

Brother Hyde faced the group and said, "I am very glad to get to know you. Brother Roberts has painted a pretty picture of me. I intend to live up to that picture as painted. I want to learn about each of you and plan to make this trip as pleasant as possible. We will get to know each other really well in the next nearly one thousand miles. There will be some heartaches and trials, and there is always the possibility that a few might not live to see the great basin. God forbid! When you have done your best, there are great blessings in store for you in the next life.

"Each morning, there will be a group prayer before moving out. At night, there will be a short group activity, weather permitting, some dancing, a few might bear their testimonies, singing and an evening prayer. I understand there are a few in the group who are not members of the church, but they have expressed their desire to travel with us—and we are glad to have them. They will participate with us in all we do. They will be loved and respected by all of us. We are together as one big family. Does everyone understand? Brother Roberts has made me a list of all of your special talents and abilities. I will call on you when your talent is needed. Thank you."

8

Brother Roberts came back to the front and asked if he might speak to Jed Sandalin for a few minutes. "Now all of you check your lists you have been given. Don't skip over anything. Just make sure that you have what is called for. Any questions, please take the time to talk to me or Brother Hyde. You're now dismissed."

Brother Roberts said, "Jed, we have a sister who desperately wants to be with this group. She is single lady with a twelve-year-old son. She is old enough to be your mother, but she is strong and determined. I am wondering if you would take the assignment of traveling along with her and her son. She will probably drive her oxen most of the way with her son doing some driving. He's a good lad. You'll be able to put your food things together and eat your meals with them. You can put your bedroll under her wagon at night for a little more protection for yourself and put your packs in her wagon. I have spoken to her about you, and she would love to have you travel with them. She will be a help to you. And you can be support and strength to her and her son. Her name is Tammy Wilkins, and her son is Tad. Would you be willing to do that?"

Jed thought for a minute or two and said he would be glad to do it.

"I will take you over and introduce you to Tammy and Tad."

When they approached the Wilkins wagon, Brother Roberts called out, "Hello, Sister Wilkins. I have someone I want you to meet."

Sister Wilkins straightened up from putting things away in a packing box and wiped away some perspiration from her forehead with the back of her hand.

"Sister Wilkins, this is Jed Sandalin. He is the young man I mentioned to you earlier."

"Hello, Jed. I am glad to meet you. Tad, come out here son and meet Jed."

Tad came out on the tailgate and jumped down.

Sister Wilkins said, "Tad, this is the young man who will be traveling with us. His name is Jed."

Tad rubbed the dust from his hands on his pants and extended his right hand to Jed. "I'm really glad to meet you, Jed. It will be like having an older brother to work with. This will be great."

Jed smiled and said, "Hello, Tad. I'm looking forward to going along with you and your Mom. I'm sure we'll get along great."

Brother Roberts said he had more things to attend

to, and he left them to get better acquainted and to make sure they had everything they needed.

Sister Wilkins said, "Jed, I guess we need to go over that list to make sure we have enough for three people."

They sat down on a couple of packing boxes.

Jed told her he had some of the things they needed, but he would need to purchase additional food. They went over the list, item by item, and Sister Wilkins tallied up what they had. If it was enough, she would check it off her list.

If there were things that needed to be purchased, Jed would write them on the back of his list. When they finished going over the list, there wasn't a lot that Jed needed to buy. He told Sister Wilkins he would unload things out of his packs and bring over the horses and saddles.

Tad asked his mom if he could go with Jed.

She said that it was a good idea since they needed to get to know one another.

Jed headed over to his camp with Tad at his side. He got his horses saddled and placed the packs on Chip's packsaddle, and then they went back to their wagon. Jed led Blaze, and Tad led Chip.

As they approached the wagon, Sister Wilkins looked up and thought about how Jed would be a great help.

Jed put down his canvas pack cover near the front wheel of the wagon, and they unloaded most of his things. He asked Sister Wilkins if she knew of a store where he might go for the purchases they needed. She wasn't sure, but Brother Roberts could tell him.

Jed stepped into the saddle and took his foot out of the left stirrup so that Tad could put his foot in it, and Jed gave him an arm up to sit behind him. Jed figured the packsaddle on the other horse would not be comfortable for Tad to ride on. Jed walked the horses over to Brother Roberts's tent.

Brother Roberts stepped out and asked what he could help them with.

Jed explained the need to buy a few extra food items and wondered if he could direct him to a store where he might obtain them.

Brother Roberts said he knew of just the place to go. He told Jed the owner and operator of the store was a member of the church and always seemed to be stocked with commodities the for wagons crossing the plains. He gave Jed easy directions to the store.

Jed headed out to the road with Tad holding onto his belt. They only had to go a couple of miles, and it didn't take long get there. As they rode along, Tad kept a steady flow of questions for Jed. Jed was amused at his range of interests.

When they pulled up at the store's hitching rail, Tad slid off with a hand from Jed, and then Jed stepped down. They tied the horses to the rail and went in.

The owner had just finished with another customer and asked what they needed.

Jed handed him the list.

The owner said, "Are you headed out with a wagon train?"

Jed answered, "Yes, we will be headed out Tuesday morning if all of the wagons are properly supplied and ready to leave. By the way, my name is Jed, and my partner here is Tad."

The storekeeper said he was glad to meet both of them. "My name is James Scribner, but people just call me Jim. Who is the wagon master?"

Jed told him it would be Jeremy Hyde.

Jim smiled and said, "You couldn't have a finer man for a wagon master than Jeremy. He's the best in my book. He's a sensible man, and he will take good care of the folks in his wagon trains. He just loves people and it shows." The storekeeper led Jed and Tad out to a special storeroom in the back where he kept cured meats. "Your list calls for six slabs of bacon, here young man, you take one, Jed can grab two, and I'll bring three."

Back inside the store, the storekeeper looked at the list again. "Twenty pounds of dry beans? The beans are on that shelf behind you, Jed."

Jed set a bag of beans on the counter.

"Twenty pounds of rice? That's over on the next shelf. Two pounds of salt?" He reached up on the shelf behind him. "Let's see, your list calls for five pounds of dried fruit. We have both apples and prunes, What would you like?"

Jed said, "Make it three pounds of each."

"The next thing is dried vegetables. We don't have a

great variety of those. We have potatoes, carrots, and peas."

Jed asked Tad what he liked.

Tad said he liked them all.

Jed told Jim he would take six pounds of dried potatoes and three pounds of carrots and peas.

Jim commented that people don't seem to use them that much. He guessed that people didn't know how to use them. Jed told him that his family dried lots of vegetables and fruits every year, and his mother was a great cook and knew how to use them.

Jim said, "That takes us down to flour. How much do you need? There are five-, ten-, twenty-, and fifty-pound bags."

Jed said, "We'll take two fifty-pound bags. I think that will take care of us and get us to the valley."

"And that completes your list." Jim started to total up the order.

Jed said, "How about a bag of that hard candy there?"

Jim replied, "That sounds like a sweet thing to add to your list." He gave Jed a wink.

Tad smiled.

Jim said, "Your total comes to $56.50."

Jed dug into his pocket and pulled out two twenty-dollar gold pieces, three five-dollar gold pieces, and some other coins.

Jim counted out the coins on the counter. "That is exactly the right amount. Thank you for coming in. I'll help you out with your things."

Jed and Jim each took a bag of flour, and Tad picked up the beans. Jed put the flour in the pack bags, one on each side and the bag of beans on one side.

Tad hurried back into the store and returned with the rice, which was put on the other side.

Jim was back with three slabs of bacon, and Jed slid them down into the pack.

Tad came staggering out with three slabs of bacon, and Jim rushed to help him walk down the steps.

Jed loaded them on the opposite side of the horse. Jim and Tad came back with the fruits and vegetables. He was able to work them down into the packs.

Tad was holding the bag of candy, and Jed asked what they should do with it. He was just teasing.

Tad shrugged, and Jed held the bag open for Tad, he put a piece in his mouth and Jed took one and put the bag down into the pack. He lashed things down and looked it over to make sure things were right. He turned to Jim and thanked him.

Jim thanked Jed and Tad and wished them well on their trip.

Jed stepped into the saddle, and Tad climbed up behind him, and they were off to the encampment.

Sister Wilkins was standing out by the wagon with her hand shading her eyes. She saw them coming and went back to the fire as they pulled up. She had started to get worried when they were gone longer than she had expected.

Jed thought, *I think I have joined up with another real*

mother. She sounded just like his own mother back in Illinois.

Tad slid off the horse, went to his mother, and gave her a kiss on the cheek. "You don't have to worry about me. I was with Jed."

That gave Jed a great feeling.

Sister Wilkins told them she had food ready for them. After they tied up the horses, they would eat and then store the things away in the wagon.

After they had eaten, the three of them went to work and stored the new supplies away in the boxes that filled most of the floor of the wagon. They found a place to put Jed's things from his packs. There was room for Sister Wilkins to have her bed up on the boxes in the wagon. There was enough room on the floor where she could stand to dress. There was space where they would store the grub box and little cookstove, which they would set out on the ground when she needed to do some baking.

After three hours of work, they felt ready to be on the trail. Brother Roberts had asked that each of wagon leaders report to him when they were prepared to leave. One by one, he was informed of their readiness. It was late in the evening when the last wagon leader reported that they were ready. Brother Roberts sent word to all of the wagons that the wagon train would pull out at eight o'clock in the morning. There would be a short meeting before leaving for final instructions and a prayer.

Jed, Sister Wilkins, and Tad talked about all that

they would have to do in the morning to be ready to pull out. The oxen had to be brought in and yoked. Sister Wilkins said she would have breakfast ready when Tad came back in with the oxen. Jed would get his horses watered, his riding horse saddled, and his packhorse tied to the back of the wagon.

As they sat there, Jed picked up a piece of wood and begin to carve.

Tad moved over next to Jed and asked what Jed was carving.

Jed held up the piece he was working on. "What do you think it might be, Tad?"

Tad studied it for a minute. "A chipmunk?"

"Yes."

Tad seemed to be awed by the way Jed was working with his knife. The chips just seemed to fly. He asked Jed if he thought that he might learn to do that.

Jed assured him he could if he wanted to badly enough. Jed had learned to cut away from the grain and not into it. Jed handed Ted the finished product.

Tad held it and studied it. "That's really nice!" Tad handed the chipmunk to his mother, and she was impressed.

It was getting dark, and there was a big day ahead. Tad and Jed rolled out their bedrolls under the protection of the wagon and crawled in. Sister Wilkins stepped up into the wagon and closed the canvas for privacy. The wagon swayed and creaked a little as she moved around. Then all was still as they went to sleep.

At first light, there was two load blasts from a

trumpet. It was a signal for everyone to be up and get ready to pull out. Tad rolled up his bedroll, dressed, and headed for the oxen. Jed got his horses and took them to water. Sister Wilkins started to prepare breakfast. When the boys returned, bacon was sizzling in a pan over the fire, and the pancakes were mixed and ready to put in the skillet. They started their day with a blessing on the food and a prayer for safety during their day. The pancakes were fried and eaten.

Sister Wilkins washed up the metal dishes and put them in the grub box. With things stored away in the wagon, they were ready to be on the road. The three worked like a well-greased machine, and things were ready in good time.

Sister Wilkins said, "That went fast. The three of us are going to make a good team!"

They had to wait half an hour before they heard the single blast on the horn for everyone to assemble. They headed over to Brother Roberts's tent, arm in arm, Tad on the left and Jed on the right. They were happy to be with each other.

Jed thought, *I feel like I have been adopted into a loving family. It feels great.*

9

They were among the first to assemble. Jed looked back toward the other wagons. People came from all directions and headed for the gathering place.

At the proper time, Brother Roberts stepped up in front. As he looked out over the group, he said, "We'll wait a couple of minutes for the few who are still coming this way."

Two minutes passed, and he spoke again.

"We welcome you this bright, beautiful morning. This is a big day. You are on the final leg of your journey to Zion, to the new homes you will build in the Rocky Mountains! All of you who are happy, let's hear it. Let's give a yell of 'Hip, hip hooray' three times. All together now, Hip, hip, hooray. Hip, hip, hooray. Hip, hip, hooray!"

Everyone joined in, and it created some enthusiasm.

Brother Roberts said, "Brother Jeremy Hyde, the wagon master, will now give some final instructions."

Brother Hyde stepped up and said, "Welcome,

everyone. There are a few more things that I want to tell you. There will be some camp signals you need to memorize. As you heard this morning, two loud blasts with a trumpet is your wake-up call in the morning. That should be plenty of time to be up, get your morning meals and animals taken care of, and reload your wagons. If we all work together, helping one another, we can get early starts. Early starts mean a few more miles closer to our goal. A few more miles each day, after about four or five days, we have gained a day in travel time. There are fifty wagons in this train and about two hundred people. Everyone cannot be first in line. We will rotate so you will not always be last or first. However, if you are consistently slow in getting ready in the mornings, you might always be last. If you are struggling because of your abilities or physical strength, talk to me about it. Maybe others will be willing to help.

"Now, for emergency signals. If, by chance, we are raided by Indians, this signal will be given. I'll raise my hand above my head and swing my arm in a circular motion, which means circle your wagons for safety. The lead wagon will pull off from the trail and make a circle that is large enough for all the wagons. Pull in tight to one another, unhitch your oxen or teams, and turn them loose in the center or tie them to the inside to your wagons. By hand, roll your wagons up close to the next with the tongue going up under the wagon in front of you. The tighter the wagons, the more protection you'll have. Men, always have your guns loaded but not a shell in the chamber. That's unsafe. Just a warning, be ready at all times. We may never see any Indians that will raid our wagon train, but don't count on it. We'll probably be safe at least halfway across Nebraska. My arm held up straight means stop. Be alert always so your teams and oxen don't bump into the wagon in front of you. Keep a safe distance. If you encounter problems and have to stop, pull over as safely as possible and then signal an outrider with your problem. Outriders are riding horseback, one every four or five wagons, to be there for help when needed. One last signal, when I raise my arm straight up and then wave it forward, it means start moving each wagon in turn. I'll try to cover a few more signals and instructions in the next few evenings in camp. I am ready to roll, are you?"

The group cheered.

Brother Hyde said, "Let it be recorded that today, May 17, 1864, a wagon train of fifty wagons and two hundred people pulled out from the encampment near Omaha, Nebraska Territory, at about eight ten in the morning. Let it so be."

Brother Roberts came up and called on Brother Adam Myers, a former branch president from Ohio, to come up and offer the day's starting prayer. He gave a heartfelt prayer and asked for a blessing for all on that day's trip. When he said amen, most uttered an amen with him.

Brother Hyde said, "To your wagons, people."

They quickly went to their wagons.

Sister Wilkins's oxen were waiting calmly. Jed tied his packhorse to the rear of the wagon and stepped into the saddle on his horse. All the wagons were ready for their turn to move out.

Tad started the day by walking beside his mother as she drove the oxen. Sister Wilkins didn't sit on the wagon seat to drive them with lines. She walked beside them and called out signals they had learned.

They became the tenth wagon to roll out onto the road, leaving the encampment area. Everyone was excited, and they could feel it in the air. The sky was clear, and a gentle breeze stirred the grass and leaves. They were still in May, but the weather was warm and could get hot in the middle of the afternoon. The horses and oxen had enjoyed a few days of rest and feeding on the lush grass by the encampment area, and they were a little frisky and were feeling their oats, as the saying went. That first day, they traveled about fifteen miles. They stopped for lunch and then traveled another eight miles before making camp for the night. They had gone slower to get the teams used to the steady pull and so many wagons and people around.

They circled the wagons for the night. The animals were unhitched, taken to a stream for water, and then turned loose within the circle of the wagons. The grass would take care of all the animals for the night. Campfires were built, and meals were prepared.

At dusk, the trumpet sounded one blast, signaling all to come to the large campfire at the side of the circle. As people gathered, Brother Hyde addressed the group with words of encouragement, and he praised them for the first day's travel. He said that they would try for about eighteen miles tomorrow since the roads ahead were normally good and easy. He made assignments for the men to do guard duty. Two would be on watch until midnight, two until three in the morning, and another two from three until wake-up call for the camp. Each man going off from guard would wake his replacement. He asked that they get acquainted and find out where each would be sleeping so they would know where to find them. He found out who played the fiddles and mouth harps and had them ready to play for a few dances. Then all sang a couple of songs, an evening prayer was offered, and they all went to their own wagons for the night. During the day, Tad and his mother had taken turns driving the oxen, and Jed had been called on to be an outrider for a few hours. All three were tired and eager to crawl into their beds. There had been no time to visit much as they traveled along. Sleep came quickly after they were in bed.

The trumpet sounded two blasts at first light. Everyone was up and moving. The horses and oxen were caught, taken to water, and brought up to the wagon. Sister Wilkins had breakfast ready. After eating, the cook box and stove were set back up into the wagon, and the bedrolls were put in the back. They were ready to roll out. The wagons were rolled back until the tongue of the first wagon was free to turn out and free the others. The oxen and horses were hitched, and all was ready.

The horn blast called the people together for group prayer. Following the prayer, they went back to their wagons, ready to get out on the road. Brother Hyde gave the signal to move out. Tad started the day by driving their oxen. Sister Wilkins was up on the seat. Jed was on his horse, and the packhorse was tied behind. The morning air was cool and refreshing. The animals were fresh and moved well.

About an hour down the road, Jed traded off with Tad driving. When Tad mounted the riding horse, a big smile came to his face. He was looking forward to riding Jed's horse. Blaze was a nice, strong animal.

Sister Wilkins sat on the wagon and smiled with approval. She had reservations as to Tad's ability to adjust to the trail, but with Jed there and their bonding so quickly, her worries had left her mind. She was proud of both of them.

Another hour passed, and the wagon train pulled to a stop for a ten-minute breather. The drivers had a chance to trade off and have a drink of water.

Sister Wilkins got down from the seat and walked around to stretch her legs. She told the boys she would take the next few miles driving the oxen.

Jed asked Tad if he would like to ride the packhorse bareback. Tad said he would love that. The other bridle was put on Chip, and Jed gave him a leg up onto the horse. Tad took the horse around in a little circle. The horse responded well to him, which made his day. Jed told him to stay a behind or to his mother's side so the horse wouldn't step on her if she happened to stumble.

Tad assured him he would be careful. The signal was given, and the wagon train began to move again.

Jed rode over to an outrider and visited with him for a while, and then he dropped back to check on Tad and his mother. He asked if Sister Wilkins needed a change. She told him she would walk for a while. The drivers of oxen normally walked at the side of the oxen, carrying a walking stick. If an ox starts to lag back a little, leaving more of the load on the other oxen, the driver would reach over with the stick and tap the oxen to encourage it to move up. When a stop was made, the walking stick was stuck into the ground in front of the oxen. This told the oxen to stand until the stick was removed.

Another half hour passed, and Sister Wilkins decided to take a rest. Tad asked if she wanted to ride the horse. She told him she would like that. Tad slipped off the horse and led the horse. While the wagon was still moving, he retrieved the saddle blanket and placed it over the horse's back for his mother. While the oxen kept moving, Tad held the horse as his mother gathered her skirt. Tad gave her a leg up onto the horse, handed her the reins, and hurried to catch up with the oxen.

The oxen just plodded along and probably didn't even miss the driver. After a little while, Jed rode back over to them. He was stunned to see Sister Wilkins up on the horse. He had not given a thought to her riding a horse. *How did they manage to make the change without stopping the wagon? If one wagon stops, it causes all the wagons behind them to stop also.* No wagons had stopped. Jed realized that they were more resourceful than he had thought. Jed commented on their change and asked if everything was OK. They assured him everything was fine.

He told them Brother Hyde had asked him to be an outrider for a while, and he ended up being gone longer than he thought he would be. They assured him that they were doing well. Jed asked Tad if he needed a change. Tad assured him he was doing OK and that he could last until the lunch break.

When the sun was straight up and ahead, there was a grove of trees with lots of shade. Brother Hyde sent word back that they were pulling over for a break. Brother Hyde rode ahead and found the best place for the wagons to pull off from the road. He stopped his horse, and as the wagons came up, he directed them to line up fairly close together, making three or four rows of wagons in the trees. He told them to watch their wagon bows so they didn't catch on a branch. Everyone was careful, and there were no accidents.

Sister Wilkins asked that the grub box be set out for her. She had prepared lunch that morning. She set out fried bacon strips and dried fruit. She also had some jerky. They sat in the shade and ate. While they were eating, she asked the boys if they would set out the oven when they stopped tonight. She had some sourdough starter in the grub box, and she wanted to bake some sourdough bread for tomorrow's sandwiches.

Tad told Jed that his Mom made the best bread, and Jed said that sounded great to him. After Jed had finished eating, he and Tad took the oxen and horses over to a stream to let them drink. Others were doing the same thing, and they had to stand in line for their turn at the stream. When the animals had their fill, the boys led them back and hitched them to the wagon. The grub box was put back in the wagon.

Jed asked Sister Wilkins and Tad if they would like him to take the first shift driving the oxen. They could choose to ride a horse or ride in the wagon. Tad said he would ride Jed's horse, and Sister Wilkins said she would ride in the wagon for a while and then drive the oxen. The word came down the line that it was time to move out. The packhorse was tied behind, and they were ready. The wagons started moving back toward the road.

After an hour and a half, there was a brief stop so drivers could change positions if they wanted to. Sister Wilkins climbed down from the wagon and told Jed she would drive for a while. Tad got off Jed's horse and climbed onto the packhorse.

One of the outriders asked Jed to be an outrider for a while, and he said he would be glad to. He rode out to the side and took his position.

10

The wagon train started up again. They traveled on for a while, and a scream was heard coming from a wagon that was close to where Jed was riding as an outrider. Jed turned his horse and was quickly at that wagon. A little girl had been climbing over the seat when the front wheel dropped into a chuckhole and jolted the wagon. The little girl toppled to the ground, but she rolled away from the wheel rather than toward it. Her left arm appeared to be broken, and her hands and face were skinned up pretty badly. She was frightened, hurt, and crying uncontrollably.

Her mother, fearing for her child, had jumped from the wagon and sprained her ankle. All the wagons stopped.

The train doctor was called to come to their aid. It took a few minutes for him to get there. He examined the little girl and saw the extent of her injuries. He said he needed some white strips of cloth and a small flat piece of wood for a splint.

Jed said he would get the wood. A lady came running up with the strips of cloth needed. The arm had to be set. With one person holding the little girl's legs and body still, another person held her arm and head still. The doctor gently pulled on the arm with a little twist, released the arm slowly, and slid the bone back into its proper position.

By the time the doctor had the first wrap on, Jed was back with the splint.

The doctor looked at it and exclaimed, "You have it the right size and shape! You must have done this before!"

Jed admitted he had done it several times.

The wagon train needed to be moving again, and the wagon with the little girl moved up and over, allowing the other wagons to pass. The doctor cleaned her other abrasions and put on a little antiseptic. The little girl only sobbed a little bit. The doctor took a look at the mother's ankle, and it was just a sprain. He took some of the white cloth strips and bound her ankle so that it would be immobile. This allowed her to gently walk on it. The mother was helped up into the back of the wagon so she could lay on the bed, and her daughter was placed beside her. With things taken care of, the doctor was able to board his wagon as it rolled by. The wagon with the little girl and mother pulled in behind the doctor's wagon.

Jed mounted his horse and trotted along the wagons until he was back with the Wilkins family. He inquired if everything was OK with them. He was told they were doing fine. They asked about the child and mother. He told them all that had happened, and he moved back over to assume his position as an outrider.

The rest of the afternoon went well. There were no more accidents, and the road was good. They were making good time. As it approached evening, the wagon master signaled to pull off the road and make camp for the night. As they were in safe territory, they would make a loose circle tonight. The wagons would not be quite as close, but the tongues would be put up at night to create a barrier to keep the livestock inside the circle. The grass was plentiful, and a stream was close by.

When in position, the teams were finally unhitched and taken to water.

Tad and Jed set out the grub box and the oven stove. They also took out another box with baking supplies. A small folding table was set up for Sister Wilkins to mix her bread on. Wood was gathered and brought back to camp. The campfire and a small fire in the stove were started.

Sister Wilkins mixed her bread, set it out, and covered it to rise. Jed went to his pack in the wagon and dug out a small carved bird. He was going to see how the little girl was doing. Her wagon was across the circle from them. The mother hobbled around as she tried to fix supper for her husband and little girl.

Jed asked about the little girl and how she was doing.

The mother told him the doctor had been by to check on her. He had gently tied her little arm across her stomach so she wouldn't attempt to move it for a few days. It didn't seem to be hurting her very much now. At least she wasn't crying.

Jed asked if he could see her for a few minutes, and the mother said that would be fine. She took Jed to the back of the wagon and said, "Lilly, you have company."

Lilly sat up in bed.

"This is the young man who helped the doctor fix your arm."

Lilly asked, "What is your name?"

"My name is Jed, and I have brought you something to help you feel better." He stepped up into the wagon and handed her the little carved bird.

Lilly reached out with her good arm and took it. "It is so cute!" She held it up to her cheek.

The mother said, "Jed, that is so thoughtful of you. Did you carve this?"

"Yes, I did."

"Jed, you have a real talent, and you are so kind to bring this to her. She really loves birds. This will be a treasure for her."

Jed said goodbye to Lilly and told her he would come see her again.

Lilly said goodbye and blew him a kiss.

Jed stepped down and told the mother to take care of herself and her sweet little girl. He also shook the father's hand. As he walked back to the wagon, he thought, *It so much fun doing things for other people!*

When he got back to the wagon, Sister Wilkins had just put the bread into the pans to rise before going into the oven. She had fixed other things for their supper. They ate and then set to work washing the pans and dishes. Tad dried as she washed, and everything was clean and put away. The bread was ready for the oven. Sister Wilkins put her hand in the little oven to test the temperature, and then she put the bread in.

The trumpet sounded for people to gather for the evening fireside. She told the boys to go on over, and she would tend to the bread until it was done, and then she would come over. The two boys walked over to the fireside.

Brother Hyde told them they had done well today and had made nineteen miles. A very good day. He commented on the accident with the little girl and cautioned that parents needed to be in constant training with their children to keep them safe. He realized that accidents could happen, and that this one could have been worse, but it was a lesson to all. He told the group that the little girl was doing well, but her arm was broken. He acknowledged that children normally mend quickly, and he hoped that this would be the case with little Lilly.

Brother Hyde announced some dancing and a couple of songs before prayer. The little band started to play, and people went out to dance. The fireside ended with songs and a prayer.

Sister Wilkins walked up to the boys as they sang. When they headed back to their wagon, Sister Wilkins walked between the boys with her arms interlocked with theirs. They got back to the wagon, and she offered them a slice of warm bread with little jelly on it. She had brought a few bottles of jelly from home. She cut three pieces and put jelly on each one. She handed the boys a piece, and took one for herself, and they had a bedtime snack.

The boys complimented her on the nice warm bread.

She climbed up into the wagon, and the boys rolled out their beds under the wagon. They were all soon asleep.

The next day, things went along in routine from morning until late evening. They had their fresh bread sandwiches at noon. That day, they made a full twenty miles. The next day was Sunday, and they stayed at the camping spot and made it a real day of rest. With a couple of men as herdsmen, the livestock were turned out of the circle to graze near the wagons. They had at least two men with them at all times to see that none strayed away. The livestock had bonded and stayed close together.

In the morning, an assembly was called, and the people gathered and had a worship service. They passed the sacrament in remembrance of our Savior and had a couple of sermons from two of the brethren, a song and prayer. They were dismissed and admonished to have a restful day.

Monday morning came early when the trumpet sounded. Everyone in the camp was up and doing what needed to be done to get ready to leave. The horses and oxen were brought in, watered, and hitched. With breakfast finished and boxes stored in the wagon, they were ready to pull out. The trumpet sounded again, and the people gathered for short instructions and prayer.

The wagons began to line up and headed out onto the road. The Wilkins wagon was about two-thirds of the way back for the day's travel. In the afternoon, Jed noticed that clouds were beginning to gather off to the north. By late evening, they could have a thunderstorm. With the threatening storm headed toward them, they made camp earlier that evening.

Brother Hyde sent word down the line to either block the wheel wells or stake them down since the wind can blow so hard that it could roll a wagon and cause damage. Someone could be hurt, especially if they were in their bedroll under the wagon. Everyone took the extra precaution and prepared for a storm. Meals were eaten quickly, and those things that were normally left out at night were put back into the wagons. Those who slept in the wagons got in early and tied down the canvas in the front and back. Those who slept outside laid down their rain slickers, the beds on top, with an extra canvas over them.

As everyone settled in, the storm hit with all of its fury—with loud thunder and bolts of lightning. Then the torrents of rain hit. Many in their beds feared for those on guard duty that night. After an hour or so, the storm let up, and the rain slowed to a sprinkle. In two hours, the storm had stopped altogether. The guards had worn their rain gear and were pretty dry for all they had been through. The rest of the night was peaceful, and everyone got their rest.

The next morning, they were on the road again. They had camped just a couple miles east of Columbus. There were just a few houses and one little store. The little settlement was only three years old. The road was a little muddy at first, but it dried out fast. They made good time, and things went smoothly for them.

Just before they stopped for the evening, they had to ford Silver Creek to make camp.

The next two days went well, and there were no accidents or sicknesses.

At the campfire, Brother Hyde told the group that they would be passing through a new settlement, Grand Island, in the morning. If they had forgotten to stock up on any particular item, they might be able to purchase it there. He asked if anyone need to stop, but no one raised their hands. He assumed that nothing was needed. The spirit of the whole group was good, the people were happy, and Brother Hyde was pleased. They were dancing and singing and bonding as a group.

At ten in the morning, they passed Grand Island. The area was mostly barren, and there were only a few trees along the Platte River. At noon, Jed took a few minutes to check on Lilly. Her mother was fixing lunch when he walked up. She was hardly favoring her ankle at all. He asked about Lilly, and Lilly came running around the wagon with her little bird. She threw her good arm around his leg and gave him a hug, which gave Jed a thrill.

Jed said, "Lilly, it looks like you're doing really good. I'm so glad." Jed picked her up and held her, being careful with her arm.

Lilly's mother told Jed that Lilly would hardly let her take the carved bird out of her hand to wash or eat. "She just won't let the bird out of her sight."

Jed put Lilly down, said goodbye, and walked back to the wagon.

Sister Wilkins had lunch ready.

After lunch, Jed took a piece of wood from the wagon and carved another small bird. Tad watched in awe as the bird just seemed to crawl out of the stick of wood. With the bird finished, they hurried and watered the animals and hitched up the oxen and were ready to roll out when the word came down. That night, they forded the Wood River. The roads were good, and they were averaging eighteen or twenty miles per day, which was really good for slow-moving oxen pulling wagons.

On Saturday night, they found a really nice campsite with plenty of grass and good water. On Sunday, they rested up from their week of travel. They held a worship service in the morning and a fireside that evening to sing quite a number of songs. A lady in the wagon train had a beautiful singing voice, and she sang two songs for the group. They all seemed to enjoy her talent.

11

On Monday morning, the wagon train was back on the road. It seemed like they were constantly fording streams that came down from the north and emptied into the Platte River. The next day, they had some bad luck when one of the wagons broke a wheel. When the wheel collapsed, it nearly tipped the wagon over. It really scared the mother and two children who were riding in the wagon. They were thrown around a little, but no one was seriously hurt.

Most wagon trains that traveled west had a plan, and each wagon carried one or two extra parts to repair a broken-down wagon, including wheels, axles, tongues, and yokes.

The wagon train was held up for about thirty minutes while a new wheel was brought to the broken wagon. Each wagon carried a wagon jack, and one was placed under the wagon. The wagon was raised up, and the broken wheel was replaced. The wagon train rolling again in less than thirty minutes.

Jed had been there to help change the wheel. He surveyed what was needed to repair the wheel, and he knew that he could make it like new again. He just needed the right wood. That evening, he walked around in the trees in the area and found some hickory trees. He took his ax with him, and he cut off a piece and took it back to camp.

Over the next two evenings, Jed made replacement parts. On the third evening, he built a larger campfire, assembled the wood parts, heated the iron rim to expand it, and placed it over the wooden wheel. Tad poured a bucket of water over the hot rim, shrinking it and drawing the wood very tight together. The wheel was just like new again. Tad was really impressed, and he told Jed that he would like to learn how to do all of that someday. Jed assured him he could learn, and he would try to teach him all he knew. After they ate, they went to the fireside. Jed found Brother Hyde and asked him who had provided the new wheel to replace the broken one. Brother Hyde said he would find out.

When the fireside opened that evening, Brother Hyde asked for the man who had provided the wheel to raise his hand.

Jed recognized the man and went over to him. Jed told him the broken wheel was repaired and was ready to go back in his wagon.

The man seemed surprised to have it fixed so soon. He told Jed they would get together afterward and take the wheel to his wagon.

Immediately after the prayer, the man came over

to Jed, and they walked over to the wagon. The wheel was leaning against the side of the wagon. Jed rolled the wheel out to the man. Tad had the fire blazing for more light.

The man examined the wheel and said, "It certainly is solid. And it looks true as well. You fixed this wheel yourself? This is amazing!"

Jed assured him that he had done the work on it.

Tad said, "I know he did because I watched him do it."

The man offered Jed his hand and said, "Young man, you do excellent work. Thank you very much. How much do I owe you?"

Jed told him that he owed him nothing because he had signed on for the trip in hopes of being of service to others in repayment for his being able to travel with them. Jed pointed out how it was safer to travel in a group than to try to cross the plains and mountains alone. "It is my thanks to you."

The man took the wheel and rolled it over to his wagon.

During the night, a light rain started to fall. When the camp awoke in the morning, the light rain was still coming down. Tad, Sister Wilkins, and Jed still had to get breakfast and bring the horses and oxen over to the wagon. The spirit in the camp was not the best, but everyone was ready to roll out on time. A light rain fell off and on all morning. At lunch, there was no rain, but it started up again a little while after getting back on the road. The road was starting to get muddy, and walking with the oxen became more difficult as the mud deepened.

The wagon train was still about four miles from the North Platte River. Brother Hyde decided they had gone far enough in the wet conditions. The wagons pulled off the road and made camp.

At the Wilkins wagon, the boys hung a canvas to create a dining fly so they could be out of the rain. Their campfire was safely on the outer edge of the dining fly, and there was no chance of it catching fire. The heat of the fire radiated under the cover they had created and warmed them. The group was called to gather for one song and prayer. The person offering the prayer asked for a blessing that the rain might subside and that they could roll out in the morning on time, after a good night's rest. The boys rolled their bedrolls out under the dining fly, hoping for more protection from the rain. A short shower in the night woke up Jed. When the rain stopped, he went back to sleep.

The trumpet didn't sound as early the next morning, but most were awake by habit. Brother Hyde had gone out early, checked the road conditions, and found them quite muddy. He decided to not leave until later in the morning, which gave everyone a little more rest. It was getting light, and those who were up could see that the clouds were rolling away from the area, which meant the sun would soon be exposed and the roads would start to dry out.

At ten that morning, Brother Hyde decided they should give it a try. He sent word out to the wagons to hitch up and prepare to leave. At noon, they saw where the North and South Platte Rivers came together. A little way up the North Platte, they had to ford the river. It was the scariest crossing. With proper direction, the wagons went across one at a time. Only one or two of the wagons got any water in them. They plodded on for another hour before the lunch break was called. They made it a shorter break this time because the oxen had not pulled for long. They were back on the road in about a half an hour. The farther west they went, the drier the roads became. Their spirits were lifted, and they were happy as they traveled along. After lunch, they traveled another ten or eleven miles before pulling off for the night's camp.

On Sunday, there was no travel. The cattle grazed outside of the circle, and they had an extra man with them on each shift to watch after them. They had a good sunny day, and everyone dried out. For the next couple days, the road was very rutted. The wagon train had to slow down and ease the wagons slowly through the bad places, which cut their average daily mileage down to about fifteen miles per day.

On Thursday, they had to ford the North Platte River again. The river wasn't high and the river bottom was solid, so they crossed without difficulty. At the deepest part, the water was well below the wagon boxes. When all were safely across, they camped for the night.

The next day, they were confronted with a new adventure. One of the outriders spotted a lone Indian on a horse on a high bluff to the north. This brought fear to some of the travelers.

Brother Hyde told them that he had already seen him. When they stopped for lunch, Brother Hyde called a meeting for all of the men. He explained that this Indian was just a scout to keep an eye on them. They would see an Indian on a bluff like that for another day or two. They were instructed that no one was to shoot at the Indian. That would only provoke them. If a group of Indians approached them, they would stop the wagons. If they should come at them on the run, yelling and making a lot of noise, he would signal to circle the wagons with all animals inside. The men were to get their guns and prepare to defend the wagons. Other wagon trains had found that not shooting at them unless fired upon was the best policy. Usually the Indians would want a gift of food or something else to pay them for allowing the wagon train to cross their land.

Brother Hyde said, "Play it smart and let me give the orders because one false move could make everyone in the train pay dearly."

That night, they made a tight circle. The cattle and horses grazed outside the circle for about two hours and then brought into the circle of wagons for the night. An extra man was put on guard for each shift as well. It was unlikely that the Indians would bother them in the night except to steal some oxen.

At the fireside that night, Brother Hyde told the group that if the Indians came peaceful tomorrow, he would ride out and talk with them. "They will probably want an ox or two, but usually they will accept flour instead. So, women, if you will take out three or four pounds of your flour and put in a cloth bag, we can go from wagon to wagon until we have twenty or twenty-five pounds in each bag. That way, each Indian brave will have something to carry away for their efforts. Hopefully, that will satisfy them."

The night was peaceful, and nothing happened. At ten the next morning, nine Indians came down from the bluff to the north. They came slowly with an arm signal that they came in peace.

Brother Hyde and one other man went out to talk. He had guessed right; they wanted meat. He explained that they needed the animals to pull the wagons off their land. He offered flour instead.

The Indians talked it over among themselves and decided they would accept the offer.

Brother Hyde came back to the wagons and asked for the flour. Four men started collecting flour, and they came back with two hundred pounds of flour. With the help of the outriders, the flour was taken out to the Indians. The men rode among the Indians, giving a bag or two to each.

The Indian chief made a friendly gesture to Brother Hyde, and the Indians turned and headed up over the hill.

Brother Hyde signaled for the wagons to start moving again.

That night, at the fireside, Brother Hyde thanked the people for sharing and making the Indians happy.

Peace with the Indians was a valuable thing for wagon pioneers. "If we had refused in any way, they would have given a signal for warriors over the hill to come down upon us, and we possibly would have all been killed—or at least severely damaged." He told them they might see one or two more groups, but they likely would not see more. He explained that the cost for each wagon was less than the price at a toll bridge or a ferry crossing.

On Sunday, they stayed in camp.

Monday and Tuesday were good days, but the travel was shortened to give the livestock more time to graze in the mornings and evenings since the grass was not as plentiful. They were still making nearly fifteen miles per day.

On Tuesday night, the cattle grazed along the banks of the North Plate River. At dusk, one of the men herding the livestock heard a strange sound in the willows along the riverbank. One of the oxen had gotten into some quicksand and was in desperate need of help. The other riders were called over. They threw their ropes over the head of the ox and pulled. Slowly but surely, the ox inched toward good footing and came out of the sand. If the ox hadn't been found in time, it surely would have died. The men realized the importance of staying close to the livestock and looking after them.

On Friday night, they camped near the border between the Nebraska Territory and the Colorado Territory. Jed expressed his pleasure to Sister Wilkins and Tad that another goal on his list had been reached.

With them being in camp a little longer each evening, Sister Wilkins decided to bake something special for the occasion. She baked a cake and two more loaves of bread. To have the cake—even with no frosting—was a treat.

Sister Wilkins was baking, Jed was carving, and Tad was watching every cut.

Jed said, "Sister Wilkins, what are your plans for when you get to the Salt Lake Valley?"

Sister Wilkins looked at Jed and said, "My husband was killed in an accident about a year ago. We had just joined the Mormon Church, and there was talk of going west to get away from the persecution and find peace. My husband was all for the idea, and we were making plans to go when his life was taken. Our plans for leaving were put on hold until I could settle our affairs. Tad and I got things ready and made our departure. As far as plans when we get there, we have made none. We have a few friends who went out last summer, but we do not know where they are, and we really have no plans for looking them up. I guess we will just wait and see."

Jed told her his father had met a family in a settlement who he really liked. "There might be place there for you and Tad. It's just something to think about."

The next morning, everyone noticed that the colors of the trees and the brush and the rocks and the soil were changing. In the matter of a few miles, it had changed to gray-green. At that point, they were climbing. The oxen and horses had to work a little harder to pull the wagons. They could see snow capped mountains in the distance, and there was a chill in the air—even during the day. They had to dig out warmer coats.

Sister Wilkins commented that she hadn't thought that it would be so cold in the later part of June.

That evening, Brother Hyde explained that they were on a relatively new route. It had only been used for a couple of years. The road was not worn from as much traveling as the roads back in the Nebraska Territory. The new route cut off two hundred miles.

Sunday was a day of rest. The oxen needed extra time for grazing and rest.

A couple of days later, they made camp by a cold stream. When a couple of men went with their buckets to get water, they noticed the stream was full of fish. They used one bucket to dip fish out of the stream. When they returned to the camp, they showed off the fish they had caught.

People grabbed buckets and ran to the stream. By damming the stream with rocks, they corralled the fish into a section—and everyone got a mess of fish for supper. In the camp, fish were frying at every fire. What a welcome change it was to have fresh fish.

The next morning, as they pulled out of camp, they forded the stream. The streams were smaller, and the creek bottoms were gravel or rock. They were not threats to the travelers. In the mountains, they saw an occasional deer.

Some of the men asked Brother Hyde about trying

to obtain some fresh meat for the wagon train. He felt it was safe for them to venture away from the road at this point. Two outriders were given permission to try their luck. They asked Jed to bring his horse and packhorse so they would have a way to haul the meat back if they were successful.

The hunting group went up into the trees on the north side of the road. They stayed abreast to the wagons and traveled slowly and in as much cover as possible. After forty-five minutes, they spotted several deer. They tied their horses up and slowly moved toward the deer.

After fifteen minutes, they were within shooting range of the deer. The two men readied their rifles and took aim. They fired, and two deer went down. The fun was over, and the work began.

Jed brought the horses over to where the men were, Jed had tied their two horses to the packhorse, and rode his horse while leading the others. When he got back to them, they nearly had the deer dressed out and ready to load. After getting them loaded, they headed back down to the road, and at the road, they quickened their pace. When they caught up with the train, it had pulled over for lunch and a rest. They hung the deer in a tree, and people were encouraged to take some meat for their families. When everyone had a chunk of meat, there was nothing left but bones. Quite a number asked for some of the bones to boil for broth. When finished with the deer, there wasn't much left to feed the coyotes. In camp that night, fresh meat was cooking on every fire. When the fireside was called, the people were so full that it took some encouragement to get them to dance. But dance they did.

For two days, the wagons traveled uphill and downhill. There were no level roads in the mountains.

On Saturday evening, Sister Wilkins, Tad, and Jed ate the beans Sister Wilkins had cooked. Sister Wilkins said, "Jed, I have thought about what you were telling me the other night, and where did you say your father was?"

Jed told her it was somewhere in Arizona. He wasn't quite sure where, but it was in a new settlement—and he assumed it was all Mormons.

Sister Wilkins said she kind of liked the idea of a warmer climate instead of the harsh winters.

On Sunday afternoon, Sister Wilkins brought up the idea of going to Arizona again. She asked, "How are you going to get there from Salt Lake?"

Jed had heard that wagon trains occasionally traveled from Salt Lake to the Arizona Territory, taking supplies and people to join the recently created colonies. He was going to spend a few days in Salt Lake and ask for an opportunity to travel with a group.

Jed stood up and decided to check on Lilly. He hadn't seen her for about a week. He went to his pack and took out another little carved bird. He didn't want to spoil her, but she was a cute little girl. When he got over to their wagon, the mother and father were resting by their wagon. He greeted them and asked about Lilly.

She was in the wagon.

"Is that you, Jed? Did you come to see me?"

Jed answered, "Yes, it's me all right. How are you?"

She crawled toward the back of the wagon, leaped into his arms, and gave him a hug.

Jed was almost overcome by her expression of joy toward him. She had the first little bird in her hand. With her in his arms, he stepped back around to where her parents were sitting. He told her parents he was sorry for waking her up.

The mother said she was probably awake anyway.

Jed sat down on the ground and asked Lilly how her arm was doing.

Lilly replied, "It is doing OK, and it doesn't hurt any more. The doctor thinks he can take the bandage off in a little while."

Jed told her that he was worried that her little bird was getting lonely.

Lilly said, "He's not lonely because he's got me."

Jed replied, "Yes, but maybe he needs a friend that looks like him—and then you would have two little friends."

Lilly said, "But where would we find one?"

Jed reached into his pocket, brought out the new bird, and held it up. "How about this one?"

Lilly squealed and reached for it. "Is that for me?"

Jed assured her it was for her to keep and to be a friend to her other bird. Jed told the parents that he hoped he wasn't out of line to bring her another carving.

They assured him it was fine and very thoughtful of

him. The first little bird kept her mind off her broken arm, and she had been happy in spite of her injury.

Jed put Lilly down and said he needed to leave.

Lilly gave him another hug and thanked him for the new bird.

Jed headed back to his wagon.

That evening, there was group singing and prayer, and then the camp settled down.

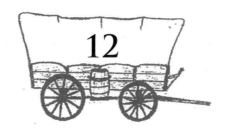

12

The next day, they passed by rock cliffs on the north side of the trail. When they got closer, they could see that many pioneers had stopped and carved their names on the sandstone. The wagon train stopped for almost an hour for people to go over and carve their names on the rocks.

Jed carved Sister Wilkins and Tad's names as well as his own. When he looked at other names on the rock cliffs, it occurred to him that maybe his father had carved his name there as well. He kept looking and hoping that his dad would have done it too. Just as he was ready to give up, he found his father's name: "Jake Sandalin, 1861." This was a great thrill. It was almost like seeing his father in person. He called to Sister Wilkins and Tad, and they came over and admired the carefully carved name on the rock.

The blast of the trumpet called everyone to prepare to get back on the road.

After a few miles, they came to a nice place to stop for the night.

Two days later, they neared Fort Bridger and spent the night. They had never camped near a fort. They had passed within a mile or two of a military fort, but this was their first time to camp by one.

The next evening, Brother Hyde told the group that they would be passing into the Utah Territory tomorrow. From there, it would be three and a half days before they would be pulling into the Great Salt Lake Valley. A big cheer went up. Everyone was elated with the news.

The dancing that evening was more vigorous, the men skipped a little higher, and the women's dresses swung out just a little farther. They were so happy about the news.

The next two days were good, and they traveled mostly downhill.

On Saturday evening, they camped in a little valley on the edge of the Weber River. The Sunday-morning worship service was a happy and tearful meeting. It turned into more of testimony bearing than having speakers. Many stood and expressed their thanks to God for their safe trip to the mountains.

Jed stood and expressed his appreciation for the friendship of this wonderful group of people. He was sure there was a God in heaven and that he had helped them in their endeavor to travel nearly one thousand miles with such good conditions. When he sat down, Sister Wilkins patted him gently on the back, and Tad interlocked his arm with Jed's. They truly had been like family.

On Monday evening, Brother Hyde spoke for a few minutes and thanked all of them for their cooperation and for making the trip as pleasant as could be expected. "Tomorrow morning, we will drive down into Salt Lake City. In the center of town, there is a center block where a new temple is being built. There is also a bowery where people gather. We will circle our wagons around this block and meet together under the bowery. We will have our last meeting together. Brigham Young, our prophet and president of the church, if available, will come and speak to you. Instructions will be given where you can camp until you decide where you want to go to establish your new homes. Some may decide to travel farther west to make homes and farms or other businesses. There will be those there who will direct you to where you can learn more about certain areas. Now, it would be nice to dress in your better clothes— not your dress-up clothes, but at least be clean and not look heavily trail worn. I am sending one of my helpers ahead to the valley to announce our arrival, so that they will be expecting us." Brother Hyde called for the band to start playing, and people stepped out to dance. There was a lot of excitement.

The next morning, the trumpet blast came at the same time as always, but everyone was already awake and stirring around. They were ready to pull out ahead of their normal time. The single blast of the trumpet sounded about twenty minutes earlier than usual. They gathered for prayer, and then the signal was given to pull out.

As they came over the hilltop, just before their last descent into the valley, the people in every wagon was jubilant. From this overlook, they could see a huge lake glimmering in the sunlight. They could see buildings and homes and streets in the city. It was so exciting for them. They had come a long way for this beautiful view.

It was a couple more hours before they pulled up by Temple Square in the center of town. There was something different when they stopped their teams of oxen. There were posts in the ground with rings at the top to tie up their oxen or horses. The adults thought this was very nice. After climbing down from their wagons, they tied up their animals and brushed the dust from clothes. The women combed their hair, straightened their bonnets, and brushed their skirts. They took off their aprons and left them on the wagon seats. The men put their hats up on the seats and stomped their feet to knock the dust from their boots. Then, hand in hand, they walked over to the Bowery.

Jed, Sister Wilkins and Tad walked over together and found seats. None of them had seen a prophet of God before. They were excited. Jed saw Lilly and her parents coming over to the bowery and waved to them.

Lilly saw him and started waving back. She pulled at her daddy's face and pointed to Jed. The parents waved to Jed.

When all were assembled, Brother Hyde stepped up

to a little pulpit and said, "Let it be recorded that this wagon train of fifty wagons and two hundred people has reached its destination. We left Omaha on the May 17, 1864, and have arrived in Salt Lake City in the Territory of Utah on the July 16, 1864. We have had no deaths, very little sickness, and all wagons and people are accounted for! So be it."

Everyone cheered.

President Brigham Young came up to the front and said, "First, let me congratulate each of you on a job well done. You have crossed the plains and mountains with the least number of problems of any other wagon train to date. That is wonderful. That in itself will give courage to those many saints who will follow you. You have been a fine example. We welcome you to Salt Lake City. We hope you can soon find places to build homes that will increase your happiness. You have been on the Lord's errand. He wants you here in these mountains to create a fortress where His Word can go out from here to the whole world. I bless you that you may be successful in all of your future endeavors in righteousness. This work is truly the work of the Lord. Amen." President Young gave a hearty wave to all and headed back to his office.

Everyone sat quietly and watched him leave. What a noble leader he was. All present, including Jed, were very impressed with his words and the strength he displayed.

Brother Hyde came back to the front after a few minutes and said, "At this large campground, there are two streams of water run down through the area, one on the north and one on the south. Those thinking of going north should camp on the north side, and those thinking of going south should camp to the south. Those who have not decided or intend to stay in this area might consider the center area. There are people who will be there to answer your questions and give you information on your areas of interest. Thank you for all you have done and for the way you have treated one another. May God bless you."

The group gave him a round of applause. As they went to their wagons, they found men there to direct them to the camping area.

Jed turned to Sister Wilkins and asked, "Have you come to any decision about which direction you would like to go?"

Sister Wilkins looked at Tad and said, "Well, son, what do you think?"

Tad answered, "I want to go with Jed—as you and I talked about last night."

Sister Wilkins turned to Jed. "And so do I. Jed, if you will allow us, we'll go with you to Arizona."

Jed put his arms around them and said, "I hoped you would say that. We're family now, aren't we?"

Sister Wilkins and Tad looked at Jed, and she said, "That we are."

Jed untied the rope that was attached to one of the oxen. The horses were still tied to the back of the wagon.

Sister Wilkins said she would like to drive the oxen

to the camping place, and Tad said he would walk beside his mother.

Jed untied his horse, stepped up into the saddle, and moved up fairly close behind Tad and his mother. Wagons were moving down the street and heading west. They were soon at the huge campground. Knowing they would be heading south, they moved the wagon to the left. They saw some trees, and it looked like there was a stream there as well.

As they approached the trees, an elderly gentleman came over and greeted them.

Jed moved up to the front to talk to him.

The kindly man said, "Just find a place you like and set up your camp. There is still some good grass in that lower area along the stream. If I were you, I would hobble your horses and just turn them loose. Your oxen will stay close to them."

Jed thought that would work well.

Sister Wilkins made a big turn with the oxen and turned them to face north and a little to the west so the wagon's tall bows and cover would offer shade in the afternoon. The oxen were unhitched and turned loose, and they went to the stream to drink and then started eating the good grass at their feet.

Jed unsaddled his horse, dug the two pair of hobbles out of his pack in the back of the wagon, and led the horses to water. He hobbled them, took the lead ropes off the halters, and let the horses go out on their own to graze. Jed turned to the man who had greeted them and asked his name.

He told Jed his name was Jacob Dillinger.

Jed said, "I am Jed Sandalin, and I am traveling with Sister Wilkins and her son, Tad. My father's name is Jacob as well, but he goes by Jake."

Jacob asked where they were headed.

Jed told him of his intentions of going to Arizona Territory to try to find his father. Jed explained that he had very little to go on. He had only the one letter from his father, which was probably written eight to ten months ago. Jed reached into his pocket, pulled out the letter, and handed it to Jacob.

Jacob took a couple of minutes to read it. He rubbed his chin and thought for a few minutes. "Well, young man, my wife and I just returned from southern Utah a few months ago. We felt we needed to come back from that area to be near our family, especially our grandchildren. We went down there in 1861 to what is called St. George to help establish a Mormon colony in that area. With the wagon train that we were with going south, we had a man kind of going with us, but he stayed out more on his own and wasn't too talkative. I never got to know him, but I do believe he was referred to as Jake."

Jed's mind started to go around in circles.

Jacob said, "After our arrival in St. George, we never saw much of him. I do believe he was a gold prospector, and he would show up on occasion to purchase supplies at the store that was started up there in St. George. He kind of made friends with one of the families in the colony. I think he may have spent a little time with them. He must have found some gold since he paid for his supplies with small gold nuggets." Jacob looked at the envelope. "I do believe that smudge and the word Arizona is referring to the old stage line that went south to Tucson and then to the east. That stage line pretty much followed the old Mormon Battalion Trail, which headed northeast out of the Arizona Territory. Son, are you well?"

Jed could hardly speak. To say he was shocked would be an understatement.

Jacob said, "I need to go check on some other wagons. By the way, if you are headed south, we are getting a group of wagons together to head in that direction in a few days. If you are interested, let me know."

Jed couldn't even answer. He just gave Jacob a little wave and sat down by the wagon. He was stunned by the information he had just received.

Sister Wilkins walked over and said, "What's the matter? You don't look good."

Jed asked her to sit down.

She sat down close to him and turned so she could see his face. "Now tell me."

Tad came around the wagon and stood by his mother.

Jed went through all that Jacob had told him. "He's not in Arizona, but he is on the border of Utah and Arizona—in the town of St. George. Just think; I am only about two weeks from finding him."

Sister Wilkins leaned over and gave him a hug. "Jed,

I am so happy for you. I believe the blessing President Brigham gave to us all at the bowery today is already beginning to happen. Can't you just feel it?"

Jed sat up and let everything sink in. "I am beginning to think there is really more in your religion than I have ever thought of."

Sister Wilkins stood up and said, "We haven't had lunch yet. I'll get something for us to eat."

When things were ready, Jed filled a plate with warmed-over beans and a biscuit from the previous night. Tad asked for a blessing of the food and thanked the heavenly Father for Jed's good news.

After they ate, Jed said he was going to find Jacob and let him know they were ready and eager to be with the next group of wagons heading south. It took a little while to find Jacob. When he found him, he told him that he had thought over all he had said, and he strongly felt the man he had told him about must be his father.

Jacob explained that they were waiting for a couple more wagons to join them for the trip south. They wanted at least twenty wagons to go at the same time, which would be a show of strength. It would also detour any Indian hostility toward the travelers. They might come to the wagons for a handout, but they should have a good trip. Their names were on the list to be included with the next group going south. He went to go speak to other wagon groups, particularly those who had still not made up their minds about where they wanted to go. Jacob and his wife had been there for three years and could explain the conditions and opportunities that were there for them.

Jed went back to the wagon, and he and Sister Wilkins talked about the supplies they needed to get them to St. George and to take care of their needs for a week or two after arrival. Jed made a list and decided to ask Jacob about the best place to get supplies.

The three of them spent quite a bit of time gazing at the island in the lake and the mountains that surrounded them. They marveled at the beauty they were seeing. The next morning, Jed found Jacob.

Jacob had good news; two more wagons had signed on. That made the twenty they needed. Things were in order to head out bright and early on Monday morning.

Jed asked where to replenish their supplies and anything else they needed for St. George.

Jacob suggested bringing garden tools and maybe a plow for farming if that's what they intended to do.

Jed asked who had decided to go south.

Jacob told him their names, including Lilly's parents.

Jed was happy to have these good people going along with them. He went back to the wagon and told Sister Wilkins what Jacob had told him about who was going.

Sister Wilkins was happy that Lilly's family was going.

Jed asked about garden tools.

Sister Wilkins had a couple of items, but a rake and a hoe would be good to buy. They had hopes of getting a small farm where they could raise a little corn and wheat and feed for a few animals. She thought a plow might be a good idea. With the number of things they would be getting, they needed to take the wagon.

Tad got the oxen and put the yoke on them. The horses still had the hobbles on their front feet, but they followed behind, hopping and whinnying. They didn't want to be left behind. Jed decided to tie them to a tree so they wouldn't try to follow. With the oxen hitched, they headed out. Sister Wilkins was up on the seat of the wagon, and Tad walked beside Jed. They had to go about a mile.

At the store, Sister Wilkins went in and enjoyed looking at the merchandise, fabrics, and dresses.

Jed found a plow, which he thought was a good buy, the garden tools they would need, and a double-bitted ax. He asked Sister Wilkins about an ax, and they only had a smaller one. It was about the size of the one Jed carried with him on his packhorse. Jed added the ax to his list, and Sister Wilkins gathered the food they would need. Tad carried them over to the counter as his mother selected them.

Sister Wilkins went back to the dresses since she had never owned a store-bought dress. The one she was looking at was very pretty and dressy, and it also had a matching bonnet. She held it up to see if it might fit her. After looking at it for a moment, she hung it back up and walked over to Jed at the counter.

Jed could tell by the look in her eye that she liked it. They told the clerk that was all that they needed. Jed told him about the ax and the plow, and the clerk started adding things up. Just as he was getting to the end, Jed told him to add the dress and bonnet.

Sister Wilkins said, "No, Jed! I can't afford that. I can get by with what I have."

Jed said, "I am buying it, and if you would like to it wear sometime, I'll let you. No, really, it's a gift to you for all you have done for me for the past three months. Will you accept it?"

Sister Wilkins replied, "Yes, Jed. I would be proud to wear it. Thank you so much." She reached up and kissed his cheek. "You are a good son, and I am proud of you."

The clerk suggested that Sister Wilkins fold up the dress and bonnet the way she would like, and he would wrap it up for her. When she came back to the counter, the clerk had torn off a piece of paper that was long enough to wrap up the dress and bonnet. When wrapped he tied it with a string and handed it her.

Sister Wilkins had a big smile on her face, and Tad was smiling too.

Jed pulled some gold coins out of his pocket. Sister Wilkins placed a twenty-dollar gold piece on the counter, and Jed added the rest that was needed. After they got everything loaded, they turned the oxen around and headed back to the camping area.

When they pulled in and headed for their camping spot, the horses saw them coming and started whinnying and stamping their feet. They must have thought they had been deserted.

Jed turned the oxen and horses loose to graze again.

The horses were content now that they were back together.

Sister Wilkins prepared them a little lunch and then settled back and they talked about the move to the south.

After a while, Jed stood up and said he was going over to the two wagons that had decided to go south. He stopped by the wagon to see Lilly.

Lilly said, "Jed, where have you been? I have missed you."

Jed said, "How are you doing, Lilly. I see you have the wraps off your arm."

Lilly said, "It is all better now, and I can move it all around. See?" She moved her arm all around to show him.

Jed told her parents that he was happy to have them headed south in the same group as he was. "All of this time has passed since we left Omaha, and I am sorry I don't know your names."

Lilly's father said, "And all that we know about you is you are Lilly's dearest friend, Jed. I am Brad Sessions, and my wife is Lillian. And your last name is?"

"My name is Jed Sandalin. Since we might be living close to one another in St. George, we really need to know each other's names. I'm sorry that I haven't fully introduced myself before now."

Lillian said, "Anyone who seems to care as much about our daughter as you seem to is a great friend of ours."

Jed said, "She is as sweet as an angel, in my

estimation, and if there is anything at any time that I can do for you, let me know. Maybe we can get better acquainted on this next step of our journey. With just twenty wagons, we can become closer friends. By the way, do you know the people who will be with the second wagon that's going south from our original wagon train? I have heard their names, but I haven't formally met them. Do you know which wagon is theirs?"

Brad said, "It is the third wagon down in that second row of wagons."

Jed said goodbye and walked over to the third wagon.

The family was sitting in the shade.

Jed said, "I'm Jed Sandalin. You've probably seen me around for the past three months. I haven't really become acquainted with you folks."

The husband said, "My name is Erastous Jameson, and I have carried the nickname of Ras thus far in my life. My wife here is Marybelle, but she prefers just Mary. Our oldest daughter, Susanna, is thirteen. Our next daughter, April, is eleven, and our only son, David, is six years old. We call him Davy."

Jed expressed his pleasure at formally meeting the family. "I understand that you have chosen to go south with the small group leaving on Monday."

Ras answered, "Yes, we are planning to do just that. We were in a quandary as to what to do and which way to go from here, but after talking to Jacob and learning about the country down south, it just came to us that it would be the right place to settle. As a family, we are excited about the prospects. We are not looking forward to another two weeks on the road, but we'll do it. We are looking forward to finding a permanent home, a place to build and make special for the five of us."

Jed briefly explained his interest in going south to find his father. He explained how he was not a member of the church, but he had been impressed with all he had seen and heard.

Jed turned to Davy and asked what he liked best.

Davy answered, "I really like animals and being around them. They're fun."

Mary said, "He certainly does, and it seems that all animals like him. He has a rare talent in that direction."

Jed fished into his pocket, took out a carved horse, and handed it to Davy. Would you like to take care of the little horse for me?"

Davy took the horse, smoothed it gently, and looked it all over. "He's a pretty horse. Did you carve him?"

"Yes, I did. If you promise to take good care of him, I will give the horse to you."

Davy said, "Wow! I promise I will take really good care of him." Davy showed his Mom and Dad and sisters the little horse, and they were impressed.

Jed said he needed to go, and as he started to turn to leave, Davy gave him a hug and thanked him.

The parents and the girls also said thank you. They knew that a happy boy added greatly to making a happy family.

When Jed got back to his wagon, Sister Wilkins asked about the two families.

"They're great people, and we will enjoy their company now that we are becoming acquainted. On the trip from Omaha to the Great Salt Basin, everyone was occupied with taking care of the necessities, and they didn't have time to get to know one another."

During the next few days, Sister Wilkins and Tad got acquainted with the two families. She thought the two families were very special, and they had told her how they liked Jed.

The next four days went very slowly since there wasn't much to do. Jed and Tad took the time to jack up the wagon, remove one wheel at a time, and check the axles and hubs to make sure they were sound enough to take them another three hundred miles. They were in good shape, and they greased them and put them back on. They repositioned the load and secured the plow on the floor.

On Saturday, seventeen new wagons pulled into the campground, loaded and ready to leave on Monday.

By Saturday evening, Sister Wilkins and Jed felt that they were ready to leave.

13

On **Sunday morning,** they decided to have a worship service in the campground since there were still a good number of wagons in the camp, including the ones that had just arrived.

On Sunday evening, they had an instructional meeting. The new wagon master was introduced. His name was Robert Winslow, but he went by Bob.

Jed was impressed that Bob had made the trip to St. George and back once each year since 1861. He knew the trail and road well. He also had become acquainted with many of the Indians in the area. The Indians trusted him and respected him. He explained that the roads were reasonable for travel, and there were only a couple of rough spots.

Brother Winslow explained the camp rules and other procedures to be followed. He informed the group that the trip would take twelve days. On Sunday, they would stay in camp and not travel. Each evening, there would be a fireside with dancing and singing. There would be a worship service on Sunday morning and singing at a fireside on Sunday evening. Brother Winslow asked if there were any questions.

One brother raised his hand and asked, "When we get into camp in the evening after walking and toiling all day—and we are so tired—why are we asked to dance?"

Brother Winslow said, "Brother, you ask a good question—and you deserve an answer. It has been proven by the many wagon trains that have traveled west that when you stop for the night and your body is stiff and sore from the strains of the day, dancing before going to bed loosens the muscles. You become relaxed, and you will sleep much better than if you do not dance. I invite you to try it. One night when coming in tired, stiff and sore, just try it. Don't dance—just go to bed when things are taken care of. The next night, when you feel the same, come to the fireside and dance. The next morning, come and tell me the difference."

The brother said he would try it.

A prayer was offered, and they separated and went to their wagons.

The next morning, the trumpet was sounded, and camp began to stir. Everyone rolled out, had breakfast, and hitched their animals to the wagons. The single sound was heard for them to assemble for any final instructions and prayer.

When everyone was ready, Brother Winslow raised

his arm, held it there a minute, and then waved it forward. "Wagons ho!"

The wagons began to roll out of the campground. They went east up to State Street and then turned south.

Jed was excited to be on the last leg of his journey to be with his father. He had really missed him. The wagons went down State Street and then turned west, going down to the Jordan River. The road followed the river upstream to the mouth of a small canyon. They took their first rest stop and had lunch.

After lunch and a rest, they started up again. They followed the little canyon a few miles, and then it opened up into another large valley with a large lake in the center.

Brother Winslow sent word to each of the wagons, by way of the outriders, that this was a freshwater lake, which was named Utah Lake. They followed the lake for four or five miles, fording a couple of streams and finally came to a stream with lots of grass around it. They made camp there the first night out from Salt Lake City. They had covered about twenty-five miles. That night, the brother who had asked about dancing did not go to the fireside. Instead, he stayed at his campfire till dark and then went to bed.

The next day, they were on their way at the given time. By noon, they were at the edge of the lush valley and trees. They stopped for lunch and a rest. After lunch, they came out into the sagebrush-covered land. There were no trees around—just sagebrush and tumbleweeds all along their route. The road was dusty, and they stayed further apart to let some of the dust settle before the next wagon came along. It was tiring for people, oxen, and horses.

That evening, they camped in the shade of the high hills to the west, which provided relief from the hot sun. They had their fireside and dancing, and the man who had questioned the dancing, danced and really enjoyed himself. He danced with his wife and exchanged partners with other couples. After the singing and prayer, he went to his own wagon and into bed.

The next morning, before doing much else, he looked up Brother Winslow and expressed his feelings about dancing in the evenings when he was so tired. "The difference between the night before last, when I didn't dance and last night, was like the difference between night and day. I was so much more rested this morning. I know now that Brigham Young and his direction to dance at night when out the trail were really inspired. I am a true believer."

Brother Winslow thanked him for sharing his experience.

The man went back to his camp to prepare for a brighter new day. When word got around to everyone, they were more attentive to dancing each night, weather permitting.

The next four days passed much the same: sagebrush, tumbleweeds, and a dusty road. A couple of the nights, they camped by a stream coming down into the narrow valley through which they were traveling. There were virtually no trees besides some willows growing next to the water. The water in the streams was cool and pleasing to their taste.

The mountains, which were mostly on the east, were less than a mile away most of the time. At the very edge of the steep mountains, there were a lot of juniper and pine trees. They had a good camp on Saturday night and Sunday. There was a stream with good water. The east mountains gave them morning shade, and they had shade from the west mountains from late afternoon until dark.

On Sunday morning, they had a worship service. They had the sacrament, passed a couple of speakers, and a few testimonies were born.

After the meeting, Jed told Sister Wilkins that he had liked the meeting, and she was pleased to hear it.

That evening, the people sang at the fireside. They sang a lot of the old gospel songs and all seemed to know the words.

On Monday morning, Jed was excited to be on the move. Just four more days of travel, and he would find his father. Almost every day, the wagon train passed by small colonies or communities of mostly Mormon people. For the most part, they had only been in the area for a year or so. Many of the homes were just dugouts in the hillsides, but there were some sod homes and a few log homes. They were just getting settled.

It was not easy to make small farms in the desert.

They had to dig canals to bring the water down from the mountain streams or dam streams to raise the water up to the land. The areas that had been planted for several years were growing good crops, and it looked prosperous.

On Wednesday evening, they camped close to the relatively new town of Cedar City, Utah. It was a bustling place with a lot of people. During the evening, some of the local people came to their camp to visit and learn where they were heading. They received a number of invitations to stay in Cedar City and make homes and farms, but everyone in the wagon train had their sights set on St. George and declined the offer. A few of the local people stayed for the campfire and danced and sang that night. It had only been a year or so since they personally had been involved in campfires while on the move.

Leaving Cedar City the next day, they were in narrower valleys. It was not quite a canyon.

On Thursday night, they camped at the mouth of a narrow rocky canyon.

On Friday morning, they entered the canyon, and Jed found a tranquility that he had not found anywhere else. Voices echoed through the canyon. It had high red rock walls on each side. It was so narrow that a couple of times the wagons had to go down the middle of the stream bed in the center of the high walls. It was beautiful and very interesting.

When the canyon ended, they found a place to stop for lunch and rest. The rest was short because everyone was eager to be on their way. From the lower end of the canyon, they could see a wide valley to the south and west. They couldn't see the valley floor from there, but no mountains obstructed their view toward the southwest. The excitement was building in their minds, and their eyes showed it.

ed's eagerness was about to burst his bubble. To the east and south, all they could see was red rock mountains with canyons going back into them.

After several hours, the wagon train came over a rise and looked down into a beautiful valley where homes were being built. There were stores and other businesses. What caught Jed's attention was that a number of the homes were being built out of bricks instead of logs or lumber. There were some frame homes going up.

In the town, they saw lush gardens behind the homes. There were some strange trees that puzzled Jed. When he had the chance, he asked what they were. Jed was told that they were a type of desert palm trees that only grew in warm climates.

The wagons were directed to a large camping area for incoming wagons. They would call it home for a week or so until they could obtain property to start building their own homes.

As they pulled up to the place to camp, Sister Wilkins said, "It is so different and so beautiful. I am so surprised and thankful to be here. We have traveled nearly two thousand miles in a wagon to find this lovely place. You know, Jed, I think the Lord really loves us—to get us here safely."

Jed said, "You're right. I also believe the Lord loves us."

At a short fireside, Brother Winslow thanked everyone for their cooperation and for working closely together. He explained where they could find the land office and how the men there would help them find land and what would be needed to get them settled. That evening, they sang a few songs and had a prayer. They were formally dismissed as an organized group.

At the wagon, Sister Wilkins asked Jed about his plans and how he planned to find his father.

Jed said he had thought of several things to do. First, he would go to the post office and ask if his father had been getting any mail. The next thing was to try to locate the family his father had made friends with. Jed wanted to speak to the bishop and ask if he knew the family or anything about his father. If the bishop didn't know the family, maybe the bishop could inquire from the pulpit as to what family he should be looking for. He said he could only take one step at a time, but he had a feeling he was in the right place. He asked Sister Wilkins what she was planning to do.

She looked at Jed and said, "I am really at loss as

to where to begin. My husband always took care of business like this." She asked Jed what he thought.

Jed thought that going to the land office and finding property to look at was a good place to start. He thought it would be good for both of them to become acquainted with the area, look things over, find the area they liked, and not act in haste because they had lots of time. Jed would wait to find his father before he made any decisions. Since his father had mentioned buying property, he may have already purchased a piece of land. Jed said that maybe he could ask the land office if his father had recorded a purchase. "If he has, you may want to buy land near us."

"I would really like that," said Sister Wilkins.

Jed said, "In the morning, I'll ride into town and check with the livery stable about the possibility of renting a horse and buggy for the day. I'll go to the land office and get directions for where to look. If that turns out well, I'll come back and get you, and the three of us will go sightseeing."

Sister Wilkins was very pleased about that idea. After some more small talk, they decided to go to bed and get some rest.

Tad and Jed took their bedrolls out from the back and rolled them out under the wagon. It took Jed a long time to go to sleep. All he could do was think about his father and how close he might be to him.

When he woke up, he reviewed the things that he was going to do that day. He finally crawled out of bed and got dressed. He went to see about his horses and found them and the oxen downstream. They were doing fine.

He went back to the wagon just as Sister Wilkins was climbing out of the wagon. He asked if he could start the fire for her. She was happy to have him offer. He got busy doing that while she mixed some pancakes, sliced some bacon, and put it in the pan. When the bacon was about done, she put a couple of tablespoons of the bacon renderings into the pancake mix to add to the flavor. She stirred the batter again, took the bacon out of the pan, and poured the balance of the bacon grease into her grease container. She poured batter into the skillet for the first pancake.

Tad wasn't up yet, and she called out to Tad to awaken him.

Tad got up and went to the stream to wash his face and hands. Before he got back, the first pancake was done and out of the pan—and another was just going in. Tad apologized for oversleeping. He had really slept soundly.

The second pancake was done and taken from the pan, and the third was frying. They had the blessing, and Tad and Jed went to work on the sweet-smelling bacon and pancakes.

Tad asked what was first on the list for the day, and Jed explained that he was going to the post office, the land office, and then the livery stable. If he got good answers, he would rent a buggy and be back to take them on a long ride.

Tad asked if he might go with Jed, and if they rented

a buggy, he could ride the horse back to the wagon while Jed drove the buggy.

Tad asked his mother for permission, and Sister Wilkins told him that would be up to Jed.

Jed said it was fine with him, and they would leave at eight o'clock. That was still half an hour away. Jed went to his pack and got a couple of his carvings—so he would be ready if a child needed a little cheering up.

15

After they finished eating, Jed told Sister Wilkins he thought he would also find out if there was a nearby church, what time they held meetings on Sundays, the name of the bishop, and maybe a few other things. He said they needed to really get acquainted with the people in St. George as soon as possible since they were becoming part of this community now.

A little before eight, Jed went for his horse. He took off the hobbles and led the horse back. The horse had rolled in some dust, and he took his cloth and rubbed him down and cleaned him off as best he could. He saddled him, and they were ready to leave.

Jed stepped up into the saddle, and Tad climbed up behind him. When Tad was ready, Jed nudged the horse with his heel, and they were on their way.

As the boys headed out of the campground, Sister Wilkins said, "Jed is a good boy, and he's good for Tad. He has been a great help to both of us." She turned back to her fire and decided to make a couple loaves of bread.

Jed and Tad headed up the street and looked for the post office. It would most likely be located in a grocery and dry goods store. There were already a few people in town. It was a Saturday morning, and in Illinois, a lot of the people saved Saturdays for going to town to buy supplies. They also made it a day to meet friends and visit.

Jed decided to ask for directions to the places he wanted to stop. There were only a few businesses in this new town.

An elderly gentleman was walking towards them, and Jed pulled his horse over and stopped. "Sir, I wonder if you could help us. We're looking for the post office and the land office, and we need to find out if there is a livery stable in town. We just came in with the wagon train last evening."

The man looked up at them and smiled. "I'd be happy to be of help to ye, my friend. The post office is part of the dry goods store, but it has its own entry on the left side of the building. It's just a little ways down on your left, and the land office is just across the street from the store. Now for the livery stable, we haven't had one here up until about a month ago. But he's open now and maybe can be of help to ye. By the way, where are you from?"

Jed told him he was from Illinois.

Tad said, "I'm from Ohio."

The gentleman said, "Well, we're just glad to have

you here. If there is anything I can help you with, just ask."

Jed bid him a good day and said thank you. They headed on down the street. There was a hitching rail in front of the post office, and Jed pulled up there. Tad slid down off the horse, and Jed dismounted and tied up the horse. They walked into the little post office, but they didn't find the clerk. There was a little bell on the counter with a note: "Ring for Service." Jed gave it a ring.

A voice from somewhere in the store called out, "Be with you in a minute."

Jed and Tad waited.

In a minute, the clerk came out and said, "What can I do for you?"

"Would you happen to have any mail for Jake Sandalin?"

The clerk reached over, took out the few envelopes from the slot marked S, and glanced through them. "Well, yes, there is. Here is a letter for him. Is that you?"

"No, but I'm his son. I just got into town. And I am eager to find him. Is the name of the sender on it?"

The clerk said, "I'm really not supposed to share that information with anyone, but because you are his son, I guess it'll be OK." He held up the envelope for Jed.

"It's from my sister back in Illinois. She must have received another letter from our father, and she has answered it. Hey, this is great news. Can I leave a note on it for my dad?"

The clerk told him that would be fine, and he handed Jed a small piece of paper and a pencil.

Jed quickly wrote a note: "Dad, this is Jed. I am here in St. George. I'm looking for you. Don't leave without finding me."

The clerk attached the note to the envelope with a clip, put all the letters back in the slot, and asked if there was anything else he could do for them.

Jed said, "Not now, but you've made my day. And I'm sure we'll be doing business with you later on."

Jed said, "Well, one stop, and we hit pay dirt. Let's go over to the land office and see what we can find." Jed untied Blaze, led him across the street, and tied him to the rail out front.

A man was working on some papers at a desk. When they walked in, he got up and came over to the counter. "Well, now, young men, what can I do for you?"

Jed told him they had several things on their minds, but he wasn't sure just where to start.

The gentleman said, "Just start anywhere, and we'll just sort it out as you go. OK?"

Jed told him about coming to St. George to find his father and how Tad's mother was looking to buy land and build a home. "Then we were wondering about the church. Where do they meet and when?"

The man said, "I am Bishop Johnson, and I am the bishop of the church as well as running the land office here. What are your names?"

Jed said, "I am Jed Sandalin, and this is Tad Wilkins.

His mother is Tammy Wilkins. We are presently camped in the wagon campground down the street. Sister Wilkins and Tad are members of your church, but I am not… at this time."

The bishop shook their hands and welcomed them to St. George. "Our small church building is just down the street on your left. And we meet at ten o'clock on Sunday mornings, and all of you are very welcome to join with us.

"You said that your name is Sandalin. About three weeks ago, a man by the name of Jacob Sandalin came in to record the purchase of a nice piece of property a little to the west of here. Real good ground out that way."

Jed beamed all over and said, "That would be my father." He was about to explode. "I can't believe all of this is happening to me. Everything is falling into place."

The bishop said, "You said Sister Wilkins is widow and is interested in some property. Just observing your interest in her and her son here, she might be interested in property next to your father's piece. There is still some land available out there."

Jed asked, "Do you know the family that my father has become friends with?"

The bishop smiled and said, "I certainly do. In fact, they own the property next to the land your father bought. Their names are Saunders, and Brother Saunders is one of my councilors in the bishopric."

Jed's face felt flushed, and he asked if he could sit down.

The bishop offered him a chair.

Jed sat down and placed his elbows on his knees and his face in his hands.

Tad put his hand on Jed's shoulder.

The bishop asked, "Is there something wrong?"

Tad said, "I believe the emotion of finding where his father is and in learning all these things about him is starting to show. He has been so eager to find him. I believe it has been three years since he saw his father." Tad told the bishop what he knew about Jed's past three months.

The bishop walked over and placed his hand on Jed's other shoulder. With consolation in his voice, he softly told Jed that good things happen to people who truly love the Lord. "Jed, I have a very strong feeling that you have that kind of love in your heart for Him and others."

Jed stood up, wiped the tears from his eyes, and said, "I'm sorry. It's just that I am getting so close to finding my father. I would like to go see the property and meet the Saunders family. Could you direct us so that we might go out there?"

The bishop said, "I'll even do you one better. I have a man coming in who can take over the office for a while. I'll get my buggy, and I'll personally drive the three you out there. It's really not that far!"

Jed smiled. "I would hate to put you out, but I would truly be grateful for your help."

The bishop said, "You two go back to the campground,

and when my man comes in, I'll be on my way out to get you."

Jed and Tad went out to Blaze and headed back to the wagon. Jed felt like putting the horse into a gallop. He was so eager to tell Sister Wilkins the news, but he resisted and only put the horse into a trot, which caused Tad to bounce around a little. Tad held on to Jed's belt and stayed on.

As they pulled into the campground, Sister Wilkins was watching for them.

Tad slid off, and Jed stepped down and handed the reins to Tad. Jed stepped over to Sister Wilkins, threw his arms around her, and put his head on her shoulder. "I just can't believe it. I just can't believe it."

She pushed Jed back a little bit and asked, "You can't believe what?"

Jed wiped his eyes, straightened up, and told her everything they had learned in town.

Sister Wilkins gave him a hug and said, "I am so happy for you, Jed. I have been praying that things would turn out well for you."

Jed said, "The bishop is on his way out here to take us out to the property next to my father's. We can meet the Saunders family. Go get your bonnet on—he'll be here soon."

Sister Wilkins said, "I can't go. I'm not dressed to meet people!"

Jed assured her she was dressed as fit as any pioneer lady, and they would love her just the way she was.

Sister Wilkins took off her apron. "Do you really think so, Jed?"

"Just get your bonnet—and you'll be fine."

Jed and Tad took out the hobbles for Blaze and led him down to where the oxen and Chip were. As they returned to the wagon, the bishop was pulling into the campground. Jed waved, and the bishop headed toward them.

The bishop stepped down from the buggy and extended his hand to Sister Wilkins. "I am pleased to meet you. I'm Bishop Johnson. Jed and Tad have told me a little about you. I welcome you to St. George. This is a special place, and I am sure you will like it here. If you are ready, we'll take a drive. I assure you it is not far."

Sister Wilkins finished tying her bonnet strings, and she and Tad stepped up to the back seat and sat down. Jed sat beside the bishop.

The bishop snapped the lines, and the horse quickly stepped out into a nice trot. They went a couple of blocks and then headed west. As they traveled along, the bishop pointed out things of interest and told them about the area.

The passengers were excited about what they saw.

In a few minutes, the bishop said, "Jed, on your right is the land your father has just purchased. It's a twenty-acre parcel with a nice homesite next to the trees on the north. Across the road from it is land that is available, and there are several nice pieces of land there. Perhaps Sister Wilkins might be interested in that land. Just down the road on your left, just past your father's homesite, is where the Saunders family lives. I'll take you in to meet them."

A minute later, Bishop Johnson pulled up in front of a nice-looking home. "Well, folks, here we are. This is the Saunders place. Real good people! While you get out, I'll go to the door."

Jed stepped down and took Sister Wilkins's hand to help her down. Tad jumped out right behind her. After a knock on the door, the door was opened by a bright-eyed boy. "Hi there, Bishop. How come you are here?"

"I have brought some people to see you. Is the rest of the family home?"

"Yes, Mom and the girls are out in the garden, and Dad and Johnnie are down in the lower field. You want to come in?"

The bishop said, "No, we'll just wait out here in the shade. Why don't you run and tell your mother you have company."

The boy said OK, closed the door, and went running through the house. "Mom, Mom, the bishop is here. He has some people with him, and he wants you to come up and meet them."

"I'll be right there dear."

Sister Wilkins looked around. "They do have a nice-looking place here."

Sister Saunders came down the front steps as she dried her hands on her apron. The four girls trailed behind her. The boy came ducking in under his mother's arm.

The bishop said, "Sister Saunders, I would like you to meet some special people. They just arrived by wagon yesterday. This is Sister Tammy Wilkins and her son, Tad. This young man is Jed Sandalin, Jake's son. This is Sister Betty Saunders. Jill is five, Jimmie is eight, Rachel is ten, Joan is fifteen, and Anna is seventeen."

Sister Saunders came up to Jed, took his hands, and looked him over. "Jed, I feel like I have known you forever. Your father never quits talking about you. He is so proud of you. You've traveled so far alone to be with him. He'll be so thrilled to have you here."

Jed responded, "I haven't been all alone—not since Omaha. In Omaha, I was asked to travel with Sister Wilkins and Tad, and since we left there, we have become like family."

Sister Saunders stepped up to Sister Wilkins, took her hand, and said, "Welcome. If you have been family to Jed, you are family to us as well. Hi, Tad. It's good to have you here."

Sister Wilkins went to each of the Saunders children and complimented them on a special feature, including Jill's dimples, Jimmie's curly hair, Rachel's pretty pigtails, and Joan's bright smile. "Anna, young lady, you are simply beautiful. What a beautiful family you all are. I'm excited to get to know all of you."

The bishop said, "I hate to break this up, but I need to return to the office."

Sister Saunders said, "Bishop, why don't you go on back and leave these good folks here with us. Tom will be coming in for dinner soon, and he'll want to meet them. We'll have some dinner, and maybe Tom can drive the boys back to town and get their wagon and things and bring them out here to stay."

The bishop turned to Sister Wilkins and Jed and asked if they would like to do that.

Jed was a little hesitant, but Sister Wilkins assured him it would be fine.

The bishop bid them a good day, stepped into his buggy, and headed back up the road.

Jed called out a thank you as he left.

The bishop returned a wave and smiled at Jed.

A few minutes later, Tom and Johnnie pulled up to the barn. Tom tied up the team, and he and Johnnie walked up to the house.

Sister Saunders ran out to tell him the good news.

Tom came into the house and said, "You're Jed? I am so glad to meet you." He shook his hand vigorously and gave him a big hug. "You are going to make a special man very, very happy—and we are expecting him to arrive here this afternoon. He told us he would come out from the mountains this weekend."

Tom was introduced to Sister Wilkins and Tad, and he expressed a very warm welcome to all three of them.

Sister Saunders suggested they sit and visit while she and the girls get some dinner ready. Sister Wilkins wanted to help in a real kitchen for a change, but she did not want to get in the way.

Tom invited them to find chairs and sit down and

relax. He asked Jed about his trip and how he had gotten together with such a good lady and young man.

Jed gave him a brief rundown on his travels and his meeting up with Sister Wilkins and Tad, their travel together from Omaha, and how they had bonded like family.

Sister Saunders announced that dinner was on the table and invited them to come to the table to eat. It was a large table, and they were all able to gather around it.

Brother Saunders asked a blessing on the food and expressed thanks that Jed, Sister Wilkins, and Tad had made it safely to St. George. They visited while they were eating, and a lot of questions went to Jed and Sister Wilkins about their travels.

When they had finished eating, Sister Saunders told her husband that they needed a ride to town to get their oxen, wagon, and horses. "The bishop brought them out here, and he needed to get back. I suggested that he leave them with us and that we would take care of them."

Tom said he would be glad to take them into town. He went to unhitch his team from the wagon and hook the buggy horse to the buggy. Jed offered to go with him. Johnnie, Jimmie, and Tad went along as well.

Sister Wilkins was so excited to be inside a home for a change, and she walked around looking at pictures and other décor in the home. Sister Saunders let her enjoy herself because she had also missed having a home when she was on a wagon train for so long.

The girls cleaned up from dinner and sat down to listen to the women as they visited.

It wasn't too long and they heard the buggy coming up from the barn.

Sister Wilkins got up to go out, but Sister Saunders insisted that she stay with her and let the men and boys go for the wagon.

"But they'll need me," Sister Wilkins exclaimed.

Sister Saunders said, "I bet you have trained those two boys really well, and they can handle things themselves."

Sister Wilkins said, "I am sure they can, and I need to let them. I'll just step out and tell them I'll wait here for them to come back." The women stepped out on the porch and Sister Wilkins told them she would just wait here for them.

Tom and the boys waved goodbye and headed down the road.

Sister Wilkins walked around the house and looked at the flowers. Sister Saunders followed her and visited with her. In the back, Sister Wilkins spotted the garden. It was a neat garden with lots of things growing. She expressed hope that someday she would have a garden again.

At the campground, Jed directed Tom to their wagon. Jed and Tad went to the back of the wagon, got their lead ropes, and went to get the oxen and horses. They put the lead ropes on and headed back to the wagon.

Tom let the boys get ready to go.

When they were ready to pull out, Tad drove the

oxen, and Johnnie walked beside him. Jed tied both horses to the rear of the wagon and got in next to Tom. Jimmie sat in the back.

As they reached the road, Tom looked toward town. He stopped the buggy and asked Jed if he thought Tad could wait there with the oxen. Jed assured him he would be fine. He wondered what Tom was thinking about. Tom asked Jimmie to get climb up on the wagon seat, and he said they would back in a few minutes. Tom turned the horse toward town. He put the horse into a trot, and Jed wondered what he was doing.

In a couple of minutes, Jed saw a bearded man on a horse leading a packhorse down the street. His heart nearly jumped out of his chest. Was this his father coming toward them? In just a minute, they were up to each other. Tom told Jake to stop because he had a young man he needed to talk to.

Jed ran around the buggy horse, and Jake jumped down off his horse. They ran into each other's arms. On the street in St. George, Utah, a father and son were reunited. Tears flowed down the cheeks of both father and son. They were speechless for a minute. A few people on the wooden sidewalk watched the drama unfolding in front of them.

Jed looked up at Tom and said, "This is my dad."

Jake rubbed the tears from his eyes and said, "This is my son."

They were in the middle of the street, and several buggies had to go around them. They recognized Brother Saunders and waved to him.

Tom suggested that Jake tie his horses to the back of the buggy, and they would head back to the farm.

As Tom was turning the buggy around, Jed remembered the letter at the post office. He asked Tom to go back to the post office. Tom kept the buggy in a full circle and went back to the post office. When they pulled up in front, Jed stepped down and asked his father to come with him. Jed led his dad into the post office and rang the bell.

The clerk recognized Jed and commented about him coming back so soon.

Jed said, "This is my dad, and he has come for his letter."

The clerk reached into the slot and handed the letter to Jake.

Jake first read the note that was attached to it, then looked at Jed and said, "Can I leave now?"

Jed smiled, and they went out to the buggy. Tom asked if they were ready to go, and Jed assured him that they were. Tom tapped the lines on the horse's back, and the horse headed down the street.

Jake looked at the return address and said, "Who is Elizabeth Porter?"

Jed told him that his daughter was married.

Jake looked at Jed and said, "Really? I never thought of that."

Jed waited as his father read the letter.

Jake said, "What? I'm a grandpa! Can you believe that?"

Jed held his breath and waited to hear if the baby was a boy or a girl.

Jake said, "It is a baby girl, and her name is Sarah."

Jed had been hoping for a girl because he just loved little girls.

Jake said, "She tells me that you are on your way out here, but you might beat the letter's arrival. She says that you will have some news for me when you get here."

Jed said, "It is not good news, and it pains me to have to tell you, but this past winter, Mama came down with pneumonia. The doctors did all they could for her, but she just couldn't throw it off. She passed away peacefully with Elizabeth and me at her side. Her last words were to tell you that she loved you."

Jake put his face in his hands. "I guess I didn't do her right by leaving her and coming west. Maybe this wouldn't have happened if I had been there. I could have shielded her from so much work, and she would have had more strength to fight her sickness."

Tom pulled up and told the boys to go ahead. "Jimmie, you hold on and don't move around so that you won't fall off."

Jimmie told his father he would be careful.

Jed sat there with an arm over his father's shoulders. "Dad, just think about this. We now have another Sarah to love and look after. I'm glad she has Mama's name."

When the women heard the wagon coming, they went out to meet them. Sister Saunders hurried over to Jake and welcomed him back. Jake was introduced to Sister Wilkins and Tad. The girls gave Jake a hug and told him they had missed him.

It made Jake feel better to have all that attention. It cheered him up, and he became more talkative.

Jed came over and said, "Something is on your mind. What is it?"

"Well, son, we have work to do. We need to be building a home, barns, and fences."

Jed and his father excused themselves and walked over to the property to look things over. As they walked, Jed explained how he had traveled with Sister Wilkins and Tad from Omaha. She had been a lot of help to him, and he thought he had helped them too. "She is looking to have her own place. She is thinking of buying the ground across the road from our place to be close. She has been like a second mother to me. I respect and appreciate her friendship. I was thinking that she could live with us until she can get her own place built. She could do the cooking and take care of the house, giving us more time to work on the place."

His father looked at him for a minute and said, "It sounds to me like you have been doing some good thinking. I won't be here a lot since I am not ready to give up my gold mine yet. It is yielding pretty good so far. I have paid for this place, and I think I have enough money to pay for all the materials to build a house, barns, and fences."

Jed said, "I learned carpentry, wagon building, some iron work and wood carving. I can build about anything—from furniture to homes and barns—and I love the work."

His father turned to him with a big smile. "Son, I'm really proud of you. I was hoping you would stay with it and learn a trade. What do you think we should do first?"

Jed said, "I believe we should build a temporary corral for the animals for the nights. During the day, we can hobble the horses and turn them out to graze. The oxen are trained to stay with the horses and not stray. Next, we should build a small building that we could live in until a nice home can be built. This building could provide a small bedroom for Sister Wilkins, a small bedroom with bunks for us, and a larger room for a kitchen, a table, and a place to rest. I could use it for a workshop later. We could make a shelter for the livestock in the winter if you think we would need it."

Jake said, "Your plans sound great to me. I was concerned about who I could get to do all of this building. You are the answer to the main part. You have the know-how, and I have the money. I can be a good helper when I can be here." Jake shook his son's hand. "We're partners, and we'll work together and see it through."

Jed smiled and said, "We certainly will."

Tad showed up and said, "Sister Saunders sent me to tell you supper will be ready in about thirty minutes. Don't be late, OK?"

Jake told him to tell her they would be there on time.

When Tad headed back, Jed said, "The first thing

we need to do is get the covered wagon parked in a convenient spot. Next, we should dig a well or find a usable water source—and then a corral for the livestock. Then we can start a temporary home. Do you think that's a starting list?

Jake said, "We'd better head over to the house."

When they got to the Sanders home, supper was nearly all on the table. Jake and Jed went to the back porch, washed up, and went back inside.

Sister Saunders told everyone where to sit, and Rachel and Jimmie sat at a little table next to their mother.

When all were seated, Tom called on Anna to say the blessing. She gave a nice prayer and expressed a thank you for having such good friends—and a special thank you that Jake and Jed were together again.

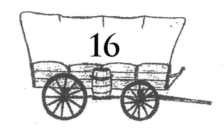

16

Bowls and platters of food were passed around, and everyone began to eat. After the meal was over, the younger kids all went outside to play.

Anna and Joan stayed to help clear the table and do the dishes.

Tom, Jake, and Jed sat together in the corner of the big room.

Tom said, "What can I do to be of help to you fellows?"

Jed said, "Maybe you can answer some questions for me."

Tom answered, "Well, my boy, if I don't know the answers, I'll help you find them. Just ask away."

Jed started, "One of the first things we're going to need is a well... to have water on our place."

Tom said, "Under the surface of ground, around these parts, there is lots of water. Some of the wells around here have hit water where there is pressure. If you are lucky enough, you might hit one of those.

Otherwise, you need to get a pump to bring the water up out of the ground. We were lucky and got a spring. With you being this close to us, you'll likely hit that same underground water that will have pressure—and you won't need a pump."

Jake asked Tom how deep they had to go to get the water.

Tom said, "We didn't know just what we would need so we bought a length of pipe and a sand point with a valve in it. We started digging about a four-foot square hole. When we got down about eight feet, we hit soft sand. We stopped digging and started to drive the sand point with the pipe attached. At about four feet farther down, we started getting water out of the pipe. About a foot farther down, we were getting a heavy flow of water, and that is where we stopped. We filled up the hole, and we have had good water flowing continuously ever since."

Jed asked about getting lumber and poles.

Tom told him of a sawmill about five miles away. "They're cutting a lot of lumber up there. And if they don't have what you need, they will cut it for you. They try to get whatever you need in just a day or two."

Jed asked about nails and a few tools that he hadn't brought with him.

Tom said, "The grocery and dry goods store in town carry a good stock of nails, tools, and other things you might need."

Jake said, "Jed, you sound like you know what we'll need for all that needs to be done."

Jed said, "Remember, Dad, it was you who thought I should learn a trade. I have now had three years of training in carpentry and woodwork, and I love the work. I guess I'm ready to tackle what lies ahead of us. We need to take the wagon over, put it in a good place, and set up camp." He went over to Sister Wilkins and asked, "If it is all right with you, we'll take your wagon back over to the property and set up camp so that we will be set for the night and for the Sabbath tomorrow."

Sister Wilkins jumped up and said, "I'll go with you." She went to the back door and called for Tad to come and help. She thanked Sister Saunders for their kindness. "Oh, I almost forgot to ask about tomorrow. We understand from the bishop that services start at ten o'clock. We certainly would like to go."

Sister Saunders said, "We have a large buggy that seats our whole family and a second smaller one that will carry four. We'll take both of them. You folks can ride with us in either of the buggies."

Sister Wilkins smiled and said, "That sounds wonderful. I am excited to be able to get back into a building for Sunday services. It will be so nice."

They all went out of the house to the front yard. Tad had gone for the oxen, and Jake and Jed followed to get their horses, which had been tied along the fence down by the barn.

Tad was quick to get the oxen and had them about hitched when Jed and the others got back to the house where the wagon had been parked.

After thanking the Saunders family, Jed and Jake

mounted their horses and headed down the road to their new homesite. The oxen and wagon followed.

In a few minutes, they neared the property line. Jake and Jed stepped down off their horses and looked along the edge of the road for the best place to pull the wagon down. They found a good place and called to Tad to swing the oxen wide so that the wagon could go down through the small dip straight instead of at an angle, which was better for the wagon.

When they were in the field, Jake suggested they tie their horses to the back of the wagon and walk ahead to find the best place.

Sister Wilkins climbed down from the wagon and walked along with them. She took hold of Jed's arm to steady herself.

Jake suggested a place near the trees where there would be good shade most of the day. "Because, here in St. George, the days are really warm."

All agreed, and they signaled Tad to bring the oxen and wagon down. After getting it into the right place, the oxen were unhitched. After their yoke was removed, the oxen were turned loose to graze.

Jake and Jed unsaddled their horses and took the packs off the other two. Jake asked Jed if his horse was the young colt from when he left home. Jed assured him that it was. Jake walked over to the horse, pulled the horse's head down to him, and put his face against it. Jed noticed a tear in his dad's eye as he loved the horse and rubbed its neck. They hobbled the four horses and turned them loose.

They turned their attention to unloading the things from the wagon. The canvas dining fly was put up, and the bedrolls, the grub box, and the little stove were set out.

Jed's father had hardly spoken a word to Sister Wilkins since being introduced, but he seemed more at ease with her. He finally started to make conversation with her about little things, asking about the long trip and where she came from.

After the dining fly was up, the men gathered some rocks to make a firepit. Tad went out to gather wood. At twilight, they sat down on a couple of the wagon boxes.

Sister Wilkins jumped up and exclaimed, "I'm going to wear my new dress to church tomorrow. I going to unwrap it and hang it up to get some of the wrinkles out. I want it to look nice for tomorrow." She went up into the wagon, and they could hear her rattling the paper it was wrapped in.

When she got down from the wagon, she asked Jed if he had clothes in his pack that needed to be taken out and hung up. He dug them out, and she took them into the wagon to hang them up.

Sister Wilkins said she would fry some bacon and make pancakes for breakfast in the morning.

Jake said, "I guess we don't have to worry about water for the stock. Tom told me that there's a seep by the trees. There's good water, and the oxen and horses can find it themselves."

Jed commented about how the horses and oxen had bonded and stayed close together to graze, and the horses didn't go too far from the wagon with their hobbles. He said, "Dad, I have found that animals are really smart, and if you treat them well, they'll respond in a very intelligent manner."

Jake said, "The horses out on the gold claim are like having two extra people with me. I talk to them, and they just seem to understand what I say. They will stand close to me and nicker a little and nod their heads. Having them there certainly gives me a good feeling."

At bedtime, Sister Wilkins went up into the wagon, and the fellows rolled out their bedrolls under the dining fly.

The next morning, they were awakened by the birds singing their hearts out. This had been a normal part of Jed's travels since he slept under the stars nearly every night.

Sister Wilkins moved around in the wagon, and the guys rolled out and dressed. They were rolling their bedrolls up as Sister Wilkins got down out of the wagon. The bedrolls were moved under the wagon to have them out of the way.

Jed started a fire, and Sister Wilkins sliced the bacon and put it into the frying pan.

Before long, the aroma of frying bacon was in the air. It always had such a pleasant smell for so early in the morning. The pancakes were fried, and she gave the first one to Jake, which brought a smile to his face. He said his were not a pretty golden color as hers were. Sister Wilkins had brought a couple of jugs of maple syrup with them from Ohio, which she had made herself, and she still had half a gallon left. To Jake, it was special. He hadn't had maple syrup for a long, long time.

After all had eaten their fill, Jed stood up and said he would like to walk around for a little while and survey the area. Jake said he would go with him.

Sister Wilkins and Tad washed the few dishes, put the camp to order, and sat down to relax for a few minutes. It was so pleasant to just sit and look around.

At nine o'clock, Jed and Jake came back to camp. Jed announced that they needed to change their clothes if they didn't want to keep the Saunders family waiting. Jake told them the clothes he was wearing were the best he had, and he would have to go as he was.

Sister Wilkins handed the clothes to Tad and Jed to change into and said she would put on her new dress.

Jed and Tad quickly changed, and Sister Wilkins came down from the wagon and modeled her new dress. It appeared to fit her fine. She even had her hair fixed nice.

Tad exclaimed, "Mom, you look great in that dress."

Jed told her he was glad she had decided to take the dress since she was very attractive in it. Jake rather shyly acknowledged her appearance.

Tad stood out at the side of the wagon and said, "They're coming. Let's go out to meet them."

They got to the road just as the Saunders family pulled up.

Sister Saunders asked Sister Wilkins to sit beside her

on the second seat. Anna was up by her father on the front seat, and Joan, Rachel, and Jill sat between them on the back seat. Johnnie was driving the other buggy, and Jake and Jed sat in the back seat with Jimmie, and Tad sat in front with Johnnie.

As they approached the church, a large number of buggies and a few wagons were already there. They pulled up to the hitching rail, and Tom and Johnnie tied up the horses. Everyone climbed out.

Sister Saunders looked at Sister Wilkins's new dress and told her how pretty it was on her.

Sister Wilkins was a little embarrassed, but she thanked her for the compliment.

They all walked into the building, and it was already filling up. Johnny told Tad that he would be up front to help pass the sacrament. He would talk to him later. Tom went up front to confer with Bishop Johnson. The women and girls, Jake, Jed, Tad, and Jimmie found seats and sat down.

The people continued to file into the building. When all the seats were filled, Jed offered his seat to an older sister. Jake also gave up his seat.

A couple of minutes later, a young couple with a little girl came in. The little girl pulled at her mother's face and pointed at Jed. It was Lilly and her parents, and she had seen Jed the moment they came in. She said, "Mommy, Mommy, it's Jed. Can I go see him?" Lillian tried to calm her down, but she kept trying to get down from her mother's arms. When her mother put her down, she pushed and squeezed between people, working her way toward Jed.

Jed reached down and picked her up, and she gave him a hug and a kiss on the cheek. "I was hoping I would see you here."

Jed whispered, "Lilly, this is my father, and I have come a long way to find him."

Lilly said, "Hello, are you going to be my friend like Jed?"

Jake told her he would like to be her friend.

Jed put her down, and she pushed and squeezed her way back to her mother.

The bishop stood, stepped to the pulpit, and welcomed everyone. He acknowledged all the new people and spoke about the wagon train that had arrived on Friday evening. He asked everyone to help make them feel at home, announced the program for the day, and sat down.

There was an opening song, a prayer, and another song, and then the sacrament was passed. There were two inspirational sermons, a closing song, and a closing prayer. Everyone sang enthusiastically.

The bishop stepped back to the pulpit and encouraged everyone to get acquainted with the newcomers.

Everyone started filing out of the building, and the visiting continued for near an hour.

Brad and Lillian came up to Jed and asked, "Is this your father?"

Jed was proud to introduce his father to them.

Brad and Lillian shook Jake's hand and said, "We

are so glad to meet you, and we are very happy that Jed has found his father and that you're together again. We have known Jed since we left Omaha on the same wagon train. He is a great young man and has been a big help to us even though he may not realize it. Our little daughter had fallen out of the wagon and broken her arm, and your son was there to help. He gave her a gift that took her mind off her arm and gave her peace. She just loves Jed."

Lilly said, "Mommy, Jake is going to be my friend too."

They told Jake that they hoped to see him often and went to their wagon. As they walked away, Lilly waved goodbye to Jed and Jake.

The Jameson family walked up and asked Jed who was with him.

Jed said, "Dad, this is Ras Jameson, his wife, Mary, his daughters, Susanna and April, and their son, Davey. They were on the wagon train from Omaha as well."

Sister Jameson said, "We are so surprised you found each other so quickly. It must be a miracle. Better yet—a blessing from above."

Jake said, "It must be a miracle. He didn't know where I was when he left Illinois, but he came straight to St. George—where I only show up every few weeks or so."

Ras said, "We're just glad that you have gotten together. I'm sure you are excited as well."

Jake said, "Who would have thought that I would see my son right here in the center of the street in St. George. I left him as a much smaller boy back home, and the next time I see him, he has really grown into a fine-looking young man who has learned a trade as well."

Other families introduced themselves and acknowledged having seen Jake a few times over the past three years without formally meeting him.

Brother Saunders came out of the church and was ready to head home. They all loaded up in the same arrangement in the buggies, and they were on their way.

Jake had never said much, but he began to open up and speak freely with his neighbors.

On the way home, Sister Wilkins spoke of what good people they had met at church. She was excited to get better acquainted with all of them.

As they turned down the road toward their home, Sister Saunders said, "Now you are coming to our house for dinner today."

Sister Wilkins started to protest.

Sister Saunders said, "Now, now, we have already started dinner, and I would be disappointed if you did not come. We're going to have roast beef, potatoes and gravy, corn on the cob, a green salad with vegetables from the garden, and strawberry shortcake with whipped cream."

Sister Wilkins exclaimed, "What a wonderful meal. I guess I can't say no to all of that. And I'm sure my menfolk will love it too."

Sister Saunders had put the roast in the oven in the morning, and it was about done before they went to church.

Tom and Johnnie pulled the buggies up in front of the house and let the women and girls off. The boys, Jed, and Jake said they would go down to the barn and walk back with them.

When the ladies walked in, the aroma of the roast in the oven permeated the house.

Sister Wilkins said, "What a lovely smell."

Sister Saunders put on her apron, rekindled the fire in the stove, and boiled water for the corn. The younger girls set the table, and Anna and Joan cut up the vegetables for the salad. Sister Saunders took the roast out of the oven and poured the drippings into a large skillet. She put it on the stove in front of the pot of water to make the gravy. When the girls finished cutting the salad, Anna made a salad dressing with bacon grease, cream, sugar, and a touch vinegar.

Sister Wilkins watched Anna make the dressing. It was new to Sister Wilkins, and Anna took a spoon and gave her a taste. Sister Wilkins exclaimed that she could hardly wait to try it on the salad.

Joan and Rachel came in with the husked corn. The corn was put into the boiling water, the gravy was thickened, the roast was put onto a platter and sliced, the potatoes and carrots were put on another platter, and the meal was just about ready.

Sister Wilkins was amazed at how fast the meal had come together.

As the men walked in, Sister Saunders said, "Hurry and wash up and come sit down. We're setting the table now."

As they ate, the visiting ranged from the good food to the things ahead for Jake, Jed, Sister Wilkins, and Tad.

Jed thought the first thing he would do was make a list of the materials they would need, and then he would ride up to the sawmill and see what they had. He might place an order if they didn't already have it in stock.

Tom said, "If you are going up to the sawmill, you might as well take a wagon and bring back a load. I have an extra wagon you can borrow. We hardly ever use it since we have our hay wagon now. It has a longer box on it, probably longer than your covered wagon has, and you are certainly welcome to use it."

Jed said, "Thank you. We'll take you up on that. That takes away one problem I was wondering about."

Jed said he would like to walk over to the place, and Jake said he would go with him.

Jed and Jake thanked everyone for a delicious meal, and Sister Wilkins asked Jed if he would like her to go with them. They were only going to do some planning and making a list for tomorrow. She told them she would come along later.

Tad and Johnnie walked around the farmyard. Tad stood at the chicken pen and watched them. He noticed quite a few A-shaped little houses with lattice fences and lattice over the top. Tad had never seen anything like that before.

Johnnie explained that when a hen wanted to sit on a group of eggs to hatch a brood of baby chicks, the lattice top opened and allowed them to put her in the A-frame building for three weeks until till the eggs hatched. After the chicks hatched, she would have a little lattice pen to keep her babies together so they would be protected.

Tad thought he could build his own little house and pen and raise some chickens for his mom and Jed. He asked Johnnie if he thought his dad would sell him two hens so he could start raising some chickens. Johnnie said he would ask his dad. They walked around the farmyard, and Tad asked questions and admired the things he saw.

When Jed and his dad got over to their place, they walked around and decided where to put the barn, the corral, the woodworking shop, and the home. They agreed that the first thing to do was dig the well so they would have water. Next was to build the corral to take care of the oxen and horses.

The woodshop would be used to live in until a house could be built. Jed went to the back of the wagon, dug into his pack, and found a pencil and paper. He made a list of posts and poles for fencing the corral. On a second list, he wrote down the supplies they needed from town.

As Jake and Jed surveyed the field, the position of trees, and where they would build the big home someday, they wondered where the well should be. The home would be on the higher ground, closer to the road, and if the well was on the back of the house, the water could run through a springhouse and then down to the barn to water the livestock. They decided that would be best. They placed a stake in the ground where they would dig the well. Tomorrow, if they made it back from the sawmill in time, they would go to town and get the things they needed from the store.

They sat down in the shade, and Sister Wilkins and Tad came over to the wagon.

Sister Wilkins asked if they had things planned out.

Jed gave her a rundown of what they were thinking, and she watched carefully as Jed pointed to the locations of the corral, the barn, outbuildings, the well, and the big home. He expressed the need for necessities first and then the luxuries of the big home.

She told them that it looked like a sound plan to her. "Jed, I have been thinking about the property across the road. I have brought quite a bit of money with me from the sale of my property back in Ohio. I believe that I have more than enough to buy a piece of that ground and still have money to take care of me and Tad for a spell. It might be smart to invest some of that money I have now while that land is still available. What do you and Jake think about that?"

Jake said, "It sounds like a good plan. That property will only go up in value as time goes by."

Sister Wilkins suggested walking over to the road and looking it over, and they could help her decide which piece of land to buy.

They couldn't determine the exact property lines from the directions the bishop had given them.

She said, "Maybe I can get Sister Saunders to drive me into town tomorrow, and we can go to the land office and get more information. I just have a feeling I need to act upon it right away before someone else buys it. At least I can ask the bishop to give me first chance at it."

Jake and Jed agreed with her. They walked back to the wagon, and Sister Wilkins asked if they would like a little snack since it had been six hours since dinner.

Jed was starting to get hungry again, and that sounded good to him. Tad was ready to eat something too.

Sister Wilkins sliced some of her sourdough bread and put out jelly, dried fruit, and jerky. She went to the water barrel on the side of the wagon and got a pitcher of water. The water in the barrel was getting low, and it would need to be filled tomorrow.

Jed told Tad about borrowing a wagon and going up to the sawmill for a load of poles, posts, and lumber. If he took the oxen and got the wagon right after they had breakfast, they would leave for the sawmill as soon as he got back.

By the time they had finished eating, it had started to get dark. They decided to go to bed and get an early start in the morning.

17

J ed awoke the next morning before the birds started
singing. He thought about all that needed to be done
that day. All of a sudden, a thought crossed his mind.
They really needed an outhouse. Sister Wilkins had
never mentioned it before, but he knew it was really
needed.

When it was finally light, the birds began to sing. He
made a list of the materials needed for the outhouse.
With that done, he began a list of materials for the
house, which would probably become his workshop.
He would take the list and bring all of the materials
they could haul and leave a list at the sawmill for future
loads.

Jed shook Tad and woke him up.

Tad sat up and rubbed his eyes. "Is it morning
already?"

Jed assured him it was, and if he would get up now,
he could go bring the oxen up before breakfast, which
would give them an earlier start for the sawmill.

When Tad was dressed and ready, Jed handed him the lead ropes for the oxen. Jed asked if he could bring Blaze up as well. Tad assured Jed he could, and with the three lead ropes, he was on his way down through the field. Before Sister Wilkins got out of the wagon, Jed had a fire going.

Sister Wilkins started making breakfast.

When Tad got back, Jed helped him get the animals tied up on the opposite side of the wagon.

The bacon was fried, and a couple of pancakes were done. Jake and Jed fixed their pancakes and sat down to eat. Tad got his bacon just as his mother put a pancake on his plate. After they had a second pancake, Sister Wilkins fixed her plate and sat down on a box to eat. She asked about the plan for the day.

Jed told her they would get back from the sawmill before noon. They would unload and then take the barrel from the wagon and go for water. After lunch, they would head to town for the hardware.

When Tad finished eating, he went to borrow the extra wagon. He brought a canteen to get some fresh water for the road.

Sister Wilkins asked Jed if he thought they would need to take lunch with them.

Jed thought they could just wait to eat when they got back. They hadn't been to the sawmill yet, and they didn't know how long it would take. He thought they would be back before noon.

Tad hurried the oxen as much as he could so they could be on their way.

Jake saddled the horse and had him ready to go.

Jed tossed a few ropes into the wagon in case they needed to tie down the load. He asked Tad if he wanted to drive the oxen, ride the horse, or ride on the seat of the wagon.

Tad smiled and asked if he could ride the horse.

Jed told him that would be fine.

With the canteen hung on the side of the wagon, they were off. Jed drove the oxen, and his dad walked beside him. His dad wanted to know all about his trip and what kind of man Elizabeth had married.

Jed assured his dad that Jonathon was very good to her and was a good worker and that he could be very proud of him. Jed told him about his experiences on the trail and the elderly man who knew his father.

His father remembered him and was glad Jed had met him.

Sister Wilkins finished cleaning up after breakfast as best she could because she had run out of water. She put on her bonnet and found a small bucket to get more some water. She walked up to the Saunders home and stepped up and knocked on the door. Jill opened the door and gave her a hug. The other girls came out from wherever they were to speak to her. Sister Saunders was mixing dough for a batch of bread. She told Sister Wilkins to sit down, and they would visit as she finished the mixing and put the dough in a large pan to raise.

Anna asked what Jed and the others were doing.

Sister Wilkins told her they were off to the sawmill

for lumber and poles, and then she told Sister Saunders about the possibility of going to town to see about the land across the road. She had a feeling that she needed to invest in that property.

Sister Saunders told her that the girls could take care of the bread and get it baked, and she would get ready. They would drive the buggy to town. She really needed to go to the store. Sister Saunders asked Rachel if she would run down to the barn, find Johnnie, have him hitch a horse to the buggy, and bring it up to the house for her.

Rachel happily said she would do it and was on her way.

Jimmie stepped in the back door and said, "Hi, Sister Wilkins. What are you doing here?"

Sister Wilkins told him she needed to get a small bucket of water.

Jimmie said he would get it for her. He took the bucket and went out to the well to fill it. In a minute or two, he came back with a nearly full bucket. As he brought it to her, he spilled some on the floor. "I'm sorry. I guess I got it too full."

Joan threw a rag over to him and asked him to wipe it up.

Jimmie wiped up the spill and threw the rag back to Joan.

Joan said, "Thank you."

A few minutes later, Johnnie had the horse and buggy ready.

Sister Saunders took off her apron, hung it over a

chair, stepped over to a mirror, and checked her hair. She grabbed her bonnet from a hook on the wall and put it on. She reminded the girls to take care of the bread and said, "Jimmie, you be good—and don't give your sisters a bad time, do you hear?"

"Yes, Mom, but they boss me around all the time."

Sister Saunders said, "Yes, I know, but you are always teasing them. Just be good—I love you."

As she was walking out the door, Jimmie said, "Mom, please bring me back some candy!"

She threw him a kiss as she told the girls goodbye.

When Sister Wilkins got outside, she poured a little water on the flowers because she didn't want to spill any in the buggy.

The women climbed up into the buggy, and they were on their way. When they got closer to the wagon, Sister Saunders slowed the horse, eased the horse and buggy through the low spot at the side of the road, and pulled up to the wagon. Sister Wilkins put her bucket on a box on the side of the wagon, covered it with a cloth, and went back to the buggy. The two women visited and laughed and enjoyed each other.

As the menfolk approached the sawmill, they could smell the fresh lumber, which really pleased Jed. He couldn't seem to get enough of it and breathed it in deeply.

His father said, "Son, you really like that smell, don't you?"

Jed said, "You know, Dad, if we could smell heaven, I'd bet it would smell just like this."

His dad shook his head in wonderment about his son.

They heard the sound of the saw as it sawed the length of a log, and they also heard the men calling out directions to each other. There were piles of lumber everywhere. Over to the side was a little building that looked like the office.

Jed stopped the oxen, left them in the care of Tad, and he and his dad went in.

A man was working on some papers at his desk. He stood up and came over to them. "Good morning. I'm Obed. What can I do for you fellows today?"

Jed showed him the list of things they were looking for. The first on the list was pole-fencing material.

Obed said they had poles and posts. "What lengths are you needing?"

Jed told him they needed thirty poles, sixteen to eighteen feet long, and forty-four posts.

Obed said, "We have at least that many in stock. And what else is on your list?"

Jed went down the list of lumber for the outhouse.

Obed said, "We have all of those things as well. What would you like to load first?"

Jed said, "I believe we should put the lumber on first and then put as many of the poles and posts on as we can. We don't want to overload the wagon. We'll be making a number of trips up here for more material in the next few months, and we don't want to overload the wagon today."

Jed saw a hitching rail next to the office and told Tad

to tie the horse up there, and then he could bring the wagon over to the first pile of lumber.

Obed asked about all that they planned to build, and Jake and Jed took turns explaining their plans.

Tad looked over toward the mill and saw a pile of short cut-off lumber ends and asked Obed about it.

Obed asked Tad if he could use some of it.

Tad told him he had a project he wanted to build and could use a few pieces.

Obed told him to help himself since it was just scrap.

Tad asked Jed if he could slip a few pieces into the load.

Jed wondered what Tad had in mind, but he told him he could take a few boards.

Obed had a clipboard and listed the material as it was loaded, and then the group went over to the poles. They ended up putting on sixteen poles and thirty post.

Obed went over to the office, and Jed and Jake tied down the load.

In the office, Obed totaled the bill.

Jake took out a small leather bag from his pocket and counted out the money.

Obed told them he would give them a bill, and when they came back for the next load, they could bring the money for the previous load.

While the men were settling up their bill, Tad went to the scrap pile and pulled out some boards. He took them to the wagon and poked them in where he thought they would stay put.

Jake and Jed thanked Obed, shook his hand, and then went out.

Obed reminded them to go slowly on the steep hill and apply the wagon brake. If the wagon started moving too fast, the oxen wouldn't be able to stop it. The wagon would pick up more speed and would be more than the oxen could control.

They thanked him for the advice and pulled out.

When they came to the dangerous hill, they stopped the oxen for a few minutes and let them rest. They put rocks in front of the wheels to keep the wagon from rolling forward.

They drank water and were ready to pull out again. Jake thought that it would be wise to use the extra rope to tie it to the back of the wagon and then dally the rope around the saddle horn. The horse could help hold the wagon back.

They started down the hill slowly. Jake was on the horse, Jed was on the wagon to run the brake rod, and Tad was driving the oxen. The oxen sensed the need to hold back and did their part. Before they were completely down, Jed could tell the brakes had gotten hot from the friction on the rims of the wheels. They went down slowly and arrived safely at the bottom. The rest of the way home, things went smoothly.

It was a little before eleven when they pulled into their property. As they passed the covered wagon, Sister Wilkins came over to them and said that she had just bought thirty acres across the road. "It's paid for, and I have my deed. I feel like this is really home now—and Tad and I own a piece of this valley."

Jed and Jake were very pleased for her and expressed their congratulations. Tad was as happy as his mother was.

They pulled the wagon over to the area they had planned for the corral and stopped. Jed, Tad, and Jake untied the load, took off a couple of posts, and began to stack the other posts in a pile. They placed four posts down for a base and began stacking the poles on the laid-out posts.

They drove the oxen over to where the outhouse was going to be and stacked the lumber over on a few of the fence post.

Tad took his short scrap pieces and put them out of the way. Jed was still wondering what Tad had in mind for them, but he let it go.

They pulled over to the covered wagon, got the water barrel, and put it on the wagon that the oxen were hitched to. Jed and Tad brought a couple of buckets to carry the water over to fill the barrel.

When they came back from getting the water, Jake helped Jed lift the barrel over to its place on the covered wagon. They were ready to head to town.

The men enjoyed themselves in the store and looked at all the tools. Jed had brought some tools on his packhorse from Illinois, but his space was limited.

They selected a heavy hammer for bigger nails and spikes for the fence, a bow saw, a shovel, a sledgehammer, and a couple of other things. They also looked for what they would need for the well. The store had a new tool that was used for postholes and wells. It was called a post or well auger. They decided with all the postholes and at least two wells, it would be a good investment. It came with two additional pipe sections for going deeper. They also got a framing square and two pipe wrenches.

They bought a keg of twenty-penny nails, a keg of eight-penny (a keg being a small barrel), five pounds of four-penny, and four pounds of six-penny nails. All of the nails were square. They also bought the foot valve and four, four-foot sections, one two-foot section of pipe, one drive cap, one elbow, and four couplings. If they should get a flowing well, this would give them what they needed. They paid for the things, loaded up, and headed home. It was a little after twelve when they pulled in.

Tad climbed into the wagon to see what they had bought. After he looked at all the things, he jumped back down and said he would take care of the oxen. He unhitched them and turned them loose. The oxen headed straight for the water down by the trees. The horses saw them and whinnied, and the oxen quickened their step.

Sister Wilkins called to them and said she would get their lunch ready. Jed and Jake were eager to try out the new auger. They unloaded it and the parts that came with it. They carried them over to the stake in the ground. They dug down about two feet to get the hole started. They put the auger in the hole, gave it three turns, and lifted it out of the hole. They tapped it on the ground, dumping the dirt, and put it back in again. The ground was fairly soft, and the drilling was quite fast. When they were down about four feet, Sister Wilkins had their lunch ready. They put down the auger and went over to eat.

After eating, they headed back to the well and added another section to the auger handle. It took a little longer to bring each auger load out of the hole and dump it. After about six feet, the sandy soil in the hole would not stay in the auger. They put together some lengths of pipe, the drivable foot valve on one end, and a drive cap on the top, stood it in the hole, and started driving on the pipe with their new sledgehammer. It was a slow process, and each stroke took them down about an inch. They added another length of pipe, put the drive cap back on, and drove it down some more. They added another four-foot piece of pipe, drove it down about a foot, and hit a hard layer of ground and the pipe was just barely going down with each hit of the sledgehammer..

It took another thirty minutes to go down another foot, and then it got easy again. When the drive cap was down near ground level, Jed felt like they must be in the water. They assembled the other pieces of pipe and removed the drive cap. As it was coming off, they could hear the air in the pipe escaping around the threads. When it came off, the water came gushing out. They quickly screwed on the pipe fittings, but they were getting wet with the water spraying out onto them. They had a flowing well! They were excited. Tad called for his mother to come and see.

Sister Wilkins came over and was excited to see the flowing water. "With this much water, we can irrigate a garden and have plenty of water for the livestock, the house, and everything."

Jed dug a little ditch to carry the water toward the trees.

Jake and Jed were very pleased with getting a free-flowing well. They put the tools in the wagon for the night and checked the water again. The water looked clear and inviting. They each took a sample and had a drink, and the water was really cool and tasted good.

They went over to the area where the outhouse was going to be built. Jed marked out the hole, and his dad started digging. Jed and Tad worked on making a set of sawhorses. It didn't take them long, and they were ready to be used. Tad hadn't used a saw very much, but Jed taught him how to use it effectively.

They dug the hole and cut some of the lumber and were ready to start nailing things together.

Sister Wilkins called them to supper, and they washed their hands at the well and ate. After supper, they worked on the outhouse a little longer before they had to give up because of darkness.

With darkness setting in, they prepared themselves for bed.

18

T he next morning came early, and Jed was awake
before the birds again. At first, he just thought
about his agenda. He was eager to get back to work on
the outhouse. With the cutting they had done yesterday,
it wouldn't be much longer before they could start
nailing things together. Some of the tools they would
need were in his packs, and they were in the wagon.
He would have to wait until Sister Wilkins was up and
out of the wagon to get to them. Jed continued to plan
the day. He had a pencil, a framing square, and the
saw, and he wouldn't have to wait until Sister Wilkins
was up and moving around in the wagon.

Jed got dressed, went to the open wagon box, and
picked up the tools he needed. He went to the pile of
lumber when it was light enough to see his lines on the
lumber. As he moved the first piece, a smile came on
his face. The new lumber felt good in his hands.

He put more pieces over on the sawhorses and
marked what needed to be cut. He waited until the

others were up before sawing. Finally, his father got up, and then Sister Wilkins came out of the wagon. That was his signal to start sawing.

His father came over to check on what Jed was up to so early. Jake was surprised by how fast Jed worked with the wood.

Jed made a number of cuts and stacked the material in separate little piles. They were ready to be nailed together.

Sister Wilkins called for them to come to breakfast.

Jed and Jake walked over by the well to see how the water was flowing. It seemed to flow even more than the previous evening. They were happy with the results of their well. They washed their hands in the cool water and wiped them on their pants.

Sister Wilkins commented about Jed being an early bird. She said she could tell that Jed had been up for a little while. "You are certainly eager to start working with that wood, aren't you?"

Jed told her how good the new lumber felt in his hands.

She smiled. She was as proud of him as she was of her very own son.

Jed went to the back of the covered wagon and got the extra tools he needed. As he was about to walk away, Sister Wilkins told Tad to wake up because his breakfast was getting cold.

Tad sat up in his bed and said, "Is it morning already?" He jumped up, slipped on his pants and shirt, and slid his feet into his boots. He looked at the well. "Wow, the water is still running?" He ran over and washed his hands and face. "It's cold!"

Tad's mother handed him his plate; it was all fixed and ready for him.

Jake told Jed he was going to check where the water flowed to. He got a shovel and walked along the little stream. In a few places, he dug a little dirt out or filled in dirt along the side to contain the water to a single ditch. It was flowing toward a creek that was past the trees and not on their property. He found the water had done well making its own ditch. Jake walked back to where Jed was working, sat down, and watched Jed. He seemed to have something on his mind, and Jed asked what he was thinking about.

"There are two things. First, I admire you and the way your hands work. I'm beginning to worry about my gold claim up in the mountains. There are a lot of men searching for gold in the mountains, and if you are not at your claim for a few days, they get to thinking you have deserted it—and they start to move in on you. The vein I'm working now is rich, and I'm making out real well with it. I certainly don't want to lose it to some claim jumpers. I have my claim registered, but I have to be there most of the time to keep it. I was thinking that in the morning, I would pull out and head back to the mountains. I want you to go with me to town and be there when the bank opens. I want your name to be on my account. That way, you can take money out when you need it for supplies and lumber and whatever else you need."

Jed said, "Dad, I know you need to do it, and I hate to see you leave. But you have to protect what you have worked so hard for. At least we are close, and we can see each other often. I can stay here and build the things we have planned. I love woodwork, and I'll be happy doing that. I need to write a letter to Elizabeth and Jonathon and tell them I made it, that we've found each other, and what we have been doing. Maybe they can make plans to move out here next summer, and we can all be back together. I have been thinking a lot about Mama in the past few days. I would bet that she is up there in heaven, and she has had a hand in all the things that have fallen into place to make sure I found you like I did. It's not a miracle; it's just Mama helping out where she can."

"Jed, I think you must be right. Things just don't happen like they did without heaven's help."

"I bet that Mama is up in heaven looking down with a big smile on her face."

His dad said, "It has been a blessing to be sure."

Jed finished cutting a few more pieces and was ready to nail things together.

His dad stood up and said he would go get some more nails for him. "What size do you want?"

Jed answered, "I'm ready for the twenty-penny nails. I need to start nailing the floor pieces together." He cut a few pieces and made up a couple of small boxes to bring the nails over to him.

His dad walked over to the wagon and opened the keg with the larger nails in it. The board had to be broken and pried out. He filled the boxes and came back with them.

Jed put some nails in his apron pockets and started nailing the framework for the floor.

Tad came over and asked if he could help.

Jed showed him where he could start nailing the floorboards to the framework. From there, they started nailing walls together.

Jed's dad could see what was needed and kept things in position for Tad and Jed to nail.

Jed marked out the remaining pieces for framing the outhouse. Tad cut them, which didn't take long, but Tad's arms needed a rest.

Jed's father came over and cut until Tad had rested and came back to give it another try.

They had dug the hole yesterday, and they set the floor section over the hole and started standing the walls and nailing them into position.

When the walls were standing, they took a break to get a drink and sit for a minute.

Sister Wilkins asked, "What are you building?"

Tad said, "Mom, it's an outhouse!"

Sister Wilkins let out a little squeal and danced a little jig. "No more hiding in the bushes. For this, I'll bake you something special to eat."

Jed told Sister Wilkins that his dad was planning to go back to his gold claim in the morning. Jed told her he'd be coming out more often and staying only a couple of days each time.

They were rested and went back to work. Jed saw

some young-growth trees that he thought he could use. He took his ax and cut down two trees that were about three inches in diameter. He trimmed the small limbs and took them over to the outhouse. He cut the poles into lengths; two were nine feet long, and seven were eighteen inches long.

Jed's dad said, "You amaze me."

Tad could see that it was a ladder, which they would need. Jed laid out the rafters, and Tad and his dad cut them. Jed kept giving measurements to Tad and his dad to cut siding and the roofing boards.

Jed went up on the ladder and nailed the rafters into place. Next was the siding on the front and back walls. The roof boards were also nailed into place.

Sister Wilkins called to them that lunch was ready. While they were eating, Jed told them that he had forgotten the hinges for the door. He asked Tad to ride the horse into town to get them.

Tad was excited to go, and when he had finished eating, he brought Jed's Blaze back up. Jed drew a picture of the type of hinge he wanted and a picture of the door hook they could use. They saddled the horse, and Jed gave the picture and some money to Tad. He warned him not to trot the horse too far at one time. Then Tad was on his way.

Jake and his dad went back to work cutting the remaining pieces for the siding and nailing them on. Next were the pieces for the door. Jed marked them, and his dad cut them. They had the frame for the seat ready, and it was nailed together. Jed cut out the seat, cut the hole, and smoothed the edges with his rasp. As it was nailed into place, Tad got back. Jed put the hinges on the door, and they held the door up into the opening, shimmed it to hold it, and Jed fastened the hinges. With the shims out, the door swung freely.

They cut the batten boards to cover the little space between the boards on the walls and the corner trim boards. They cleaned up, piling the scrap in one pile and the lumber on the lumber pile.

Jed said, "Go get your mother."

Tad ran and yelled, "Mom, come see."

Sister Wilkins rubbed her hands on her apron and headed over to have a look. She stepped up to the door, turned the button latch, and pulled the door open with the handle. She looked in. "Oh my! It is so nice." She hugged them all. "I have the final touch." She whispered to Tad, and he went running to the wagon. He brought back an old catalog and handed it to his mother.

She proudly stepped inside and placed it on the right side of the hole. "Now we are in business."

Everyone laughed.

Sister Wilkins told them she had supper ready. "Wash your hands—and then you can eat." She had made a stew from dried vegetables and beef jerky, and she had seasoned it just right. It smelled so good. They filled their plates and sat down to eat.

When they had had their fill, she said, "I have dessert to top off the stew." She brought out a cake and fixed a piece for each one. She put peach sauce on top of each piece.

Jake was especially pleased with the dessert. He had always enjoyed cake with sliced fresh peaches. "This is every bit as good as fresh peaches and cake!"

Sister Wilkins heated some water for the dishes. She commented on having plenty of water to use and not having to use it sparingly.

After he ate, Jed got some paper, sharpened his pencil, and wrote a letter to his sister and her family. He told her a little about his trip, his safe arrival, finding his dad and the property, digging a well, and building the outhouse. Jed told Elizabeth about getting together with Sister Wilkins and Tad and how she bought the property next to theirs for the two of them. He mentioned the good people in St. George.

It was getting dark, and he would have to finish the letter in the morning.

Jed was awake early again, and he thought about what else he should tell his sister.

When it was light enough to see, he got up, dressed, and picked up his pencil and paper. He told Elizabeth about her letter being there when he arrived and finding the people who had befriended their father. What wonderful people they were. He told her that he felt positive that their mother was in heaven and that she was looking out for them. He closed his letter by inviting them to plan to leave next May to come west—and he would have a place for them. "Sister, please keep me informed about your plans." He wished them well and told her how happy he was about her baby being a girl and giving her the name of Sarah. "Your brother, Jed. I love you."

Jed folded his letter and slipped it into his shirt pocket. When he was in town, he would buy an envelope and mail it.

Sister Wilkins was stirring around in the wagon, and he started a fire that would be ready for her to cook breakfast. She and Tad had been such a blessing for the past three months.

Jed's dad was up and dressed, and he asked Jed if he was always up this early.

Jed smiled and said, "Well, somebody has to get up to wake up the birds and get them ready to start their singing at first light."

His dad grinned and said, "I am glad you can do it. The birds need a good caretaker and music director. You're just the man for the job."

Sister Wilkins was up, said good morning, and made a trip to the outhouse. When she returned, she said, "I like it."

While Sister Wilkins fixed breakfast, Jed and his dad went over their plans for the next things that needed to be done. Jed told his dad that there were so many things he wanted to build.

Jed told his dad that he would speak to Tom about growing crops—and the best time of year to plant—so that he could have the ground plowed and ready. Jed mentioned the need for winter feed for the livestock. In St. George, there was very little winter and only a few frosty mornings. The grass would probably grow all year. They did have a short rainy season, and that would be a good time to have crops in the ground. They could plant a garden at any time since they had the well and water to irrigate with. Jed brought up the idea of fencing the whole place, or at least the pasture area, so the horses could be turned loose without being hobbled.

Sister Wilkins said breakfast was ready, and they got their plates, filled them, and ate.

Jed and his dad spoke very little as they ate. Their minds were on different things.

After they finished eating, they decided to get the horses and get ready to go to town.

They saddled Doc and Dolly, and Jake put the packsaddle on his packhorse.

Sister Wilkins handed Jake a bag with a fresh loaf of bread, a couple pieces of cake, and some of the peach sauce in a jelly jar.

Jake thanked her kindly and told her he was glad she was there, especially for all the help she had been to his son.

Jake and Jed stepped into their saddles, waved to Sister Wilkins, and headed to town.

On the way to town, Jed inquired about his claim in the mountains and what it was like up there. "Is it a mine in a mountain or are you panning for gold?"

Jake explained that it was both. He panned for gold a lot, but he found the most gold in the mine tunnel.

The bank was closed because they were a little early.

Jake said he needed some things from the store to take with him. The store was open, and they went in.

While his dad bought his things, Jed went over to the hardware area to see more of the things that were in stock. He looked at windows, plumbing supplies, and other tools that he might need. He also looked at what they had in the way of grain for livestock and seeds to plant.

Jed noticed the clerk from the post office. When his dad had finished, Jed told the clerk that he needed to mail a letter and needed an envelope.

The clerk told him he could help him at the counter. He handed Jed an envelope, and Jed addressed it to Elizabeth Porter in Johnsonville, Illinois. He put his return address on it and paid for the postage and the envelope.

They carried Jake's things out to his packhorse and put them in the pack.

The bank was open, and when they walked in, the manager welcomed Jake, called him by name, and shook his hand. Jake introduced Jed to the manager.

Jake explained that he wanted to have his son's name put on his account.

The manager smiled and told Jake he would be glad to do that for him. He invited them over to the desk and offered them a chair. He handed a form to Jed to sign, and on the bottom of the form, there was a place for Jake to sign and authorize the change.

With the papers signed, Jake thanked the manager for taking care of the matter for him. Jake told the manager they had started to build on his property. He explained that his son was trained in carpentry and woodworking—as well as growing up on a farm—and he had great faith in his abilities.

They shook hands with the banker and walked out.

By the horses, Jake gave his son a hug and told him he would see him again in two weeks. He mounted his horse, and with the packhorse trailing alongside, Jake started down the street towards the mountains.

Jed decided to go back into the store. He needed to know what all they had so he could make his plans for the buildings to accommodate what was available.

19

As he rode back toward the property, Jed thought of the most important thing to move ahead on. His first thought was to build the fence for the livestock, but Sister Wilkins's comfort—along with that of Tad and himself—was important as well.

The things on his mind included the workshop to be used for a temporary home, a springhouse that he would fix up like the Aikens place back in Missouri, an adjoining bathhouse, and outside the bathhouse, on the south side, he would place a couple of barrels to fill with fresh water, which would heat up in the sun for bathing. A barn for storing hay and for the livestock. Maybe a chicken house and a pigpen so they could raise a hog or two for meat. Maybe they could buy a cow and have fresh milk, butter, cream and cottage cheese. His mind was going wild with all the things he would like to do.

He was finally home, and he stopped at the covered wagon.

Sister Wilkins stepped out to greet him. She asked if he had gotten his father on his way.

Jed said that he did. He thought his father was a little reluctant to go, but he had a vested interest in that gold claim and couldn't just walk away from it. Besides, it provided the money to build the things they all needed.

Jed stepped to the well and got a cold drink of water. It was good water, and he was proud of one more achievement.

Jed asked where Tad was.

Sister Wilkins told Jed he was working on a little project of his own, but he wouldn't tell her what it was.

Jed saw Tad down by the outhouse—where Tad's pieces of lumber had been stacked—and he could see that Tad was working on something, but he decided not to ask. He would let Tad tell them when he was ready. Jed liked to do things and surprise others. He just called to Tad to come over. When Tad got there, Jed told him they needed to start the corral fence down where the poles were. Tad needed to bring the tools he had used and put them away so that they were protected, and he could get them out later.

Tad ran back to his project, brought the tools to the wagon box, and put them away.

Jed told him they would take the two shovels and the new auger and start on the fence. They would do a layout first and then start digging the postholes.

They set the poles out in a line where the fence would go with the proper lap and marked where the posts needed to go by taking out a shovelful of dirt.

With the layout complete, they started to dig holes. The auger was too heavy and awkward for Tad, so he went ahead of Jed and dug the holes out a foot or so deep. Jed followed and used the auger. By the time they took a lunch break, they had six posts in the holes, ready to be tamped in with dirt.

They stopped halfway to the covered wagon and looked back. It was starting to show.

During the afternoon, Jed and Tad finished digging the holes and set five posts permanently.

At the wagon that evening, after they ate, Jed asked Sister Wilkins how the food supply had held out. She said they were getting low on a few things and thought they should probably plan to go to the store on Saturday to stock up.

Jed said, "There could be someone around who has a used or a broken-down buggy for sale. If I could buy it and a buggy harness, I could repair the buggy. Chip, the packhorse, would be easy to train to pull it. I will ask around when we go to town. Tom might even know of one that might be available."

Jed hadn't talked to Tom since Sunday after they had dinner. There was still time left in the day before dark, and he decided to walk over and have a visit.

Tad asked if he could go along. Jed assured him that it would be fine. Sister Wilkins said she would stay at the wagon. As they approached, someone in the house called out that Jed and Tad were coming.

Johnnie came running around the house, and Tom came out to meet them. Tom stuck out his hand and grasped Jed's hand with a firm grip and asked how things were going.

Jed quickly reviewed all that they had accomplished in the past three days. They had gone to the sawmill, dug the well, built the outhouse, and started building a fence for the corral.

Tom was impressed.

Jed told him his dad had gone back to his claim because he was worried about claim jumpers.

Jed asked about when to plant crops and gardens. "I heard we have a short rainy season. When should we expect that?"

Tom tried to give him complete answers, and Jed tried to remember everything Tom told him.

The last question was about the used or broken buggy. "It would give Sister Wilkins transportation to get to town and back and give her an opportunity to visit other women in the area and make more friends."

Tom knew the blacksmith in town, and he might know of someone who had one that they would sell.

Jed explained that he had learned to do buggy and wagon repairs, including repairing and building wheels.

Tom said, "Young man, you are a man of many talents. You're going to do great around here. I have to make a run to town tomorrow, and I will stop and talk to the blacksmith."

Jed thanked Tom for the use of his wagon and said if for any reason he needed it, to let him know, and he would get it back to him. On Friday, he planned to make another trip to the sawmill. This time, it would be for a few more rails for his corral fence and materials to get him started on the shop that they would use for a home until a larger one could be built.

Tom told him he was doing a great job and that he would be glad to come and help raise walls or anything else.

It would be dark soon, and Jed and Tad said goodbye and headed home.

Tad was talkative on the way back. He liked being around Johnnie, and they had had fun together.

It was dark enough when they got back that they decided to go to bed.

Tomorrow, they would finish the fence and bring the livestock up to the enclosure at night from now on. There would be less of a chance that coyotes or wolves would come in and run them or kill one. Also, the horses could have time without the hobbles on.

When they had finished eating their breakfast, Jed and Tad headed for the corral fence. They planned to finish it today if possible.

They set posts tamping dirt around each post to make it solid. They set the four corner posts first and moved on to set the line post. Jed stepped back to the corner and would sight down the line of post. Tad moved them as Jed directed to make a straight line. Jed would do the tamping, and Tad would put the dirt in as needed. At noon, they had all the posts set except for the three extras that would make the up gate.

Jed and Tad took their lunch break and then were back at it. They took both hammers, nail apron, twenty-penny nails, and the spikes for attaching the poles to the post. They also took some scraps of lumber and the saw.

The four gateposts were set in pairs about eight inches apart. They would be on each end of the gate poles.

As they worked together, Jed explained why they did things in certain ways. Tad was interested in every step.

With all of the posts set, Jed went over into the trees and cut a special branch with a forked end. It would serve as a prop to hold the end of the pole being nailed. They used a brace and bit and drilled a hole where each spike would go through the pole. Tad would hold up the other end at about the right height. With one end nailed, Jed would take the prop stick to the other end and nail it. They went around and nailed all the top rails in place. Jed cut the prop stick for the height of the lower pole. They went around and nailed the lower poles in place. They were eight poles short of being able to finish.

As they picked up the tools and headed back toward the covered wagon, Tom turned off the road toward them. They hurried and got to the wagon just after he did.

Tom gave them a hearty hello.

Jed and Tad welcomed him.

Tom looked at their well and thought that the water flow was even better than his. Tom said he liked that.

He noticed the outhouse and said, "Looks like you about have the fence done as well."

Jed told him he was eight poles short. "We brought a full load and didn't want to overload the wagon to come down the steep section this side of the mill. We are headed back to the mill in the morning for another load, and we'll bring the other eight poles. The other material on our load tomorrow will start us on the building that will be our temporary home. Do you have a set of drag shoes for the wagon?"

Tom said, "Come to think of it, Jed, I do have a set. Do you think you need them?"

Jed explained the safety it would give, coming down that one hill, and that it would be better than an accident.

Tom told Jed he had bought them not long after coming here, but he had never used them. If he wanted to try them, he was welcome to take them with him.

Jed told him he would come over to his place and get them before they left in the morning.

Tom said, "Jed, you asked about a used or broken buggy that you might be able to get. The blacksmith told me of one that this fellow has. He had his horses run away with it and rolled it. It has some bent metal pieces, broken tongue, and a single tree ruined. Oh! And one wheel is collapsed. He thought you might be able to buy it for ten dollars—maybe a little less."

Jed asked if he knew where the man lived.

Tom explained how to get there. "If you should happen to buy it, you could take the hay wagon over to get it. That way, you could just set it up on to the wagon to bring home."

Jed thanked Tom for the information and for checking for him.

Tom said he had better get on home, and he was already late for supper. "You know how women worry when you are not there at the right time." Tom waved goodbye and was on his way.

Jed was excited about the information.

Sister Wilkins had supper ready for them. Jed and Tad put the tools away, washed their hands, and were ready to eat. They had put in a good day's work.

While they ate, Sister Wilkins asked what Tom wanted.

Jed said, "He just stopped to check on us and see how we are doing."

Tad caught the passive explanation of Tom's visit. He knew that Jed was planning to surprise his mom. He liked surprises too. Tad had a surprise in the making as well.

The first thing Jed did when he got up the next morning was take the lead ropes down to the end of the field where the horses and oxen grazed and bring them up. He tied the oxen and riding horse to the wagon and tethered out the packhorse near the new corral. If he didn't tie him up, Chip would try to follow them to the mill.

When Jed got back to the covered wagon, Sister Wilkins was making breakfast. She called to Tad to wake him and get him moving, and she told him breakfast would be ready soon.

Jed unloaded the nails and tools from the wagon. He told Sister Wilkins that they were going to the sawmill for another load of lumber, and it would probably be some time before lunch when they would get back.

She asked about fixing a lunch for them, but Jed thought that wouldn't be necessary. They could just eat when they got back.

Jed and Tad ate their breakfast, hitched the oxen up, and headed over to get the drag shoes for the wagon.

Anna stepped out of the front door to shake the breakfast crumbs from the tablecloth, and she called a cheery good morning to them.

Jed and Tad waved back. Jed thought, *She looks nice for this early in the morning.*

They went on down to the barn and found Tom and Johnnie doing the morning chores. Tom waved to them and told Jed he had laid out the drag shoes by the tool shed.

Jed drove the oxen around to the drag shoes. He picked one up, carried it over to the rear wheel, set it down, and checked the length of chain to attach it to the wagon box. Everything looked to be in order, and Jed set it up in the wagon, put the other one in, and tied them in so they wouldn't slide out.

Tom had never used them and didn't know how they worked.

Jed told him that a few of the heavier wagons used them when they came from Omaha. On those steeper roads in the mountains, the drag shoes had been a big help and a safety measure.

Jed thanked Tom, and he and Tad headed up the road toward the sawmill. The oxen were doing well pulling the empty wagon, and they moved along at a good pace.

They arrived at the sawmill a little before eight and went straight to the office. Jed looked in, but Obed wasn't in. They waited outside.

In a few minutes, Obed hurried over to them. "Well, what are you needing today?"

Jed showed him the list and said, "We'll put the lumber on the bottom and then the eight poles on top of the load." Jed told him that he surely was more familiar with the weight of the lumber than he was, and he asked if he would help him leave room for the eight poles on the top so they wouldn't be overloaded.

Obed said he would be glad to.

They started the load with the floor joist and the box sills. After they were on, they put on a few 2x4s, sixteen feet long, a number of 2x4s twelve feet long, and then eight-footers for studs.

When they had a number of eight-foot 2x4s on, Obed thought it would make a good load and not be too heavy. He had seen the drag shoes and asked Jed if he planned on using them.

Jed said, "The last load, when my dad was here, we dallied a rope from the wagon to the saddle of the riding horse, and I was on the wagon controlling with the brake rod. We went really slow, but we were smoking the brake shoes."

Jed asked if other haulers used the drag shoes.

Obed said that some do, and he thought it was a good idea. "You'd rather be safe than sorry."

Jed asked about other materials, shakes, planed flooring, and plastering lath.

Obed told him he didn't make shakes, but a man down in the valley, a little south of St. George, did. He told Jed how to find his place. For the planed flooring material, they had just bought a planer, which had been delivered, but it wasn't completely set up yet. They planned to be planing lumber within the next week or so. Obed couldn't cut lath with his saw, but a smaller mill was cutting lath, and he could get it from them. He told Jed where to find the small mill.

Obed gave Jed the bill for the material and reminded him to bring the money on his next trip.

Jed thanked him, and he and Tad took off for home. When they came to the hill, they stopped, put the drag shoes into place, and proceeded down the hill. This time, he didn't need the hand brake, and the oxen had to pull just a little to take the wagon down the grade. At the bottom, they stopped and backed the oxen up a little to get the wheels off the drag shoes. They put them back in the wagon and continued on home. It was near eleven when they arrived. They stopped at the covered wagon, and Sister Wilkins greeted them, commenting that they had made better time on their trip to the mill.

Jed turned to Tad and said, "Let's go on down and work on the corral."

They unloaded the poles and had the corral finished by lunchtime.

Jed said, "We'll take some of the extra posts back up here to stack the lumber on."

They loaded a few posts back on the wagon.

Tad asked Jed if they should put the horses in the corral to get them used to it.

Jed thought that was good idea.

Tad got Chip, slid the poles back that made the gate, and turned him loose in the corral.

Jed took the saddle off Blaze and turned him loose. The horses just trotted around, whinnying, and seemed to like their extra freedom.

The next thing they needed to worry about was putting a watering trough in the pen.

They were unloading the lumber when they were called to dinner. They finished the few boards they had left to unload, and Tad drove the oxen down, unhitched them from the wagon, and put the oxen in with the horses. The oxen frolicked around, and they were happy in the new corral. Tad hurried back to the well, washed his hands, and went over to the covered wagon.

While they ate, Jed asked Sister Wilkins what she had been doing while they were gone.

She had walked over and visited with Sister Saunders and the girls. "Anna said she saw you up there before you left for the sawmill this morning. Someday, that

Anna is going make some man a wonderful wife. She has all the qualities of her mother and the beauty of a princess. The other girls are just as sweet."

She thought Jed had taken it all in, but he didn't make any comment.

Jed and Tad spent the afternoon clearing off the area where they would build the small home. They staked out the house, placed strings around the outside perimeter, and got them squared up properly. They were ready for the large rocks on which they would build. Jed explained each step they would take to get things ready.

At five o'clock, Jed said he wanted to ride over to meet one of the neighbors that Tom had told him about. He asked Tad if he wanted to ride along. They would be gone for about an hour. Tad said he would stay home and work on his little project.

Jed went down to the field, and brought Blaze up then put the saddle on him. Jed headed out toward the neighbor's house, which was about two and a half miles away.

When Jed approached the house, the dogs came out and barked to announce his arrival. They were wagging their tails, so he knew they were friendly, and Blaze didn't shy from them.

Jack McMurray came out of his house and invited Jed to step down off his horse, tie him up, and get acquainted.

Jed said, "I've heard, by way of the blacksmith in

town, that you might have a broken buggy that you might sell."

Jack said, "That buggy he is talking about was a real good buggy. I was headed to town in it, and the team I was using was fairly young. They spooked at the least little thing. We were just trotting along, and a rabbit jumped out of the grass and ran right under that team. They jumped sideways and started running, and I couldn't get them under control. When they rounded the curve that's about a mile down the road, they were going too fast. As they rounded that corner, that buggy turned over, throwing me out. Fortunately, I landed in some tall grass and only sprained my ankle, but those horses ran a little farther with that buggy bouncing along behind them. They finally stopped on their own, and I was able to hobble over to them. I unhitched the buggy, dragged it off the road, and drove the team home. A couple of days later, I got some help to bring it home. So you might be interested in buying it? It is just junk to me right now. If you would like to look at it, why don't you come out by the barn and take a look?"

They walked over to the barn.

"Well, Jed, there it is. It doesn't look like much the way it is."

Jed got down and sighted the axles to see if they were straight. The wooden tongue was split a little at the smaller end. It appeared to Jed that everything was there. He figured he could use the tongue to remake the few broken wooden parts. He wanted to put a single horse on it. Jed knew he would have to see if he could buy new shafts or get the hardwood to make new shafts. Jed knew the collapsed wheel was repairable. He asked Jack what he thought was a fair price for the condition it was in.

Jack rubbed his chin and said, "How about nine dollars? Probably I should have ten or twelve for it, but if it sits in here for a while, I probably couldn't give it away. Have you fixed buggies or wagons before?"

Jed told him that he worked at it a little back in Illinois before coming out west.

Jack said, "You're just a young man trying to get started in life. I tell you what I'll do for you. I'll take just eight dollars for it. That will help you buy the extra things you might need to get it up and running again."

Jed told him he would buy it from him. "On Monday, I'll come for it and bring you the money. My property is over by the Saunders's place. I'll borrow Tom's hay wagon and come for it."

They shook hands, and Jed and Blaze headed home. Jed was pleased with the purchase. He wanted to get it fixed and then surprise Sister Wilkins with it. He would need to buy a harness for Chip and then get him trained to pull it safely so she could drive. Chip would learn quickly to pull it since he was a calm horse by nature.

When Jed pulled in toward the wagon, Tad ran out to meet him. "Did you buy it? You're keeping it a secret from Mama, aren't you?"

Jed said that he was, and it might be a week or two before he would have it roadworthy. Then he would have to train Chip to pull it. "By the way, Tad, you will have to help me find time to work on it and keep your mother from knowing about it. I'm going to ask Tom if he has spot at his place where I can put it so I can work on it away from here. We'll put Blaze out with Chip and the oxen tonight and then start to bring them in tomorrow night."

Tad said he would take him down where the others were, hobble him, and turn him loose.

Jed said he would appreciate that. He took off the saddle and bridle and put on the halter and lead rope.

Tad took the lead rope and went on a trot through the field with Blaze.

Jed took the saddle over and placed it under the dining fly to keep it out of the sun.

Sister Wilkins asked Jed if he had found the neighbor.

Jed said, "I did. He was a likeable man, and his name is Jack McMurray."

Sister Wilkins said she was getting supper for them, and it wouldn't be too long before it was ready to eat. She had made baked beans and seasoned them with bacon.

While they ate, Jed told Sister Wilkins that he needed to get some fairly good-sized rocks to use for the foundation of the small house. He thought they would be gone for about two hours. After they unloaded, they could all go to town for shopping.

Sister Wilkins said that would be fine with her.

Jed asked, "Sister Wilkins, have you ever done any

needlework, knitting, or things like that? I've never heard you speak of it."

"Well, I haven't done any since we left Ohio. I used to do a lot. I guess I am busy like you. I see you haven't been doing any carvings lately."

Jed smiled. "You're right. I really haven't been doing any carving lately."

Sister Wilkins said, "At this time, I don't have any thread or yarn to work with. I saved all my money to make the trip, but now that we are here, maybe I'll look at the store. Maybe I could find some material, yarn, or something else. I hadn't even thought about it until you brought it up. Yes, I just might do that."

20

The next morning, after breakfast, with the oxen up and ready, Jed and Tad took off for the low hills where he had seen some rock. Jed, for safety precaution, had thrown a couple of sticks into the wagon.

It only took forty-five minutes to get to the place with the rocks. Jed stopped the oxen out on the road and stuck the driving stick into the ground in front of the oxen.

Jed got into the wagon, gave a stick to Tad, and he took the other one.

Tad asked, "What is this for?"

Jed said, "I don't know if we'll need them, but there is a possibility that there could be rattlesnakes out in these rocks. As we are looking for rocks to use, we'll tap these sticks ahead of us. If there are snakes, they let us know with their rattles where they are. We'll go slow, just to make sure we don't get too close to one.

We may not find any, and I am hoping we don't. We'll just have to find out."

As they walked out into the area, Jed would point out rocks that were the right size.

Jed tapped his stick on a rock, and a snake gave a buzz with its rattles. Jed moved up a little, and the snake coiled up at the shady edge of the rock. The snake made a strike at Jed, but Jed had his stick in his way. The snake couldn't reach him, and Jed proceeded to kill the snake.

Tad was very leery of snakes and stayed back.

Jed said, "Let's see if we can get some of these rocks loaded. We'll start back by the wagon, getting the closer ones first. Snakes are known to move around a little, so we'll be cautious and tip each rock up with a stick before picking it up." One by one, the rocks were carried over to the wagon.

They just needed two more to have what they needed. As they went out a little farther, they heard another snake buzz. Jed stepped up and took care of it. Jed tipped over a rock with his stick, and there was another snake under it. It was a little more active than other two, but Jed did his thing. After the snake was killed, the rock was loaded.

Jed found a rock that was close and hoped for no snakes. He walked all around it and tipped it over, and it was clear underneath. When he reached down to pick up the rock, another snake came out from under another rock close by. The snake struck at Jed and struck the sole of his shoe. Jed turned and dropped the rock on the snake, which took care of the snake. He went ahead and loaded the rock. Jed went back to the dead snake and made sure there was not a fang in his shoe. The snake's fangs had not been broken, and he felt relieved.

Jed and Tad turned the oxen in the road and headed home. Tad was glad to be on the road and away from the snakes. They arrived home at ten and went right to work unloading the wagon, which didn't take long.

Tad told his mother about the rattlesnakes.

Sister Wilkins said, "If I had known that there were snakes out there, I wouldn't have let you go."

Jed said, "Snakes are dangerous, but if you are careful, you can work around them. The next time we need rock I will ask about a better place."

Jed and Tad washed their hands, got ready to go, and helped Sister Wilkins into the wagon for the drive to town.

Jed pulled the oxen up across the street from the store and tied them to the rail. He helped Sister Wilkins down from the wagon, and the three of them walked across the street to the store. Jed said he needed to walk down to the blacksmith's shop for a few minutes.

When Jed got to the blacksmith's shop, he introduced himself.

The blacksmith said his name was Albert, but he went by Al.

Jed told him he had bought the broken-up buggy from Jack McMurray and wanted to put shafts on it for a single horse. He told Al he would use the old hardwood in the tongue to replace the other broken parts.

Al didn't have any shafts that were already made, and thought the store might have a set available. It would be worth asking.

Jed told him he would get the buggy on Monday evening, and he might discover a couple of broken metal parts that he would need some help with.

Al said he would be glad to help wherever he could.

Jed walked back to the store and joined Sister Wilkins and Tad. Sister Wilkins had already taken some food supplies over to the counter.

Jed asked if she had looked at any sewing things. She was reluctant to spend money on any of those things. Jed assured her that spending a little money on things that would help occupy her time was a good investment.

Sister Wilkins went back to the shelves and selected a few skeins of yarn. She figured she could knit a few useful items.

Jed took Sister Wilkins over to the cast-iron cookstoves and showed them to her. She was excited about getting one to cook on.

He asked which one she liked best and thought would be the most serviceable. After she selected the one she liked best, Jed called the clerk over and told him they would like to buy it. Jed explained that they wouldn't need it for three or four weeks since they had to build the home to put it in first.

The clerk offered to hold it for him, and if someone

needed it before that, he would talk to Jed before selling it. The freight wagons came every two weeks—and sometimes a little quicker than that. When Jed was out of hearing distance from Sister Wilkins, he inquired about buggy shafts. The clerk said that he had just gotten a set a few days ago, and he quoted the price.

Jed said he would take them, but he wouldn't take them today. Jed told him he was fixing up a buggy for Sister Wilkins to drive, and it was to be a surprise for her.

The clerk nodded and walked back to the counter. He added up all the purchases for the day.

Jed handed him the money and asked if he could check if there was any mail for him or his dad.

The clerk told him there was nothing for them today.

They loaded up their goods and took them out to the wagon.

Jed glanced over toward the bank and saw that it was open on a Saturday. Jed told Sister Wilkins that he needed to draw out money for their recent load of lumber. He ran over to the bank and took care of that before they headed home.

Back at home, Sister Wilkins set out lunch for them, and they sat down to eat.

After lunch, Jed and Tad were ready to start positioning and spacing the rocks. Jed knew that a good foundation was the right way to start a building. He explained all of this to Tad as they went along.

Jed started at the lowest corner of the building and placed the first rock with the flattest side up. He made sure it was perfectly bedded in the ground. They measured the proper distance to the next rock with a board and a string and made each rock level with the others. They set the first four rocks in a row along the string. The four down the center were eight inches lower to place a double two-by-eight beam on them. The final four, on the other outside wall, were placed like the first four. Using the same technique, all twelve rocks were set.

Tad said, "That was neat. They look so nice. They are perfectly set in rows any way you look at them. I can see the importance of a good foundation and how to get it."

Jed and Tad carried the 2x6 over to make the bottom plates for the two outside walls. They cut a few of them and made up the beam of 2x8s for the center. The next 2x8s were set on the outside edge of the plates, creating the box sills, and the next step was laying out the floor joist. Jed used his six-foot folding rule to get the distance right. He used his framing square to mark where each joist would be placed. All the joists were cut to the right length.

When they had several of the joists cut and set, Sister Wilkins called that their supper was ready. They put away the tools and went to eat.

After eating, Jed said that he wanted to visit with Tom for a few minutes and make arrangements for going to church tomorrow morning. Sister Wilkins and Tad said they would like to go as well.

When they came up in front of the house, Tom

and some of the children were out on the front porch, enjoying the shade. Tom greeted them and told Sister Wilkins to go on into the house. Sister Saunders and a couple of the girls were doing the dishes and cleaning up after supper.

Tad and Johnnie went off together to talk, and Jed asked Tom to go for a short walk with him. Tom stood up, and the two of them walked slowly toward the barn.

Jed told Tom about the buggy and asked to borrow the hay wagon.

Tom said that would be fine, and they could take the team of horses to pull the wagon rather than the slower oxen. He asked Jed how much he had paid for it. Jed told him Jack had asked for nine dollars and then lowered it to eight dollars. Jed told Tom about his plan to make it a surprise for Sister Wilkins, and he wondered if Tom had a place where he could put the buggy until he could fix it up.

Tom said that he had a spot where it could be placed.

Jed said he would try to work on it for a few hours every evening, and it shouldn't take much more than a week. He would ride Chip over to work on it. He wanted Chip to get used to the buggy. He thought Chip would make a good buggy horse, and Sister Wilkins could feel safe with him.

Tom said, "I believe you have thought of everything—and I think that is great."

They walked back to the house, and Tom asked if they would like a ride to church in the morning. Jed told him that it would be very helpful and that they would be pleased to ride with them.

Sister Saunders and Sister Wilkins came outside to be with Jed and Tom, and Anna and Joan followed them out.

Anna said, "Hi, Jed. Are you working on your house now?"

Jed said that they were placing the floor joists.

Anna said, "I don't even know what a floor joist is. I'll just have to walk over and see what you are talking about."

Jed said, "You are welcome anytime. It's getting late, and we had better be going."

Sister Wilkins called for Tad to come, and Tad and Johnnie ran up.

Jed said, "We will be ready to go when you come by in the morning. Have a good evening—and thank you for all you do to help us."

After they had left, Anna told her folks that she thought Jed was a very sensible young man. Sister Saunders looked at Tom and winked.

When they got back to their place, Jed said that he and Tad should bring the horses and oxen up to the corral for the night. They threw the lead ropes over their shoulders and headed to the lower end of the field.

Tad asked, "Do you think the oxen and horses will ever learn to come up on their own?"

"Until we get the whole field fenced, I doubt that

they will. With the hobbles on their feet, the horses don't go farther than they have to."

Tad put his ropes on the oxen, and Jed caught the horses and took off their hobbles. They put them in the corral and put the poles back in place. The animals seemed to be content in the corral, and they walked back to the wagon.

The next morning, Jed went down to the corral and turned out the oxen. As they headed to their favorite area, he put the hobbles on the horses, turned them loose, and went back to the wagon.

Sister Wilkins was just getting down from the wagon. She looked at him and said, "You're always up before me, aren't you?"

Jed smiled. "I just like to be up early—that's all." He walked over to where the house was started and looked things over. He got down on his knees and sighted down the box sills. They looked good and straight, which pleased Jed. With a good day's work on Monday, they would be ready for the subfloor material. He thought they had better head back to the sawmill on Tuesday.

Sister Wilkins had hot-cracked wheat cereal and toast with butter and honey for breakfast. Sister Wilkins had bought the cereal, the butter, and the honey at the store. They visited until it was time to get ready for church. Sister Wilkins let Tad sleep in, and when he finally woke up, Sister Wilkins warmed up his cereal and made his toast. While he ate, Tad mentioned how the toast with butter and honey was special.

When Sister Wilkins went up into the wagon to put on her new dress, Jed asked her to hand down his better clothes.

A few minutes before nine thirty, they went out to the road to wait for their ride.

When they got to church, Jed didn't see the Sessions family. He was eager to know if they had settled somewhere and hear how they were doing.

Lilly Sessions and her parents got there just before the meeting began. She waved to him, and he waved back. Her mother must have told her she could see him afterward.

The meeting was a good one, and there were two excellent speakers. Jed enjoyed both of their talks.

When the meeting was closed, the people started filing out. Lilly and her parents were waiting outside for him. Lilly squealed, and her mother put her down.

Jed immediately picked her up, and she gave him a hard hug and a kiss on the cheek. She chattered so fast that he could hardly understand what she was saying. He worked his way over to Brad and Lillian and asked how things were going.

Brad explained that they had bought ground a little south of St. George, and he was working part-time for a man splitting shakes. They were getting material together to build a small house to start with.

Jed told them that he was starting on a small house to live in while he built a larger home. He had heard about the man who was splitting shakes, and he hoped to go out there in the next few days to buy the shakes he was going to need.

Brad asked how many he was going to need.

Jed told him that he would need about eight squares (a square being one hundred square feet of coverage) for the small home. Jed asked if he kept a good stock on hand.

Brad said that they were going out about as fast as they could get them ready. "If you want, I'll place your order so that you can come get them in about a week."

Jed said, "That sounds great to me. I'll see you next Sunday, and if they're ready, I'll come the following day to pick them up. By the way, do you know how much he is asking for them."

Brad told him the price.

"I'll have the money when I get there. How do I find his place?"

Brad explained how to get there. "I'm sure you'll find the place OK."

Jed shook Brad's hand and said goodbye to Lillian. As they were talking, Lilly stayed in Jed's arms with her arm around his neck. When her mother held out her hands to take her, Lilly gave Jed another hug and a little kiss on his cheek, and then she went to her mother.

Jed found Sister Wilkins and the Saunders family, and he walked over to them.

Anna said, "Well, it looks like you have a girlfriend already!"

Jed said, "I think she might be a little young for me, don't you?"

Anna said, "Yes, she might be at that, but watching her, I'd say she might just love you anyway. Someday you'll have to tell me how this affair got started."

Jed chuckled.

Tom came out of the church, and they all went to the buggies.

Sister Saunders said, "Sister Wilkins, we are planning on you folks coming over for dinner today. You'll come, won't you?"

Sister Wilkins said, "The way you put it, it would be hard to turn you down. You folks are doing so much for us, and we'll never be able to return all of the kindness you have shown us. Yes, we'll come—and thank you all so much."

The buggies stopped, and Sister Wilkins, Tad, and Jed got out and thanked them.

Sister Wilkins said, "I'll change, and we'll be right up."

Jed took out a couple of carvings, a little bird and a squirrel, from his pack and stuck them in his pocket.

Sister Wilkins was ready, and they headed over to the road. In a few minutes, they stepped up on to the porch. The door swung open, and Jill and Jimmie were standing there.

Jimmie said, "Well, come on in."

Tom was relaxing in his favorite chair. He invited Jed to come over and sit down.

Jed sat down, and he asked Jill and Jimmie to come over to him.

Both of them stood in front of him, and Jimmie said, "What do you want?"

Jed told them he had brought something for them. He told them to close their eyes and hold out their hands.

Jimmie was reluctant at first, but when he saw Jill standing there with her eyes closed and her hand out, he finally did the same.

Jed took out the two carvings and gently put the bird into Jill's hand and the squirrel into Jimmie's hand. He told them to open their eyes.

Jill said, "He's so cute. Thank you."

Jimmie said, "Wow! It looks so real. Thank you!"

Jill ran to her mother to show her and the others, and Jimmie showed his squirrel to his dad and then the others.

Tom asked Jed if he had carved them.

Jed said, "I did. I enjoyed doing them, but I enjoy them even more when I can make a child happy."

Tom told him he had a great talent and should never give up making them.

Anna came over to Jed and told him she thought the carvings were wonderful.

Jed said, "Down at the church, you asked me to tell you how my affair started with the little girl I was holding. When we were only a few days out of Omaha, Lilly was riding on the seat of their wagon at the side of her mother. She went to climb into the back of the wagon, and the wagon hit a hole or a bump in the road—and she was thrown out onto the road. I was riding as an outrider, only about a wagon's length from their wagon. Lillian, her mother, was so frightened that she jumped out of the wagon and sprained her ankle. I was first to get to them after hearing the mother screaming and Lilly crying loudly. I held Lilly still until the doctor could get to them. The father went to the aid of his wife, and I held the little girl. The doctor took care of the girl. Her little arm had a bad break, and he needed a splint for it. The doctor set the bones back together, and I cut the splint and carved it to fit her little arm. The arm was wrapped, and the splint was placed in position and wrapped some more. She sobbed for the next few hours. That evening, I went to check on her and took her a carved bird. From the time I gave it to her until her arm was completely well, she never cried about her arm or the sling that held her arm against her body. She just loved her little bird and played with it. Her mother still comments about how the little bird took her mind off the pain and what a blessing it was for her. Now you know what causes her to hug and kiss me as much as she does."

Anna was really attentive as he shared that story. When he finished, she said, "You know, if you were to help me like that and give me a little bird, I would probably give you a hug and a kiss too." She chuckled.

Sister Saunders said, "That was really nice of you, Jed."

Jed said, "I think anyone would have done the same thing. It just happened that I was there and could help."

Sister Saunders said that dinner was on the table and asked for everyone to set up.

After the blessing on the food, which Johnnie was

asked to give, the food was passed around. Everyone filled their plates.

The visiting went back to Jed and his carvings. Someone asked if he had other experiences giving carvings to children. He said that he did, and he shared a couple of those experiences.

Tad said that Jed had promised to teach him how to carve someday.

Sister Saunders announced she had apple pie for dessert. She, Anna, and Joan cut and served it.

Sister Wilkins said she was getting excited about the new house. She said that she could hardly wait to use her new cast-iron cookstove. "I love to cook, bake, and do canning. When the house is done and moved into, we'll have to try to find a cow so we can have milk, cream, and butter. Does anyone around St. George have a cow to sell? We're not ready yet, but I was wondering if they do come available on occasion."

Tom said that it was rare, but there were more available up in the Cedar City area. "You can usually buy chickens and pigs up that way as well."

Jed was pleased to hear that. It wouldn't be long before they could look for other animals for their small farm.

Tom and Jed went back to the living room area and sat down to visit some more.

Anna, Joan, and Rachel went to put things away and do the dishes.

Tad and Johnnie went for a walk down to the barn, Sister Saunders and Sister Wilkins took a walk out toward the garden, and Jill and Jimmie had their carvings to play with.

Sister Wilkins asked Sister Saunders if she had done much drying of fruits or vegetables.

Sister Saunders said she had done some drying and some canning, but with vegetables growing nearly all year around, she had gotten away from doing much drying. "We have tomatoes from late February into December. If we are careful and cover the tomatoes during the couple of months when we get a little frost, we can have tomatoes all year round too. It's the same with a lot of other vegetables. You can have one item, like carrots, coming up all the time."

Sister Wilkins said, "It's going to take some getting used to. Where I come from, they have harsh winters to contend with, and all the fruits and vegetables are just one crop a year."

Sister Wilkins asked about when to plant.

Sister Saunders said that anything she planted would yield a crop before the cooler time of year. "Since you have water running from your well all the time, you can irrigate whatever you plant."

Sister Wilkins said, "I'll have to ask Jed and Tad if they can get a small garden plowed, and I'll plant some vegetables. Do they carry garden seeds at the store?"

Sister Saunders said, "They carry a lot of seeds—but not everything you might like."

The ladies walked back into the house and sat down.

Jed turned to Sister Wilkins and asked if she was ready to head home.

"Yes, but I'm in no hurry."

Jed said, "We might as well go then."

Anna and Joan sat at the kitchen table. When Jed stood up to go, Anna asked if it would be all right if she and Joan went with them to see what he was building.

Jed told her that it would fine, and the four of them walked to the front porch.

Sister Wilkins called for Tad. He came running, and she told him they were walking back home—but he could stay longer if he wanted to.

Tad said he would stay for another hour and then come home. He and Johnnie went back to the barn area.

As they walked, Joan said, "It's great to have neighbors so close. Before you got here, it was just family. There was no one else to talk to except when we went to the store or to church. It's so nice to have you here."

The girls saw the framework of the floor for the new house and walked over to it.

Jed just followed along.

Anna said, "You spoke of putting in the floor joist. What part is that?"

Jed told her about getting the rocks, setting them to make the foundation, and preparing the box sills and floor joists. "Tomorrow we'll get all the joists in, and on Tuesday morning, we'll go back to the sawmill and get the lumber for the subfloor and the material to frame the walls."

Joan asked, "What's the difference between a plain floor and a subfloor?"

Jed explained the difference.

Anna said, "I have never given any thought to how many pieces and parts it would take to make a house. I find this really interesting."

Joan agreed with her.

Anna asked where other things were going to be.

Jed pointed to the outhouse and the corral fence, and he showed them where the barn, the pigpen, the chicken house, and the large home would be built. He told them that the house they were working on would be his workshop someday.

The girls were really interested in all he was doing. Joan said that when their dad built their house, they hadn't come down to St. George to live yet and didn't see it being built.

The girls said they should go, but if it would be OK, they'd come down every few days to see all that he was doing and how it was coming along. They said goodbye and started walking home.

Jed went over and sat under the dining fly.

Sister Wilkins said, "I do believe those girls are the nicest girls I have ever met, and I think they were sincere in wanting to know how and what it takes to build a building."

Jed agreed with her.

Sister Wilkins said, "How long do think it would take to plow a small garden spot for me. Sister Saunders was telling me that we still have time to grow a garden before the cooler weather gets here in December."

Jed said, "If we get the floor joists all set by tomorrow afternoon, we could probably plow it then."

She said, "Then the first chance we get after that, we'll buy some seed."

Jed said, "Tomorrow evening, Tom and I are going over to another neighbor's place to pick up something. He asked if I could go with him. After we eat, I'll be gone for a while."

"Oh, that will be fine," she said.

When Tad got home, he told them that he really liked Johnnie. He was a good friend, and they had a lot of the same interests.

Jed said, "Tad, when the joists are all in place tomorrow, I'll have you bring up the oxen—and we'll plow a garden for your mother."

"I'd be glad to," Tad said. "Mom always grew a big garden back in Ohio, and I used to help her a lot with it."

They spent another hour talking, and Sister Wilkins suggested fixing them something for supper.

After supper, Jed said, "We ought to go bring the livestock up to the corral."

Tad said, "Let me do it. I want to try something."

Jed said, "Have at it."

Tad picked up the lead ropes and was on his way. Before long, he was on his way back. He had the hobbles from the horses over his shoulder and a lead rope on Blaze. The oxen and Chip were following them without lead ropes.

Jed smiled and said, "You know, that son of yours really has a way with animals. If it wasn't for having to have the hobbles on the horses, I do believe he could just call to them—and they would come."

Sister Wilkins said, "That boy has always had a way with animals. He likes them, and they like him."

21

The next morning, Jed was up early, dressed, went out to the new house, measured the length of a joist, and cut it. He had marked and cut two more before he noticed Sister Wilkins was up. He carried them over and put them into place. Setting two more up on the sawhorses, he marked and cut them. When Sister Wilkins called him to breakfast, he put down his tools and went over to the dining fly.

As soon as he took his last bite, he headed back to his work.

It seemed to go fast that morning, and by the time Tad had eaten and come over to help him, Jed had cut six joists and placed and two more marked and ready to cut.

Tad remarked, "Jed, you're really working fast."

Jed said, "They haven't been nailed yet, just set in place. The one by the saw is the pattern to mark by. Go ahead and cut the others as needed." Jed began nail.

Each time Tad had two marked and cut, Jed would

239

help set them into place and get two more up on the sawhorses. After an hour, all the joists were cut and placed.

Tad went to the wagon and got the hammer that they had just bought in town. Tad nailed the outer end into place while Jed nailed the other end of the joist to the center beam. Tad's arm was not used to swinging a hammer, and he had to stop often to rest his arm. Tad was getting more accurate and bent fewer nails.

By the time Sister Wilkins called them for lunch, the joists were all nailed into place.

Jed put his arm around Tad's shoulders and said, "You know, Tad, I think we make a good team. I thought it would take us well into the afternoon to get this part done, so after we have lunch, we can plow the garden. That will make your mother happy."

They washed their hands and went over to eat.

Tad told his mother that the floor joists were all in and nailed. "After lunch, we'll plow you a garden."

While they ate, Jed thought about making a wooden frame that the oxen could pull over the garden after it was plowed and level it, which would get it closer to planting condition.

As soon as Tad finished eating, he took the lead ropes and went after the oxen.

Jed started to get the plow out of the wagon and had it ready to lift down.

Sister Wilkins stepped over and helped set it down by taking hold of the plow handles that were extending from the wagon bed. Jed had the heavier iron section, and they were able to get it onto the ground.

When Tad got back with the oxen, they placed the yoke on the back of oxen's necks and a chain attached to it extended back to the plow. They were ready to roll the ground over.

Tad walked at the side of the oxen, driving them, and Jed would guide the plow. The first furrow was down the center of the garden, and each trip down and back added a foot and a half to the garden's width. After twenty round trips, the garden was thirty feet wide and forty foot long. They plowed the ends out to make sure that all the garden soil was rolled over.

While the oxen rested, Jed went over to the sawhorses and cut some pieces of the plank that was left from the floor joist. He cut other pieces that were left from the outhouse. He put the pieces together and nailed them. He went to his pack in the covered wagon, took out his brace and bit, and he drilled four holes, through which he threaded a rope, which made a loop in front to hitch the chain extending from the ox yoke.

Jed hitched the oxen to the ground level and drove back and forth, leveling the garden and breaking up the clods of soil, and made the garden nice and smooth.

At three in the afternoon, the garden was finished. Jed had time to make a quick trip to town and pick up his buggy shafts, garden seed, and some pipe and fittings.

The oxen were hitched to the wagon, and Jed asked

Tad if he wanted to go. Tad said that he wanted to work on something.

Jed left for town, when he got there, he tied the oxen up across the street and walked over to the store.

The clerk recognized him and gave him a wave, but he was busy with another customer. Jed went to the hardware area to look things over. He found the pipe valves he wanted and the short lengths of pipe and the three elbows. He put them out on the floor and went to find the garden seeds. He selected things he thought Sister Wilkins would want: carrots, tomatoes, cabbage, melons, corn, beans, and a couple envelopes of flower seeds. Jed thought that would get things started.

The clerk came over, and Jed told him about the pipe and fittings on the floor. The clerk went over for one load of items, and Jed went back for the few remaining.

Jed said he would take the buggy shafts today as well. The clerk carried them around the outside of the store, leaned them against the hitching rail out front, and asked if there would be anything else today.

Jed said, "I can't think of anything else—unless you have some mail for me." Jed really didn't think that there would be any.

The clerk said there hadn't been any mail since Jed was there on Saturday. The clerk gave him the total, and Jed reached into his pocket and dug out the money.

The clerk took a load of things, and Jed was able to take the rest to the wagon. They put them in the wagon, and Jed hurried across the street and brought the shafts over.

The clerk asked how things were coming along at the farm.

Jed said, "It's going quite well. In fact, we are going to the sawmill in the morning for our third load of lumber."

The clerk said, "Sounds like things are moving along well for you. I just had a customer walk in. Thanks for your business, and I'll see you again soon."

Jed waved goodbye, untied the oxen, and headed home. He went on up to the Saunders's place and put the buggy shafts in the tool shed.

Tom said, "Are we still on for going over to get the buggy this evening?"

Jed said, "Yes, if that is still OK with you. I just brought the new buggy shafts and was dropping them off here."

"OK. I'll come along a little after six this evening."

They waved goodbye, and Jed drove home.

When he drove in, Tad ran up and whispered, "Did you get the buggy shafts?"

Jed nodded.

Sister Wilkins walked over and said, "I saw you coming a little bit ago, but you went on up to the Saunders's place."

"I bought something at the store that needed to be taken to them."

Sister Wilkins said, "That was nice of you to be helpful for all they do for us. Supper will be ready in twenty minutes."

Jed said, "Sister Wilkins, there is something for you in the back of the wagon."

She turned and looked in the back. "Oh, my heavens! Would you look at that? We're going to have us a garden." She picked up the seeds, headed to the wagon, and read the names on each package.

Jed pulled the wagon over to where they normally parked it, and Tad asked if he wanted him to put the oxen back down into the field. Jed said, "That would be great." He took the other parts out of the wagon and put them by the well to see if they would all work as he had planned. He didn't have time to work on it then, but he was sure that it would work fine when he got to it. He washed his hands at the well and went over to the covered wagon.

Sister Wilkins told him it was thoughtful of him to get the seeds.

Jed said there were a lot of other seeds available, and she could look over what they had and get them the next time she was in town, but those would get the garden started.

Tad got back, and they all filled their plates and ate.

Jed said, "Maybe a one rail fence around the garden spot would be a smart thing to do, and maybe a row of flowers along each side of the fence would make it look pretty."

Sister Wilkins said, "Jed, your mind is always working, isn't it?"

Jed said, "I've heard that any job worth doing is worth doing well."

They had finished eating and were talking when Tom's wagon came down the road. Jed jumped up, grabbed his hat, and said, "I'll see you later." He jumped on the wagon before it was even stopped and moved up to stand by Tom.

Tom said, "What else happened today?"

Jed gave him a brief rundown of all they had accomplished.

Tom looked and Jed and said, "Young man, you just don't let any grass grow under your feet, do you?"

Jed smiled and said, "I don't like sitting around. When there is work to be done, I just like to get at it. I like to see things progressing. By the way, do you know of a better place to get rock than that place by the hill going up to the saw mill?"

Tom stared at Jed. "You went there to get rocks for your foundation?"

Jed said, "Yes, did I do something wrong?"

Tom said, "You didn't see any rattlesnakes?"

"Well, we saw four, which I killed, but we did get the rock we needed for the small house."

Tom said, "It a wonder you didn't get bit by a rattler."

"Well, one did strike my shoe, but it didn't leave any fangs in it. I dropped the rock on him before he could strike again."

As they turned into Jack's place, Tom said, "I'll tell you a better place on the way home."

Jack stepped out to meet them and motioned for them to drive over to the buggy.

When they had stopped, Tom tied up the lines,

stepped down from the wagon, and shook hands with Jack.

Jack turned to Jed and shook his hand. "Are you ready to take on this project?"

Jed responded, "Yes, I love a challenge."

Jack said, "Well, son, I think you have one here, and I wish you luck."

Jed said he thought it would be best to remove all four wheels. That way, the buggy would sit down better on the wagon and be easier to pick up and load.

Jack said, "I've got my wheel wrench right over in the shed. I'll go get it."

When he got back, Jed removed the nuts from the axles and removed the wheels and the tongue. When they were ready to load, Jed and Tom lifted the heavier end, and Jack took the other end. They lifted it up and slid it into the wagon bed. They slid the tongue and the wheels in good positions so they wouldn't fall off. Jed and Jack looked around to make sure that all the loose parts had been picked up and loaded.

Jed took the money from his pocket and counted it out for Jack.

Jack smiled, and they shook hands. "I wish you luck in getting it going again."

Tom and Jed climbed onto the wagon, and Tom took the reins in hand, tapped the lines, and waved to Jack as they headed home.

Tom said, "You made a good choice in buying it. With your ingenuity and ability, I'll bet it won't take you too long to get it back together." Tom told Jed about a better place to find foundation rock. "As far as I know, they haven't found any snakes in that area—and it is just as close. I still can't believe you didn't get bit."

Jed explained how they tapped the sticks a head of them as they walked out in the area to wake up the snakes and get them to sound their rattles before they got too close.

Tom said, "I still think of you as being mighty lucky. That place is lousy with snakes."

They passed the Sandalin property. Jed had told Tad to keep an eye out for them and to take his mother's attention away from the road as they passed by.

They went on up to Tom's shed and stopped, and Tad ran toward them. Johnnie came out of the house at the same time, and the two boys helped unload the wagon.

Tad said, "As soon as I saw you, I ran to Mom and got her away from where she couldn't see you go by. I told her I just saw you passing by, and I wanted to go up and walk back with you. She told me to run along. Here I am—can I help?"

Jed smiled. "You're a good boy, my friend, and you sure can help."

They took off the wheels, leaned them to one side, and put the tongue next to the wheels. Finally, with the help of the boys, the buggy was set off.

Jed carefully studied each part to decide where to start. The reaches and reach braces were OK. The dash was bent over, but it could easily be straightened. The box body was OK, the surrey top frame was bent, and the supporting wooden posts had been broken. Straightening the metal and replacing the wood parts of the posts would be easy. The seat cushions were OK. The seat backs were scuffed, but they would be OK. The top fabric had a small tear, but he could patch it. The item that would need the most work was the metal parts of the tongue. He might need some help from the blacksmith. Overall, he was happy with the purchase. He decided to fix the broken wheel first and put the wheels on, and then he would straighten the dash, the top, and the posts. The shafts would be last.

Tom and the boys watched him go over it.

Jed finally stood up and said, "I believe it will turn out fine."

Tom said, "Jed, I have faith in you. If you say you can do it, I know it will come out great. Johnnie, will you put away the horses and the wagon? Take Tad with you."

Jed said, "I need to work on the house, but I would prefer to work on the buggy. I'll just have to go slow on the buggy and work it in. It won't be here too long, maybe a week or two at the most."

Tom said, "It's not in the way where it is. Don't push yourself to get it done. I would like to see a roof over your heads before we start getting fall weather. I'm sure you'll get it done."

They stepped onto the porch, and Anna asked Jed if he had all the floor joists in.

He told her he had—and that the garden was plowed

and leveled. He'd been to town and picked up some garden seed for Sister Wilkins.

Anna said, "I ought to go down and help her in the morning. She said it was more fun when two people work together. Why don't you tell her I'll come down at nine in the morning and help her?"

Jed said he would do that, and it was nice for her to offer. He knew Sister Wilkins would be happy to have her there to talk and help plant.

Tad and Johnnie said the horses were unharnessed and in the corral.

Jed said, "We had best be going then. We have a big day planned for tomorrow." He thanked Tom again for his help and for the use of the team and wagon. He said goodbye, and they headed down the road.

Sister Wilkins asked if they had finished helping Tom.

Jed and Tad both answered at the same time: "We sure did!"

Jed said, "He seemed to be happy about it. By the way, we saw Anna, and she said to tell you she is coming down in the morning to help you plant the garden. We need to walk out, and I can show you where to start your rows. I'm going to put a ditch across the head end to water from. Let's walk over to the garden, and I'll show you where the ditch will be."

All three of them walked over, and Jed scratched a line on the ground to show how far out the ditch would be and where to start the rows of vegetables.

Sister Wilkins was pleased that he had taken time to show her where to start.

Jed showed her the pipes that he was going to attach to the well pipe with the valves. He explained that it would make watering the garden much easier by controlling the water flow.

It was starting to get dark, and Tad went to bring the horses and oxen up to the corral.

When Tad got back, he had a big smile on his face. "I did something different tonight to bring them up. This time, I just took off the hobbles and told the horses to come on. I didn't put the lead ropes on either horse, and they just followed me back to the corral and went right in. I am so glad that animals aren't dumb."

Early the next morning, Jed went to the corral and tethered Chip. He led the oxen and Blaze to the wagon. He tied up the oxen, saddled Blaze, and put the tie-down ropes and drag shoes in the wagon. Then he went for the pipe wrenches. He started to put the pipes and fittings into place along with the two valves. He planned to dig the ditch when he got back from the sawmill.

Sister Wilkins called out that breakfast was ready. He put the tools away, washed his hands, and went over to eat. Tad was just getting out of bed.

Jed told Sister Wilkins that the pipes were put together, but he would have to dig the ditch when they got home. When he had finished, he took the canteen over to the well, rinsed it out, and filled it with fresh water.

Tad hitched the oxen to the wagon, and they were ready to head out. Jed said that he would drive for a while, and if Tad wanted to, he could ride Blaze. Tad liked that idea, and he climbed into the saddle, and they were on their way. They were just a little earlier getting away today, and they would probably he home well before noon.

It seemed like they got there more quickly than before, but they could just be getting used to the road.

When they pulled up to the office at the sawmill, Obed said, "Well, young men, are you ready for some more lumber."

They told him they were.

"Well, what do you want first?"

Jed told him they needed 480 board feet of subflooring on the bottom. He could take it in eight-, ten-, or twelve-inch widths and twelve- and sixteen-foot lengths, whichever he had in stock.

Obed replied, "Well, my good man, we have all width and lengths. But probably more twelve-inch widths right now since we have some really good logs coming in."

Jed said, "If it doesn't matter to you, we'll take the twelve-inch width. If my figures are right, it would mean sixteen sixteen-footers and twenty twelve-footers."

Obed directed them to back up to the sixteens and then to the twelves. "What's next?"

Jed said, "2x4s for the walls. I am using eight-foot studs for the walls. Do you have eight-footers?

"Sure do," said Obed. "How many?"

Jed told him eighty, and they backed up to that

stack and loaded them on. Next were eighteen sixteen-footers and twenty-six twelve-footers.

Obed said, "It looks like you have a little room left if there is something else you'll be needing."

"Let's put on ten 2x6 twelve-footers, and four more 2x4 sixteen-footers."

Obed said, "That looks like you have good load. Let's go to the office, and I'll make out a slip for you."

On the way over, Obed asked how the drag shoes had worked on the last load.

"Great," Jed said. "I'm glad we had them."

Obed added up the bill, and Jed threw the drag shoes and ropes into the wagon. He didn't feel the need to tie down this load. He went into the office, took out the money for the last load, and handed it to Obed. "On our next load, we'll be needing material for more rafters and roofing lumber. Do you have the planer running?"

Obed said they had run it a little but still needed some adjustments before they started really planing the lumber.

Jed told Obed about his friend who was working part-time making roof shakes. "I placed and order with them for what we will need." He put the bill in his pocket and thanked Obed for the material.

Tad climbed up on Blaze, and they headed home. At the top of the hill, they stopped and put on the drag shoes and slowly went down the hill. They stopped at the bottom, removed the drag shoes, and put them up on the load. They took a drink of the cool water in the canteen and went on their way.

They pulled into their place just a little after eleven.

Anna was about to go home. She asked what the lumber would be used for.

Jed told her the bottom material was for the subfloor and the next up was the wall framing for the outside and inside walls. The few pieces on the top were to start the roof framing.

Anna was impressed, and it was all very interesting to her. She needed to go, but she would be coming by every day to see the progress.

Jed assured her she was welcome anytime she wanted to come by.

Tad unhitched the oxen, and Jed unsaddled Blaze. They got Chip and the hobbles, and Tad took the oxen and horses out to graze. He hobbled the horses and headed back to the wagon.

Jed stopped at the garden to see the progress Sister Wilkins and Anna had made. They had planted about half of the garden and had made corrugations to run the water down.

Jed grabbed a shovel and started digging the ditch at the top end of the garden. He would like to have it dug before lunchtime. He worked fast, and Tad took the other shovel and went to work with him. They finished the ditch by piling the dirt along the sides to make the banks higher. Jed turned the water down the pipe into the ditch. They washed their hands, and Jed turned off the other valve, which sent all the water into the ditch.

As the water in the ditch filled up, Sister Wilkins called for them to come to lunch. Jed closed the upper valve so only a small amount went into the ditch. He wanted the ditch sides to soak up good—but not run over the sides.

As they ate, Jed asked Sister Wilkins if Anna was a good help for her.

Sister Wilkins couldn't say enough about Anna. She said Anna had worked hard for the two hours that she was there. "She knows her gardening, and she seems to enjoy every minute doing it. It made me hurry to stay up with her."

"I'm glad that she came to help you," Jed said. "It was probably nice to have Anna around just for a little female company. All you have had for the past three months is Tad and me."

Sister Wilkins said, "It was nice to have her here, and I really enjoyed her."

Jed got up and said, "I had better check the water in the ditch. I don't want it to overflow. I'll be right back."

When Jed got back, Sister Wilkins had some cake with a sweet sauce for them.

When they finished eating, Jed said, "Well, we have some lumber to unload and a floor to put down—so we had better get at it."

Jed and Tad went to the wagon and took off the drag shoes and ropes. Jed rearranged the posts on the ground, and he started pulling off the lumber and stacking it by size. Soon, they were down to the flooring material.

Jed told Tad to carry a few at time and stack them on the floor joist.

Jed took the first twelve-foot 1x12, cut a forty-five-degree cut on each end, and each cut was opposite of the other. He positioned it and nailed it down. Jed explained that he put the subfloor down on an angle to add strength to the floor system and give support to the finished floor.

Tad was eager to learn about building with wood.

One board was placed at a time, and the floor took shape.

They took a break, and Jed went to check the ditch. It was soaked, and the ditch banks had settled. It was time to send a little water down each corrugate.

Sister Wilkins came over and asked if the ditch was ready Jed said that it was. She said she would take over of setting the of water in each row, so they could go back to the floor.

Jed and Tad worked on the floor, and by evening, about two-thirds of the floor was cut, laid down, and nailed in place.

Jed looked over the floor, and he was pleased with what he saw. "By noon tomorrow, we'll be nailing walls together. We can have Tom and Johnnie come down in the evening and help stand the first wall sections and brace them."

Jed decided to work on the floor that evening and not go up to Tom's. He felt an urgency to get the house done.

Sister Wilkins called them to supper at six. Jed ate

quickly and he and Tad went back to work on the floor. By the time it was too dark to see clearly, there wasn't much floor left to put down.

Tad had already gone and brought the horses and oxen up to the corral, and Jed called it quits for the night.

Early the next morning, Jed was up and laying out the top and bottom plates for the first wall. When it was light enough to see well, Jed went back to sawing and nailing the floor. When he was called to breakfast, the remaining floor was almost finished. He didn't linger after he ate, and he went back to work on the floor. Tad was there to help. About thirty minutes later, the floor was finished.

They cleared the scraps of wood from the floor, and Jed went back to work on the wall plates. He cut the lengths and marked the front long wall. This wall would have two windows and a door. He marked the headers and plates for the windows and a header for the door.

Jed and Tad took turns cutting the needed pieces.

Tad carried over the 2x4s for the wall studs and put them in place as Jed directed him. Tad nailed the studs into place, and Jed did the corner post and window area. Within an hour, the first section was nailed together for the front wall. It had one door and one window. The second section had just one window and went a little faster. The third and fourth sections were for the back wall and were the same as the front sections. Tad was catching on fast. They had just started on the fourth section for the back wall when they were called for lunch.

Sister Wilkins commented that it looked like they were moving along fast.

After lunch, they finished the fourth section, and they were able to drag the two bedroom sections back to make the end wall for the bedrooms. At four in the afternoon, they finished the first end wall.

Jed said, "Are you liking carpentry work?"

Tad said, "I am enjoying it. It's fun to put things together and see them turn into something good."

Jed suggested that they get four 2x4s and put one at each corner of the building to use for temporary braces to hold the walls vertical and true until the siding was put on.

It wasn't long before Sister Wilkins called them to supper. They went over to the well and washed their hands.

As they finished eating, Jed suggested that Tad go see if Tom and Johnnie could come down and help raise the walls.

Tad said he would be glad to go. He quickly finished and hurried off.

When Jed finished eating, he said, "Sister Wilkins, I'm going to lay out the rafters and maybe cut some of them." He put three two-by-sixes on the sawhorse, cut the first one, and used it as a pattern for the next two. As he finished cutting, he saw the whole Saunders family and Tad heading over to the new building.

Jed said, "When I sent Tad for help, I hadn't intended to route out the whole family. You're our friends, and we're glad to have you."

Tom said, "What can we do to help?"

Jed said, "Let me make one mark on the floor where this end wall will go, and we'll raise it up."

Jed and Tom got in the center of the wall, and Tad was on one end with Johnnie on the other. Jed told them to all lift together and to be careful not to push the wall off from the floor. They lifted the wall, and Jed told them to hold it steady while he positioned it and nailed it down along the bottom. Jed asked Tad to hand him a brace, and Jed placed it in the center of the wall and down to the floor.

They took the back corner section and pulled it over so that it could be stood up. Being a little shorter, it was a little lighter. By shifting it a little, they got it into place and nailed it to the floor and the corner. They raised the second section of the back wall and braced it.

They stood and nailed the two sections for the front wall. Once the walls were properly braced, they were done for the evening.

The women clapped their hands.

"It looks like the beginning of a building," Tom said. Jed and Tad you have put all of this together really fast."

Jed said, "Tad is really good help, and he's learning fast. I'm glad he's my partner."

Tad looked down and blushed.

Anna asked her family to come over and look at the garden. It looked nice and, the straight rows had just been watered.

Tom looked at the well and said, "You folks have

been here less than two weeks, and you have a well, a garden, a corral, an outhouse, and a small home that is growing by leaps and bounds. You are doing really well, I must say. If your dad comes out from the mountains this weekend, he won't know the place. I'm sure he'll be proud of you for all you have done."

Sister Saunders said, "We had better be heading home."

Anna stepped over to Jed and said, "Jed, you're doing a great job, and I am proud of you." She reached over and gave his hand a little squeeze.

He returned her gesture with a smile and a thank you.

Sister Wilkins, Tad, and Jed said thanks and bid them good night.

After they had gone, Sister Wilkins said, "You know, Jed, we could have looked this whole world over, and I am sure we could not have found better people to be neighbors to."

Jed said, "I agree. They are special."

Tad went to bring the livestock up to the corral for the night.

Jed said, "Sister Wilkins, With the way things are looking, we'll get the other three walls put together in the morning. I'll ride Blaze into town and get the money to pay for the last load of lumber that we picked up at the mill. If there are other seeds that you want, I'll stop at the store and get them if they are available."

Sister Wilkins said, "Cantaloupe, turnips, beets, and more corn."

Jed wrote them down and said he would look.

Tad came back as it was getting dark, and Jed and Tad were tired since they had put in a full day.

Everyone went to bed.

22

The next morning, Jed was up and at work when it was just light enough to see his lines on the wood. He was doing the interior walls. He had one twelve-foot wall and two twenty-foot walls to lay out. A twenty-foot wall had two doors in it for the bedrooms, and the other long wall had no openings. When he saw that Sister Wilkins was up, he sawed them to length. He brought over the seven eight-foot 2x4 studs for the twelve-foot wall and started nailing. It didn't take long before that wall was complete.

Jed was carrying a load of studs over for the twenty-footer when he was called to breakfast. He put down his load, washed his hands, and walked over to the covered wagon.

Sister Wilkins said, "Well, early bird, what have you done already?"

He said he had the shorter wall nailed and the other two laid out and was nearly ready to nail. He filled his plate and sat down to eat.

Tad got up, dressed, and washed his hands, and when he got back, his mother had filled his plate. She handed it to him, and he sat down to eat.

Jed told Tad the plans for the day. They would finish the two walls, and then he would ride Blaze into town and get the money for the last load of lumber. If he could have the oxen hitched and ready, they would head out to the sawmill for another load. He hoped they could get to the sawmill and finish loading before lunchtime.

After breakfast, Jed and Tad went to the building to do another wall. Jed told Tad that he needed nine more studs brought over. While Tad got them, Jed cut the studs to go under the headers and four pieces for the headers, which would carry the weight over the doors and windows. They laid the studs in place and started nailing. With that wall done, they started on the last wall. They needed eleven studs for the last wall. It had no doors or windows. Jed and Tad hurried along and nailed it together.

Jed went down to the corral and brought Blaze up and saddled him. Since he didn't need to leave yet, he took out the few boards left in the wagon out and stacked them, and then he loaded the drag shoes and tie ropes in case he needed them. He planned to go to the store and then the bank.

At the store, Jed was able to get all the seeds except for the beets, which was OK by him since he didn't care very much for beets. He asked the clerk what time the bank opened. The clerk told him usually by eight thirty.

That meant the bank was probably open by now. Jed paid for his purchases and walked over to the bank. The door was still locked, but as he turned to walk away, the banker walked up.

"Hello, Jed," said the banker. "You are up early this morning, aren't you?"

Jed replied, "Well, not really. I've already got a couple of hours in on the house, and we're headed up to the sawmill for another load of lumber as soon as I get back to the place. Just needed to get the money to pay for the last load."

The banker told him to come in and went to get him what he needed.

With the money in his pocket, Jed headed home.

As he pulled in, Tad stood by the wagon with the oxen hitched and ready to go. Tad had hung the canteen from the side of the wagon.

Jed stepped down from the saddle, and Tad climbed on. They waved to Sister Wilkins as they pulled past the covered wagon.

It was a few minutes before ten when they pulled into the mill yard.

Obed walked over and said, "You fellows must have a pretty good crew to be ready for more lumber this soon."

Jed assured him that it was just the two of them doing the work. "We did have help to stand some walls last evening."

"What do you need today?"

Jed read the list. "We'll put the 1x6s on the bottom, then the ten-foot 2x4s, and then the twelve-foot 2x6s."

He directed them to the 1x6, and they backed up and started loading. They went from one stack to another until they had all the listed items.

Obed said, "You can add a little more if you know what you will need next."

Jed told him they would finish up the load with as many ten-foot 1x12s as they could get on.

They pulled over to the 1x12 and were able to get fifteen of them on. They went to the office, and Obed added it all up and gave Jed the bill.

Jed took out the money and paid for the previous load. "Could you tell me again the directions to the man who made lathe." After receiving the directions, he asked about the planer and how it was coming.

Obed told him they had it running now and would be building up their stock of planed lumber.

Jed asked about dry sawdust or shavings. He had seen a good idea for a springhouse and the plan called for dry sawdust or dry shavings.

Obed assured him he had plenty whenever he needed it.

"If I build the sides up about three feet higher, I think I can get what I need in one load." Jed went out and checked to be sure he had the drag shoes on the wagon. He waved goodbye to Obed, and they were on their way home.

At the hill, they stopped and put on the drag shoes,

and they stopped at the bottom to place them back on the load. At that point, they were halfway home.

When they passed the snake-infested rocks, Tad said he didn't want to ever go there again.

Jed responded, "Tom told me about another place for getting rock, and as far as he has heard, there are no snakes."

Tad said that it sounded really good to him. He hated snakes of any kind.

They finally pulled into their place at twelve thirty.

Sister Wilkins jumped up and hurried to fix their lunch.

Tad unhitched the oxen, and Jed unsaddled Blaze, and they walked down to the corral. Chip trotted around and whinnied. He was glad to see them. They put the lead rope on him, and Tad took the hobbles and the other stock down to the field to turn them loose.

By the time they got back to the wagon, Sister Wilkins had their lunch out and ready for them. "Anna came down while you were gone, and we planted some of the seeds you brought home this morning. I watered them, and now we have a big garden growing. It will be nice to have fresh vegetables again."

Tad asked Jed what they were going to work on next.

Jed said, "Because the rafter material is near the top of the load, let's cut them and stack them. You might run up and tell Tom that we have the other three walls ready to stand up, and when they are available, we could use their help. Make sure you tell them to come only when it is best for them because we have other things to be doing in the meantime."

Tad was on his way.

Jed set up two of the cut rafters on the lower wall plates to see if he had them cut right. They were cut just right, and he set them back and out of the way. He went back and marked and cut and marked and cut.

When Tad came running back, there were only a few left to cut. Tad reported that Tom and Johnnie were about to finish their own project and they would come down when they finished.

Jed cut some of the top plates that would go on right after the three walls were standing. They unloaded the material from the wagon down to the 1x6 roof sheeting on the bottom. Jed cut one of the 1x6 boards and marked it the ridge board for the rafters to attach to at the very top.

Tom and Johnnie came, and they stood up the three walls and nailed them into place.

Tom said, "With these three walls up, it is really taking shape. Anything else we can do to help?"

Jed told him that this would allow them to continue building the roof and get it ready to put on the shakes. He told them he really appreciated them breaking into their work to come give them a hand.

Tom said he was glad to be of help, and with that, he and Johnnie went home.

Jed sent Tad over by the outhouse to get the ladder, and Tad went after it. When he got back, Jed had cut the first top plate to go on top of the twelve-foot bedroom wall. They went on to put on all the top plates, which tied all the walls together.

Jed worked from the ladder to lay out the places for each rafter on the two outside walls. He needed to put a temporary support on the outside to hold up the first rafter at the top and then one on the center wall at the end of the bedroom. Jed saw the need for a second ladder, so they took time and built a taller ladder. It was ten feet long and made from 2x4s and one-by-four steps. Jed taught Tad how to toe nail so he could nail the rafters down on the top of the outside wall plates as he nailed the rafters to the ridge board.

One by one, the rafters went up, and by suppertime, half the rafters were up and nailed. They took time to eat and then went back to work. By the time the light had faded, they only had a few rafters left to go up.

Tad left to bring the oxen and horses up for the night, and Jed cut a few of the ceiling joists until it was too dark to work.

On Friday morning, Jed was up working at first light. He carried the 2x4s in to make the ceiling joists, and he was starting to nail them into place when Sister Wilkins called him for breakfast.

He went to the well, washed his hands, filled his plate, and sat down to eat.

Sister Wilkins asked what he hoped to accomplish today.

Jed said he would like to get all the roofing boards up and nailed, but that might be pushing it. He would certainly try. Jed quickly ate and got up to go.

Sister Wilkins said she hadn't called Tad yet, but she would in a little while. She said, "Tad tries to keep up with you, and he is starting to wear out."

Jed assured her that letting him sleep a little longer was the right thing to do.

Jed went back to work. He took the smaller ladder and went along the twelve-foot wall between the bedrooms and marked where the ceiling joists would be nailed into place. As the building was twenty feet wide, it took two ten-foot joists to cover the width. One by one, he carried them up the ladder and nailed them flush on the outside. He did the first half over the one bedroom and then worked on the other half over the second bedroom At this point, he had half of the joists up and nailed.

To put the others up over the living room/kitchen area, he would need Tad's help. He went back to the sawhorses and cut the last four rafters. These four would be nailed on when the roof sheeting was all nailed. They would be the trim for the outer edge of the roof, which were called barge rafters.

Tad came over after breakfast and was ready to help. They finished putting up the last of the regular rafters. Next was placing the support braces from the bottom of the ceiling joist up to the rafters, which would strengthen the joist.

"Tad, if you would like to take the horses and oxen down and turn them loose, I'll cut the braces." Jed cut a piece of 2x4 to go between the floor and the bottom of the joist as a temporary support to hold the joist while nailing each brace.

By the time Tad got back, the braces were cut and ready to nail into place. They went right to work on them, and it wasn't long before the last of the joists were in place and the braces to the rafters were nailed.

They put the 1x6 roof boards into place as sheeting. The bottom row took more time since it extended over the end of each rafter by one and a half inches. Jed cut little pieces to keep in their pockets to check the spacing. The sheeting boards would hang over fourteen inches on each end and would splice at the center of a rafter where the two boards came together.

Jed cut ten four-inch spacer blocks. One would go in their pockets as a movable spacer, and the others would be nailed in, overhanging the outside rafter about two inches. This would keep bugs and birds from getting into the attic.

They put the first row in, and then it was one board at a time until they had four rows. They worked from the ladders and leaned a number of boards up to the roof where they could pull them up as needed. They took the saw up with them and worked from there to the top. They were a little over two-thirds done on the back side when they were called to lunch.

After Jed and Tad climbed down, they stood for a minute and observed their progress on their house.

They washed, filled their plates, and sat down to eat.

Sister Wilkins admired their work and the accomplishment.

After they finished eating, they rested a little longer and went back to work. It took about an hour and a half to finish the back side.

They moved their ladders around to the front and put the first row on. Tad had gotten the hang of it, and he was doing his fair share. Jed admired how quickly he had caught on. It wasn't long before the first four rows were on. They carried lumber to the front and leaned it against the roof. They refilled their pockets with nails and went up on the roof to cut and nail them. They went even faster on the front side as they worked together as a team. They hardly spoke to one another since they knew what to do. A couple of times, one or the other would go down to get more lumber and lean it against the roof.

They nailed the last board on and were called for supper. After supper, they would nail the barge rafters into place under the fourteen-inch extensions, and then the roof would be ready for the shakes. Jed would see Brad at church on Sunday and find out if the shakes were ready.

After supper, they nailed the four barge rafters into place. They started cutting the blocking between the wall studs. Jed asked Tad to get the scrap down close to the outhouse and bring back all the 2x4s that were at twenty-two inches long. There weren't many of them.

Jed measured the distance between studs and started cutting. He cut up all the short scraps, and then he cut the longer boards. As he got an armload ready, he carried them over to the house and placed them in the proper place. He showed Tad how to nail them—flat side out and flush on the outside—by using the marking stick Jed had cut. When the last one was cut, Jed went to work nailing with Tad. In less than an hour, they were all in place.

They had brought a few siding boards from the mill on the last load, and they started to put on the siding. These one-by-twelve-inch boards went on vertically, and it was not necessary to be placed tightly since they planned to use a one-by-four to seal the cracks or spaces between the twelve-inch boards. The ten-footers were the exact length needed, and they only had to cut a notch at the top end to go around the rafters and cut the proper lengths at the windows and doors and the sloped ends of the house.

When they had the fifteen pieces in place, Tad asked, "When do the windows go in?"

Jed said, "When the window and door openings are finished with siding, like this window opening is, we can put the windows in."

"Wow!" Tad said. "It's coming right along, isn't it?"

They had used up all the material they had, and that was all that could be done on the house until they went for another load on Monday. On Monday, they would go to the sawmill, to the shake yard, and to get the lath for the interior walls and ceilings.

They would take the wagon to town to get the four windows, nails for the shakes, the lathe, and the siding. They could also get the butt hinges for the four doors.

Jed planned to ask the clerk if he thought they could pick up the lath on saturdays.

Jed thought he had enough money for the lath and things from the store, but on Monday morning, he would have to go to the bank to get more money.

Tad told Jed he would bring the animals up to the corral.

Sister Wilkins admired the building and the progress of the day.

Jed said, "In the morning, I think we'll go to town to pick up the windows and some other things we'll be needing real soon. If you would like to ride along, you would be welcome."

Sister Wilkins said she would think about it.

Jed asked if she had a lantern in the wagon.

She had brought a glass-based lamp and a metal lantern from home, but to avoid the possibility of spilling it in the wagon, she had emptied the coal oil. "If we want to use the lamp or the lantern, we'll have to buy some coal oil for them."

Jed said, "Maybe with a light inside the house, we can work and extra hour or so each day."

Sister Wilkins said, "Jed, you wanting to work more hours each day doesn't surprise me, but don't you think you are putting in enough hours per day as it is?"

"The extra work I can do inside would not be heavy work like we have been doing in framing the building. I'll look into buying some coal oil when we're in town."

Tad came up from doing his evening chores with

the animals, and Jed asked him what he thought about carpentry work now.

Tad said, "I really like it. I think putting things together and seeing it develop into something is great. Once you show me what to do, I love to get right at it."

Jed said, "You're doing great. When we get things done here, maybe we can hire out to build homes and buildings for other people."

"Really, Jed? Do you think we could that? I think I would like to do that."

It was getting dark, and they all went to bed.

J ed **thought about** building some long lower
sawhorses to put planks on so that they could walk
on them while they worked on the ceiling and upper
walls with the lath and plaster work. In the morning,
he would see what materials they had and what he
could do with it. With those thoughts on his mind, he
went to sleep.

The next morning, when he opened his eyes, his
mind went right back to thinking of the need for
sawhorses. He got right up and dressed and went out
to see what they had to build them with.

Jed knew that they didn't have the planks, but he
did find enough material for the sawhorses. He would
build four—six feet long and twenty inches high—with
six legs on each. This would allow them to completely
set up once in each bedroom and two times in the big
room. This would make the work so much easier and
faster.

He gathered the material and went to work cutting.

He cut the four 2x6s in six-foot sections. He cut the angle legs, eight left and eight right, and he nailed one set together and then measured the length of the straight center legs and cut eight of those. Next was cutting and nailing the twenty-four braces. As he was starting to nail, he was called to breakfast.

He washed his hands and went over to eat.

Sister Wilkins asked, "What are you building? I thought you said you were out of material?"

Jed explained what he was doing and how it would make the inside go faster.

She smiled. "If anyone can think of how to make things better and easier, I'm sure you're the right man for the job."

When he finished eating, he headed back to his project. He heard Sister Wilkins calling Tad as he walked away. He finished the nailing and put the sawhorses in the house.

When Tad finished his breakfast, he came over to find out what they needed to do.

Jed told him they would leave for town at eight and would take the oxen and wagon. "When you go for the oxen, just leave the horses in the corral until we get back."

At quarter till eight, Tad went for the oxen. He had them up and hitched to the wagon by eight.

Jed asked Sister Wilkins if she wanted to go. She said she would pass.

Jed and Tad went off to town. They stopped at the store first and took the list to the counter. Jed selected the nails, hinges, and door latches, and then he talked to the clerk about the windows. He had just three in stock, but more were due in the coming week. Jed said he would take the three, and then he asked about the plaster.

The clerk said he usually had about thirty bags in stock.

Jed asked how many square feet of coverage per bag. He was told about eighty square feet, and he would have to add the sand.

Jed said that he would need about twenty-three bags. "By the way, where can I get the sand?"

The clerk told him.

Jed asked about mortar mix to lay up the chimney, and they always had plenty in stock. He also asked about coal oil.

"Do you have your own can?" the clerk asked.

Jed replied, "No, I don't."

"We have one- or two-gallon cans that we can sell you. I'll fill it from my barrel."

Jed said he would take one of the two-gallon cans.

Jed asked about a nail apron, and the clerk said they had them. Jed asked him to get one and put it in something to keep it hidden from Tad. He was going to make a gift of it.

The clerk put it where Tad wouldn't see it, wrapped it in paper, and tied it up with a string.

Jed said, "That will do it for today."

The clerk added everything up, and Jed took out his money and paid.

Jed pulled the wagon around to the back. They put the windows in first and fixed them so they wouldn't get broken, and then they put the other things inside. Jed went back to the bank, but it was still closed. They would head over to the sawmill and stop on the way back.

As they started to pull out, the banker walked up. "I'm sorry for being a little late this morning. I saw you go up to the door. If you want to come back, I will help you with what you need."

Jed backed up the oxen and wagon to make sure he wasn't on the street, and he asked Tad to stay with the wagon.

Jed went to the bank and got the cash for Monday's two loads. When he came out, they were on their way to the sawmill, which took them about twenty minutes from town.

The man was glad to help them. Jed told him they needed some lath. The man said he had plenty on hand.

Jed said, "It's for a small house, and I need about eighteen hundred square feet."

"There are forty square feet per bundle," the man said.

Jed said, "In that case, I'll take forty-seven bundles. That will give me a little extra. My name is Jed Sandalin. What's your name?"

"Joseph Tague—but most people just call me Joe." He directed them to back up to a pile.

Tad drove the oxen around and backed them up

to the pile. They were able to get them all in, and the bundles seemed secure.

Joe gave Jed the total, and Jed paid him. It was a little before eleven when they pulled in.

Sister Wilkins came out and said, "Well, it looks like you got a full load again."

Tad unhitched the oxen and said he would take the horses down to the field.

Jed dug out the nail apron and showed it to Sister Wilkins. "Could you sew Tad's name on it? Maybe in black thread?"

Sister Wilkins looked at it and said, "I think I can do that. Jed, it was really nice of you to do this for Tad. He'll love it."

Jed said, "When you have good help, you have to treat them well. When you get it done, we'll give it to him as a surprise."

Sister Wilkins said, "I can hardly wait to see his face. He'll really be thrilled to have it." She hid it in the covered wagon.

Jed started to unload the lath, and he found he could take four bundles at a time comfortably. By his second load, Tad was back. He started stacking them in a neat pile. When the lath was all stacked in the house, they brought in the nails and other things they had bought along with the two gallons of coal oil. They brought the windows over from the wagon and stacked them in the house. When they had all three neatly stacked, they put a couple of layers of lath bundles over them to make sure nothing would damage them.

Jed took a couple of the long sawhorses into Sister Wilkins's bedroom, and he put two five-foot 1x12s on the lower sawhorses. This gave him a small place to work. He got his nail apron and changed the nails to lath nails. He had Tad bring the saw and two bundles of lath into the bedroom. Jed nailed one lath across two studs, three feet off from the floor, and he leaned the rest of the open bundle against the lath on the wall. He told Tad they were ready to start. He held one lath up and marked it and asked Tad to cut five that length. He told him to take four more and lay them together—with the marked one on top—and cut all five at once. They leaned them up by the uncut lath. Jed marked another one of the five.

Jed explained how they would alternate the splices on the ceiling joists. The spacing of the lath was not to be more than three-eighths of an inch between each lath. It was not to be less than a quarter of an inch, but trying to maintain the three-eighths distance would be ideal. This allowed the right amount of plaster to ooze between the lath to help adhere the plaster to the wall or ceiling.

Tad paid close attention to all that Jed showed him and told him.

In a couple of minutes, eight square feet of ceiling had been covered. Jed marked another and asked for five that length. Tad cut them. Jed started to nail down the wall one lath at a time, alternating where the splices were.

Jed explained the rhythm: cut, nail, cut, nail. That

left just the cuts at the ends of each run of lath. He stopped and moved the boards and sawhorses he was standing on. "On Monday, when we go to the sawmill, we'll bring some long boards we can use as planks. We'll be able to work the full ceiling and the walls down about one-third the height without having to move the scaffold plank. In the big room, we'll only have to move the scaffolding two times to do the whole room."

Tad took it all in and tried to commit it all to memory.

They worked for another fifteen minutes before Sister Wilkins called them for dinner.

Before they left for the wagon, Jed told Tad that he was going to work on the buggy for the afternoon.

Tad smiled and said he would cover for him.

After they had eaten, Jed told Sister Wilkins he was going to help Tom with a project.

She said, "That would be nice. Maybe that will help repay them for all they have done for us."

Tad asked if he could stay and nail some lath.

Jed said that that would be great and to remember to maintain the proper spacing and keep the rows of lath straight.

Tad said he would remember and gave Jed a wink.

Jed picked up a few tools and headed out.

When he got to the buggy, he brought out the broken wheel to work on it. It had bolted hubs and four broken spokes. Jed took out the bolts that held the broken spokes and removed the four broken ones. He cut some new pieces out of the discarded tongue and shaped the new spokes with his drawknife. Being skilled at making spokes, it didn't take him long to shape them. The next broken piece was two sections of the felloes, the outer wooden pieces of the wheel. Another section of the tongue was cut off to give wood for the felloes. He shaped them with his drawknife. He removed the bolts holding the iron rim of the wheel and took off the rim. He had his brace and bit to drill with and his tenon cutter. He prepared the end of the spokes and drilled the felloes to receive them. He knew he would have to heat the rim to expand it to put it over the outer circle of the wheel.

Tom came along at just the right time and asked if he needed any help.

Jed told him he needed a ring of fire to heat the rim to expand it enough to go over the wheel, and if he also happened to have a couple of pairs of blacksmith tongs, it would be a great help.

Tom got the little blocks of wood and chips for the fire. Jed gathered up the shavings he had made from making the spokes and felloe pieces and spread them around the ring. Tom had a little coal oil in his shop and dribbled it on the wood.

Jed said, "Before we light the fire, we need to get everything in order so we'll have it at our fingertips when we need it. I need some wood blocks to set the wheel on, so it will be solid when I place the hot rim around it."

Tom said he had just the thing in the firewood pile he had gotten from the mill. He went and returned with some short pieces of 2x4. Tom didn't have any tongs, but he did have three shapes and sizes of pliers. With longer handles, they might work. He brought them over, and Jed started the fire.

When the fire was burning evenly around the ring, they set the rim into it and watched. Jed remembered that they needed a bucket of water to cool the rim.

Tom went for the water and came back shortly.

The rim neared the right temperature and would soon be ready to set. Jed said, "You don't want it red-hot. That would burn the wood too quickly. Nearing white-hot is ample. Once the rim is ready to move, we must work fast. You take one pair of pliers, and I'll take the other two. We'll pick it up and set it in position, and then I'll tap it with the hammer to get it in the right position. I'll have you pour a little water along on the rim. Just follow me around the wheel. Remember to just pour a little water as we go around."

"OK, let's grab it."

In a minute, the rim was set and cooled—and the wood wasn't even scorched.

Tom had heard about setting rims, but he had never seen it done or helped with it. Needless to say, he was impressed.

The wheel was nice and tight and true.

Jed asked Tom if he could help get the wheels on.

Tom answered, "I sure can."

They took off the nuts from the axles and got the two front wheels close at hand. Jed lifted the front end, and Tom slid a wheel on and rushed around and slid the other wheel into place. They put on the nuts and tightened them. The back end was heavier, and they got it up on blocks just about to the height needed. With a lever and a taller block, they finished lifting it up and put on the wheels and the nuts.

The next thing would be to put the rim bolts into the rim of the repaired wheel and bolt them to the felloes. That would finish the wheel.

He straighten the dash so the front looked good again. After that, Jed worked on the post for the surrey top. He had only enough wood from the tongue to make one post, but he needed three more. Jed would like to have hardwood for them if possible.

Tom told him that down on the edge of his property, there were a couple of hardwood trees, and there might be a couple of dead limbs that would yield what was needed.

Jed took his saw and headed down there. He found one dead limb that had a straight section that would probably work. He went to work sawing. Before long, he had a piece of good wood about eight inches in diameter, and it was long enough to do the job. He piled the scrap he had cut off in a neat pile and took his straight piece back to the buggy. He split the log into four pieces and then split off small pieces until it was down to where he could finish up with the drawknife.

He was nearly through with the final shaping when Tom came back and inquired if he had found something.

Jed showed him the neatly finished pieces.

Tom said, "Jed, you really know how to work your tools, don't you?"

Jed said, "I love to work with my hands, and the tools seem to fit them. They just seem to work really well together. Thanks for your help, Tom. It is truly appreciated."

It was late in the evening, and Jed knew Sister Wilkins would have supper ready. He picked up his tools and headed home.

Anna came out and asked if she could walk with him. She wanted to see how the house was coming along, and she been down for three days.

He said sure, "I'll be glad for the company."

As they were walking, she asked about the buggy and how it was coming along.

He told her about the progress. "And with another hour, the surrey top will be done—except for the patch on the leather top. Then I only have to get the shafts ready and change the mountings on the axle. Then it will be ready for paint."

"Jed, could I do the painting for you? I love to paint."

"Anna, the next trip to town, I'll get the paint and a paintbrush. You can do the finishing touches—if you would like to."

Anna said, "Jed, I'd love to. Wow! Your house has changed so much, and it looks so good. Jed, this is exciting. You will soon be sleeping indoors."

Jed explained they would be going to the sawmill on Monday to get the rest of the material for the outside walls. "I'll find out at church tomorrow if the shakes are ready to be picked up on Monday."

Anna said, "Jed, you're doing so well at this. I'll bet you really enjoy this work, don't you?"

He admitted that he did.

Anna said she had to get back. They were getting ready to eat supper when she left. As she ran up the road, her skirt flew. It was the first time he had really noticed her.

Sister Wilkins stepped over to Jed and said, "That was Anna, wasn't it?"

Jed told her that she had seen him heading home and walked home with him to see the house.

Sister Wilkins smiled and said supper would be ready in a few minutes. She had waited for him to get home. She asked how things were going for the Saunders family.

He said it was going well, but he would need a couple more hours to finish the work he was doing there.

She said that was nice of him to be of help. "Tad has gone to bring the stock up to the corral."

Jed stepped up into the house and walked to the bedroom where Tad had been working. It was nearly done, and he had done a neat job too. He thought, *That boy is learning fast. He'll do well at woodwork with the way he is going.* He went back to the wagon.

Tad asked, "Did you see what I got done while you were gone?"

Jed assured him he did—and that he was doing a good job too.

Tad smiled and admitted that his arm was getting

tired from all of the nailing and cutting. His mother had come out and handed him the pieces as he needed them, which had helped.

They washed their hands and went over to eat.

Rachel and Jimmie came running up and told them they had been sent to tell them that the folks would pick them up in the morning for church.

Sister Wilkins and Jed thanked them, and they ran home.

As they ate, Sister Wilkins said, "When I go inside, it is starting to feel like a home."

After they finished eating Jed said, "I think I'll go over to the house and nail some more lath on."

Tad said he would go with him and cut and hand pieces to him. "Maybe we can get the first bedroom done."

When they got to the house, they moved the sawhorses to the other bedroom.

Jed went to work and marked the pieces for the patterns Tad would use to cut the four or five of each length needed. In thirty minutes, the room was complete.

It started to get dark, and Jed suggested that they fill the lantern and see how much light it would make for them.

They filled the lantern, being very careful not to spill any. They put the can away and lit the lantern. When they carried it into the finished bedroom, they were pleased that it created enough light to work by. When the siding was on and shakes were on the roof, the lantern would create enough light to be able to work after dark. They blew out the lantern and headed for the wagon.

On the way over, Jed asked Tad if he had ever been around plastering before.

"No," said Tad. "You'll need to explain it to me."

Jed said, "We'll need to make a mixing vat to mix the plaster in, a hod to carry the plaster into the house, a mortarboard and a stand to pour out the plaster. We'll make a darby to smooth and flatten the plaster on the walls and ceiling. I'll see if they have a plaster trowel at the store. If not, I'll have to make one. Oh, and we'll need a hawk as well."

Tad said, "It takes all of that to plaster the interior of a house?"

Jed said, "It may sound complicated, but it is quite simple once we start. Then you will see how it is done."

On Sunday morning, Jed woke up with the birds at his normal time. He hoped that he would receive good news from Brad about the shakes. He wanted to get the house sealed in as soon as possible and get the next load of lumber from the sawmill on Monday. In a couple of days, they could have the shakes on the roof and maybe the siding on. In a couple evenings, he could make the front and rear doors and set them and put the windows in place. In less than two weeks, they could be moved in. He had almost forgotten about the chimney. He would have lay the bricks for it. He would have to ask where the brickyard was. All of these things were tumbling around in his head. He was excited and overwhelmed by all the things that needed to be done.

24

Jed **heard Sister** Wilkins moving around in the wagon, and he got right up. He had barely dressed when she stepped out of the wagon.

She said, "Good morning. You didn't roll out quite as early today."

Jed answered, "Yes, I was just going through all that needs to be done tomorrow."

She chuckled. "Jed, you're going faster than I ever thought possible as it is. Don't worry yourself over it. We're doing just fine as we are."

Jed hurried and started a fire for her.

"Jed, do you like hot cereal for breakfast?"

He said that he had hot cereal for breakfast most of the time back home, and he liked it.

She told him she was going to make a change this morning and make hot cereal and toast.

Jed responded, "That sounds great to me."

"Hot cereal takes a little longer to cook than bacon and pancakes—if you boil it properly."

Tad was still asleep.

Sister Wilkins asked "Jed, what do think of Anna?"

Jed paused and then said, "I think she is real nice, and I like being around her. She doesn't make me feel uncomfortable when she's here."

Sister Wilkins said, "I think Anna would like to help on the house if there are things that she could do to be of help."

Jed told her that he hadn't thought about that. He would have to think about it and see if he could come up with something she could do to help.

Sister Wilkins said, "Maybe if she was invited down here when you are working, she would learn by watching—and then she would know how to help. I don't think she has been around when a house was being built before."

Jed thought about it and said he thought it would be a good idea. He mentioned that he would be gone a good share of Monday, hauling materials home, but if he found the right moment today, he would ask if she would like to come down to work.

Sister Wilkins was stirring the cereal and had her back to Jed, but a little smile came on her face. "Tad, wake up. Breakfast is about ready." She toasted some bread on the stove and set out some jelly.

Tad crawled out of bed, got dressed, washed his hands, and was ready to eat.

Sister Wilkins dished up the cracked wheat cereal for the three of them and had the toast ready. As they ate, Jed and Tad commented on how good the cereal was with the toast.

"Well, then, I'll fix it more often," she said. "Jed, do you like honey?"

Jed said, "I enjoy honey, especially on biscuits and toast."

Sister Wilkins said, "Then the next time we go for groceries, I will ask if they have honey."

The dishes were done and put away.

Tad went down and took the stock out to graze.

For the next hour, they sat and talked. It was time to get ready for church. When Sister Wilkins got up into the wagon, Jed asked her to hand him his better clothes to change into. She handed him both his and Tad's clothes.

When they were ready to go, Tad stood out and watched for the buggies. When he saw them coming, they hurried to the road, got in the buggies, and took off.

The younger children chattered between themselves and laughed from one buggy to the other.

They pulled up in front of the church, pulled the buggies up to a hitching rail, and started getting out. The horses were tied to the rail, and they all went into the church together.

A good feeling came over Jed as he entered the building. He felt he needed to whisper if he needed to talk at all.

The bishop came over to Sister Wilkins and whispered that they hadn't received their membership records from Salt Lake yet, but they should be here soon. He went back to the front.

A good sister played the prelude music on the pump organ. Sister Wilkins thought it was good to hear the hymns played, and it prepared her for the service.

The room was packed, and even the aisles were filled. There was hardly room for the deacons to move around and pass the sacrament to everyone.

Brother Saunders stood to conduct the meeting. He welcomed everyone and announced the program. The meeting proceeded as announced with two very good speakers. It surely would give a spiritual lift to everyone present.

When the meeting concluded, everyone started filing out. Jed hadn't seen little Lilly's family yet. When he finally stepped outside, Lilly said, "Jed, over here— here we are." Lilly held out her arms and gave Jed his usual hug and kiss on the cheek.

Anna came over and stood next to Jed.

Jed said, "This is Anna. She lives next to where we live, and this is my sweetheart, Lilly."

Lilly gave him another hug. "Anna, will you be my friend too?"

Anna said, "I would love to be your friend." She took Lilly's little hand and kissed it.

Lilly turned to her mother and said, "Mama, Anna is going to be my friend too."

Brad told Jed that his shakes were ready, and he had personally split them and made sure they were the best available.

Jed thanked him and said he would come first thing in the morning because the roof was ready for them.

Brad remarked, "You have been here just two weeks now, and you have your home that far along. It sounds like you're doing great."

Jed saw Tom coming out of the church, and he said that they needed to go since they rode in their buggies.

Lilly gave Jed another hug and reached over and gave Anna a hug as well, and then she went to her mother.

They said goodbye, and Anna and Jed turned and started for the buggies. Anna took hold of Jed's hand and said, "Jed, I can see why you like that sweet little girl. She is an angel for sure."

Jed squeezed her hand, and she looked up at him and smiled.

They got into the buggies and headed home.

The buggies stopped in front of the Sandalin property and let Sister Wilkins, Tad, and Jed get off.

Sister Saunders reminded them that they planned on seeing them for dinner, which would be ready by twelve. "We'll see ya then."

Anna said to her family, "That little Lilly is certainly a sweet little girl. I can see why Jed thinks so much of her. You only have to be with her a few moments before she'll have you loving her. When Jed said we had to go, she gave Jed a hug and a kiss on the cheek—and then she reached over and gave me a hug too. Then she went to her mother. She is really sweet."

The buggies pulled up in front of their home, and

everyone got out except the two drivers. Tom and Johnnie took the buggies to the barn, unhitched the horses, and put them away. They rolled the buggies back into the shed—where they were kept out of the sun and the weather and walked to the house.

At the Sandalin place, Sister Wilkins changed out of her Sunday dress and into a recently washed and ironed dress. She hung up her Sunday dress and smoothed it with her hands; she loved that dress.

They visited for a little while and then headed to the Saunders's home.

Following dinner, the girls took over cleaning up and putting things away. The women, Tom, and Jed went over and sat down to visit. Johnnie and Tad went off to be by themselves.

When the dishes were done and the kitchen was straightened up, Anna headed out back. She hesitated at the door until she caught Jed's eye and motioned for him to come.

Jed excused himself and went out the back door a minute behind Anna.

Anna was standing over in the shade under a tree. "Jed, I hope you didn't mind me joining you when you were visiting with the Sessions family at the church today, but I had the urge to meet Lilly. I am glad I got the opportunity. She is so sweet." She slyly looked up at him and smiled. "I'm not really jealous of that little girl."

Jed said, "I didn't think that you would be. You seem to be interested in the house we're building. I was wondering if you would like to come down and watch what we're doing."

Anna said she would just love to do that, and if she could be of any help, she would like to learn. "I have a real interest in doing things outside, but my Daddy thinks I should be helping Mama in the house. With three other girls, there is not a lot for all of us to do. Mama tries to keep us busy, but there is only so much to be done. I'm sure Mama wouldn't mind my coming down when you are working."

Jed told her he planned to go get the load of shakes the first thing in the morning and then go to the sawmill for a load of lumber. They should be home by midafternoon to start to put shakes on the roof.

Anna asked if she could get up on the roof and help in some way.

Jed was a little hesitant. "It wouldn't be safe for you to be up on the roof in a dress. You could trip on your shirt and fall off the roof."

Anna said. "I already thought of that. I took a pair of my father's old work pants and altered them. I patched them where they needed it, and now they fit me halfway decent. I will just wear them."

Jed looked at her and said, "Do you really want to?"

She assured him that she really wanted to work at something besides housework all the time. It wasn't that she didn't like housework. She liked doing other things too, but she had never had a chance.

"OK. But make sure it is all right with both your

parents. I don't want them to be unhappy at me if you fall off the roof or get hurt."

She laughed and said she'd be careful. Anna then asked Jed what things do you like to do for fun?

Jed confessed that he hadn't done much of anything just for fun, especially since his dad had been gone. He had been left as the man of the house and he done all the chores and took care of the farm. He enjoyed his work, and he enjoyed his carving. He told her his greatest thrill was giving a carving to a child and seeing the glow that comes into their eyes.

They found many things in common that they both liked.

Jed finally said he needed to go. He told her he would look forward to her coming down tomorrow.

She told him she would be there when he got home from the sawmill.

Jed said, "I hope you coming down to help won't upset you parents."

She winked at him and said, "Don't worry about it."

Jed followed her into the house and told Sister Wilkins they needed to go.

She stood and thanked Tom and Sister Saunders for the ride to church and the fine meal.

Jed also thanked them, and they walked out to the porch.

Sister Wilkins said, "Just send Tad home later. He does enjoy being with Johnnie, and he needs a friend and a little time to be just a boy."

Sister Wilkins and Jed headed home. They walked

over to the new house and went in the back door. Jed pointed to the area where the kitchen would be and asked where she thought the best place for the cookstove and the cupboards would be. He was thinking of having a wood box on the left side of the cookstove, a small space for proper distance, lower cabinets, which would give a workspace, and cupboards on the wall.

Sister Wilkins just stood there and took it all in.

Jed pointed out where the dinner table would be here. He said he had thought of making the table expandable for when they had company. "The table would have to seat at least ten people. Or we could have a second table that would set over on the wall between the two bedroom doors, and it could be moved over when there is company."

Sister Wilkins said, "Hold on a minute, Jed. This is your house, and you need to do it as you would like. While I am here with you, I will enjoy it however you fix it. OK?"

Jed said, "Maybe you are right, but you have become like a mother to me, and it didn't come to my mind that you wouldn't always be here."

She looked at him and smiled. "Maybe the one you should be asking is Anna."

It kind of embarrassed him when she said that. "I guess that I will marry someday, and then maybe I would want to build a home just for her, whoever that might be.

Sister Wilkins said, "Jed, I think that the ideas you have and have shown me are well thought out, and I don't know how they could be improved upon. I believe you are heading in the right direction."

Before going out, he showed her that the bedroom he had planned for her was ready for plaster. They would lath the full house, put the shakes on the roof, and add the siding before they did the plastering. They were only about four days from being ready for plaster. "With the new help I just hired, maybe things will even go faster."

Sister Wilkins stopped and looked at Jed, "New helper? Hired?"

Jed smiled. "Yes, I talked with Anna, and she was hoping she could come and help. She has even altered a pair of her father's old pants. She put a few patches on them, and she said she would be here when we get home from the sawmill tomorrow."

Sister Wilkins clapped her hands. "I had a feeling that girl wanted to do that. I am so glad for her. I think she'll really enjoy it. I think the two of you will work well together. Just be patient—this will all be new to her. She might have a natural ability to work with her hands that will surprise you."

They walked over to the wagon and sat down in the shade of the dining fly. A little breeze was blowing, which made it a comfortable evening.

As they sat and visited, Jed brought up an idea he had been thinking about. He said that when the house was finished, and they had built a few small animal shelters like a chicken coup, a pigpen, and maybe a shelter for the stock at the side of the corral, they should plan a trip to Cedar City to buy some livestock. He could build crates for chickens, and they could buy three or four wiener pigs and a milk cow. The cow could be led home, the pigs could ride in the bottom of the wagon, and the chicken crates could be suspended over the pigs. The trip would take approximately five days: two days going up, one day there, and two days coming home.

Sister Wilkins said, "Jed, I think that is a great idea. Maybe we could inquire around here to see if anyone knows of someone up there who will have livestock for sale—and maybe you could find something around here in the meantime."

Jed said it would be about a month before they would be ready—maybe a little longer—and they could keep it in mind.

Tad finally came home and said, "You know, Mom, I like Johnnie. We like a lot of the same things. Thank you for letting me stay longer." Tad said that he would bring the stock up to the corral. He headed down to where the stock were grazing, took the hobbles off the horses and told them to come with him, and they got in line and just followed him back. When they got to the corral, the horses and oxen just went in and never gave him any problems at all. Tad just smiled at them and told them that they were good animals. The horses nickered back at him as if they were saying thank you.

When Tad got back up to the wagon, Jed said, "If we can leave here a little after seven to go get the shakes, we should get back before nine thirty. Then we'll unload and head to the sawmill. Hopefully, that will put us up there by ten thirty, and then we can be loaded—and home by noon or shortly thereafter. By the way, Tad, we have a helper who is coming to work with us starting tomorrow afternoon."

Tad asked, "Who?"

"Anna."

Tad looked over at Jed and said, "Anna? What does she know about woodwork?"

Jed said, "Probably not much, but she wants to learn—just like you wanted to learn."

Tad replied, "I guess that will be all right. But it will hard for her to work in dress, won't it?

Jed said, "We'll just have to wait and see."

Sister Wilkins gave Jed a little wink and said she would set out some supper for them. They got their plates and sat down to eat, but no one was very hungry since they had had a big dinner and hadn't done any work.

When the Saunders family set up for a light supper, Anna announced that she was going over to work with Jed and Tad on their house tomorrow afternoon.

Her dad said, "You're going to do what?"

Her mother looked at her with a question on her face.

Anna explained that she wanted to do some outside work besides gardening. She was fascinated by watching them work on the house. Jed had invited her to come and watch if she would like. She said she wanted to help and learn.

Her dad said, "But, Anna, you can't work on the house in a dress!"

Anna answered, "I know that. I took a pair of your old work pants that you don't wear anymore and altered them. I patched them, and they fit me pretty good. I'll just wear them and one of my older blouses."

Her dad sat there in awe for a minute and then said, "Anna, you're a sweet young lady, and I guess it is time for you to do the things you would like to do. But remember to do this for the right reason and be of help and not to be a bother to them."

Her mother nodded in approval.

Anna said, "Thank you. I'll do my best."

Volume II of "Determined and with Courage": "Building and Growing Together" continues the story of Jed and his friendship with Anna. It will be available soon. Please watch for it!

Made in the USA
Middletown, DE
19 October 2022